# EROTIC ACCOMMODATIONS

*Volume 1*

## KATRINA JACKSON

ISBN: 9781673230451



Editor: A.K. Edits

Created with Vellum

# ROOM FOR THREE?

# CONTENT WARNINGS

Mentions of child abuse, racism
Allusions to disordered eating

# PROLOGUE

## The Interview

Precious had been trawling the Craigslist ads for roommate listings for days, growing more and more despondent with each page. When she'd finally responded to the ad from a couple seeking a roommate, she'd been a glass of wine in, starting to throw caution to the wind. She'd been hoping to find another student in need of a last-minute roommate like herself. Instead, she'd found a lot of old men advertising for a roommate but describing some terrifying hybrid between a maid and a sex slave. At first, she'd been certain she was reading the ads incorrectly, but when she showed up at a luxury apartment, and her potential roommate had answered the door in a too small silk robe, she'd turned and run away, terrified that she'd end up back in the university dorms before she found a roommate that wasn't a terrifying cliché from her favorite detective drama.

The ad was simple, no big red flags; at least, none that she could spot after reading it four times.

Young couple (late 20s) looking for a roommate (no gender prefs) to rent a small single bedroom. Looking for roommate only. All sexual propositions will be deleted without reply. Rent must be paid in American dollars, not Bitcoin or trade in kind.

They seemed alright, she thought, and muttered to herself that everything would be okay while typing her brief response to their ad; because she needed everything to be okay. She needed this small second bedroom in Manhattan that was close to campus and under $1000 a month. She needed it too bad to let herself freak out about living with not one, but two strangers. She didn't have the luxury to be too picky; not while she was practically squatting in what was supposed to be her new apartment, full of unpacked boxes, with her stomach full of knots and her brain still unable to accept how she'd come to this place.

Normally, Precious was the most prepared person

she knew. She was a problem solver by nature and could see issues from one hundred feet — or three bad decisions — away, and start course corrections early. She had to; she had too much riding on her shoulders to be anything less than capable, and almost no safety net to catch her if she fell. Her brother was all the way in Vienna and her mother was back in Georgia; she only had herself.

That's why it more than stung when Laura, her best friend in graduate school, called her up the day before they were set to move into their new apartment to announce that she was going to move in with Dr. Friedlander, the chair of their department, instead. Caught completely off guard didn't even begin to explain how she felt; betrayed was closer to the truth, but still not enough.

Also shocked by the news — unconfirmed gossip aside — was Precious and Laura's entire graduate cohort, the Sociology department, the School of Arts & Sciences, and Human Resources. The University of Manhattan had very progressive and strict codes of conduct governing faculty fraternization with *any* student, which meant that on top of needing to find a new apartment asap, the department and university HR had hauled Precious in to grill her on what she'd known about Laura and Dr. Friedlander's relationship for a pending disciplinary review. Those were peak apartment hunting times, eaten up by her friend's foolish decision. Precious would have told Laura that she was being foolish months ago if she'd bothered to disclose that the hot older nerd she was dating was the chair of their department. She also would have told her that he wasn't hot, but he was definitely married with kids.

But Laura had chosen her path, and Precious was almost homeless; she didn't have time to save a friend who apparently didn't think she needed saving. They could handle the fallout from Laura's decision when Precious had a guaranteed roof over her head. Sometimes you have to prioritize yourself, her brother Andre would have told her.

That their almost landlord had let Precious break their lease and stay for a month while she found a new place to live had been a miracle. Costly and total dynamite to her very carefully managed budget; but a miracle nonetheless. And when she finally received the invitation for references and an interview from "modelcouple_123" three days after she'd sent an inquiry for their spare room, she'd hoped it meant that her luck was finally improving.

She tried to keep a positive mindset as she walked tentatively down the dimly lit hall in an old, but fairly well-maintained, walkup just two subway stops from her university. The lobby was clean, the elevator was old but seemed to be running smoothly, and the hallway seemed quiet. These were the bare minimum of things she was looking for in a new place to live, but good signs nonetheless. But she couldn't stop her practical brain from compromising as her move-out date in her old apartment loomed ever closer. She decided that so long as her roommates weren't living in a hard-core hoarder situation, she was going to take this room if they offered it to her. And if the couple seemed creepy, she'd just invest in an extra lock for her door. She didn't have the time or the money for any other options.

She stepped in front of 6F, took a deep breath, raised her hand to knock, cursed, and then pulled her phone from her purse instead.

She opened her text messages, shared her location with Andre and then sent a message:

Going into the interview. Best case scenario, I'll text in less than an hour with a place to live!

She pressed send, took another deep breath and knocked timidly on the metal door. The clanging sound made her jump.

Her phone beeped with the notification of Andre's surprisingly prompt reply.

And worst case scenario, you're dead. Got it.

Precious rolled her eyes and muttered, "asshole," just as the door swung open.

Precious had imagined some very vivid possibilities for what Mike and Cali would look like. She was an avid fan of too many detective and true crimes shows; she'd listened to the podcasts, she watched all the terrifying documentaries. If there was anything she'd become uncomfortably used to, it was the fact that people could be very creepy, and the creepiest ones of all were the ones that seemed very normal. And scary roommates in New York had to be its own true crime subcategory. Her guard was way up, but her options were very few, so she was prepared to put on her fakest smile and hope for the best. The best in this case would be a clean apartment and no strange vibes.

But when the door opened, her imagination's best felt very small indeed, because the man and woman crowding the doorway looking at her with warm smiles on their faces weren't old, or creepy, or unkempt; they were beautiful.

They looked like models.

Like... she'd-seen-their-faces-before models.

And then it hit her, exactly where she'd seen them before. Her mouth fell open and she blurted out, "Oh my god, you two are on that billboard in Times Square," before she could stop herself. "I had a dream about you two!"

She was definitely not getting this apartment.

---

Mike laughed louder and harder than he had in days. A real big, lose your breath but in a good way, type of laugh.

That laugh felt like a miracle, because less than an hour ago, he and Cali had been yelling so loudly at one another he'd been out of breath but in a bad way. They'd been having an old fight — as old as a fight could be, even though they'd been together for just over two years. It was a fight that made him, and their relationship, feel ancient and not long for this world, and that made him feel tired and sad because this wasn't the relationship he wanted, but his desire to be with Cali overrode all that exhaustion and sadness; at least for now. But that didn't mean they were in the right mood to interview a new roommate.

They'd considered calling Precious and rescheduling their interview, because this fight had all the makings of an epic blowout. Mike had been ready to make the call, but Cali had squashed that idea, in the ice princess voice he both hated and loved.

"If this," she'd gestured nonchalantly between the two of them as if their relationship was an inconsequential thing, "doesn't work out, I'll still need a roommate." It had broken his heart and made his blood boil with an anger only Cali could inspire.

How could she be so dismissive of him and their relationship, he'd wondered? But hadn't she always been? Hell, hadn't he been wondering how long their relationship could survive for months? The uncomfortable questions followed by the obvious answers made his lower back ache with stress.

But Cali was right; someone would have to cover his portion of the rent if they broke up and he moved out. The realization had sat between them in their quiet apartment, the air still ringing with the echoes of their shouting voices, and they'd retreated to their corners with heaving chests and stinging wounds. They'd stayed like that — seething at one another, stomping around the apartment like children — while waiting for their potential new roommate. They'd lost track of time in their anger.

And then a small, tentative knock broke the stalemate between them.

They'd walked to the door, the tension so thick between them, Mike could feel it. He'd pulled the door open and there she was, exactly as her name had promised, and he felt certain that the balloon of anger around them hadn't quite burst so much as it slowly began to seep away as they'd stared at her, adorable and flustered and beautiful.

"Come in," Mike said quickly. He reached out to softly place a hand on her shoulder and was shocked at the feeling of his own gut tightening at that contact.

"Please," Cali said, touching Precious's other shoulder. He wondered if she felt it too.

They'd practically had to drag her through the door, she was so embarrassed at her outburst. He couldn't see why she should be embarrassed, and he told her so, as did Cali. She'd looked at them with a shy, incredulous look on her face that made him want to cup her cheeks and kiss her, and he didn't know what to think about that, so he didn't.

They left their hands at Precious's back as they walked her into their living room. They settled Precious on the couch, and Mike was surprised when Cali sat next to her and started rubbing soothing circles across her back to console her. His shock was mostly because he'd never seen Cali nurture anything that wasn't one of the million plants all over their apartment, not even him. But it didn't make him jealous, or not for the reasons he might have expected. *He'd* wanted to sit next to Precious and console her. He'd wanted to rub circles on her back. He'd wanted to touch her.

He offered to make tea instead, and used the minutes it took to calm himself, pushing down the surprising shock of desire that seemed to blossom from nowhere.

"So, what do you do?" Cali asked nonchalantly, a cup of tea in one hand while the other played with Precious's ponytail. Mike watched as Cali gently wound the small curly ends of their potential roommate's hair around her delicate fingers. All his hard work in the kitchen was slowly undone at the sight.

"I'm a student at the University of Manhattan."

"How old are you?" Mike asked, the lust in his brain coming to a screeching halt.

Precious laughed. His back tensed with desire. He noticed Cali's fingers stop moving in Precious's hair and her hand grip her teacup just a bit tighter.

"Oh, I'm twenty-five. I'm a grad student in the Sociology program. Sorry. It's my second year, I'm still getting used to it all. I'm not an undergrad."

Mike and Cali visibly relaxed.

"Good. I don't think I could live with a college student again. I didn't go to college, but I lived with a bunch of undergrads when I first moved here. I hated it. I don't want to go back," Cali said nonchalantly. Or at least she was trying to sound nonchalant, but Mike could hear the strain in her voice, even if someone who didn't know her as well as he did might have missed it.

They all laughed politely.

"I'm the same. I didn't even want to live in dorms when I was an undergrad. I lived in the grad dorms last year but... I hated that. But I'm a good roommate, I think. I'm really quiet and clean. I like books and studying and this kind of sad Swedish detective show. You won't even notice I'm here," Precious replied, her laugh more nervous than polite. And then she pressed her lips shut as if she was afraid she'd said too much.

She was so fucking cute, Mike thought as he chuckled. But then he swallowed the thick ball of lust seeming to clog his windpipe, he wanted her so much. He wasn't sure why he was having this reaction to her, and he didn't have a clear head to pinpoint exactly what it was about her that was turning him on, but with Cali sitting right there in the room he felt uncharacteristically out of control. It was inappropriate, but he didn't hate it.

"We'd notice," Cali said in that slightly superior accent that offended most people. It offended Mike at times. But Precious just smiled at her, open and innocent. "We'd notice," Cali said again, but this time in a kind of breathless, dreamy huff that reminded Mike of what she sounded like when they made love first thing in the morning.

"How old are you two?" Precious asked. She took a sip of her tea, her eyes darting between them.

"We're both twenty-seven," Cali answered for them.

Mike sometimes hated when she spoke for him, but his brain felt sluggish, so he nodded.

His eyes landed on the blunt rounds of Cali and Precious's bare knees touching, a surprisingly erotic sight that made his gut clench even tighter, and a thought intruded into his brain. They shouldn't offer her the room, he thought. It would be a mistake. No one who could make him feel this way within minutes of meeting her could be good for their relationship.

He needed to use his veto.

He and Cali had decided on a simple system when they started looking for a roommate; they each could veto any candidate without discussion, and whoever they offered the room to had to be someone they both agreed upon fully. There was no other way they could imagine this arrangement working.

Cali had already used a veto on another model Mike knew from auditions. Rick and Mike had met on the commercial athletics model scene. They both liked to work out and play first-person-shooter video games. Cali had hated him as soon as he'd walked into their apartment. Mike still didn't know exactly why she'd said no to Rick, but a deal was a deal. He was happy he'd never pushed her about Rick and hoped that when he said no to Precious, she'd extend him the same courtesy.

Mike was about to ask Cali to follow him into their bedroom for a second so he could tell her that Precious was a no-go, when his eyes snagged on Cali's hands. Cali pulled him from the depths of an existential sexual crisis and his eyes followed her movements as she put her tea on their coffee table. He watched with bated breath as she placed that hand, probably still warm from her cup, on Precious's skin just above the knee; so close — too close? — to the hem of Precious's short dress.

He watched a shiver run up Precious's body and felt it in his own. Mike watched as Cali's other hand moved the tip of Precious's ponytail over her shoulder to rest across her chest. His heart started pounding as he saw his girlfriend's slender fingers caress that neat lock of hair as if Precious was the most precious thing in this room, and he didn't disagree.

They were speaking, Cali and Precious, but he was only nodding and humming in probably odd spaces. He didn't know what they were talking about, and he didn't quite think he cared; nothing could be more important than how close their bodies were, how much Cali seemed to enjoy touching Precious, and how ecstatic Precious seemed to be at being touched.

Eventually, Cali and Precious stood from the couch, and Mike followed because he wanted to be near them. He only vaguely realized that Cali was showing Precious around the apartment. He was grateful that she'd managed to keep her head about her since he hadn't.

And then he heard it, Cali's voice coming to him from what felt like a million miles away.

"I think, I mean, if Mike agrees, that we'd like to offer you the room," she said in that same breathless whisper.

They both turned to him with wide, expectant eyes and dilated pupils that probably mirrored his own.

His brain was screaming, "This is the worst idea." But when he opened his mouth, his voice said, "Absolutely."

---

Cali had a reputation for being stuck up. Everyone thought she was stuck up. Even Mike had, when they first met. He knew now that she wasn't — or at least she thought he did — but first impressions were a bitch. Her modeling agency leaned into her reputation to move her into the editorial modeling world because high fashion loves a diva. Fashion designers and photographers loved a model who was in control of herself, especially her body, and that's who they all thought Cali was.

On the one hand, Cali loved the work and the money, but a part of her hated that people had such an egregious misconception about who she was. She wasn't stuck up; she took modeling very seriously. She was also shy and, like so many models, desperately insecure. And she hid all of her sore spots behind armor so thick that Mike had only just cracked a hole in it after three years.

But the armor was as much about control as protection. Cali had learned early that the only thing she could control was herself. And hiding herself away from people who didn't know or love her was the safest she could be. The problem was that she'd mastered how to keep people away, but she was still a novice in how to let people in.

Also, it wasn't exactly true that she was always in control of herself. Too often, she had to hide how out of control she felt behind her armor. She had to, but sometimes she couldn't. Sometimes she struggled to hold herself together, but she'd never had to struggle so hard as she did during this interview.

She did all the normal things she was supposed to when interviewing a potential roommate. She asked all the right questions: references, deposit, move-in date, etc. She'd even managed to tell Precious that their offer was contingent on them speaking to her current landlord, which was bullshit. The man could tell her that Precious had burned down his building and she'd still offer to arrange Precious's movers, because, from the moment she and Mike had opened their front door, something inside Cali had broken free. It was a small thing, but it had grown stronger over the half hour of their interview.

Cali felt wild. Very out of control. So out of control that she hadn't been able to stop herself from petting and stroking Precious whenever and wherever she could. There had been that voice in her head that always sounded suspiciously like her grandmother, telling her that this was inappropriate, and she needed to get herself under control. But for once in her life, she ignored it, because only she knew that she wanted to do so much more.

And then there was Mike.

Or, maybe more accurately, there was always Mike, just at the edge of her vision, tall and strong and warm where she was sometimes so cold. Touching Precious and knowing that he was right there... Cali wanted to sigh at how much she loved that.

She'd expected Mike to step in, to pull her away from Precious and ask her just what in the fuck she thought she was doing. She wasn't sure how she might have answered that question, but it never came up, so it didn't matter because when she managed to drag her eyes — but not her hands — away from Precious, she immediately saw a familiar desire in Mike's eyes. It was even more perfect than she could have imagined, and she suddenly stopped fighting it.

She wondered if Precious felt it too.

Getting through the rest of the interview felt like beautiful torture; Precious's hand in hers, Mike's eyes roaming over her skin. She wanted more.

When Precious finally left, every part of Cali's body felt raw. She pressed her overheated back against the cool metal door, the thin fabric of her dress barely providing a barrier to her overheated skin.

Her eyes were closed, but she knew he was watching her.

"Should we... talk about this?" His voice was gentle, and that made her want to weep. Anything louder might have hurt, and of course, he realized that; he was so heartbreakingly perfect for her, and it broke her heart that it was so hard to express that to him.

She knew they should talk about what she was feeling; what they were both feeling. They should talk about this and their families and the future and all the topics he was always trying to carefully broach with her, and she was always trying to run from. They'd start fighting, if they did that, and she couldn't bear that right now. She never wanted to fight with Mike, but she didn't know how to stop it; not yet.

Cali shook her head, "Please, not now." A familiar plea. The "later" was always implied, even if it never came.

She opened her eyes, and her nipples ached at the desperate hunger in his face.

She smiled. Finally, they were on the same page.

"I'm so wet," she said, her voice strangled with barely contained need.

She clutched at the hem of one of the tight, sleeveless body-con dresses she liked to wear around the house. She wasn't wearing anything underneath. It maybe wasn't the best outfit to interview a potential roommate in, but it had felt right sitting next to Precious in barely any clothing, wanting her and wanting Mike.

He watched as she pulled the fabric of her dress slowly up her thighs, over her sex, finally resting just above her slender hips.

She didn't need to tell him to come to her. He might have made her wait longer if she had, just to draw this out for as long as he could. Maybe she would have liked that another time, but not tonight.

His steps were slow and measured, and each footfall only cranked up her desire. Cali thought it felt amazing. When he was finally in front of her, he reached out to run two fingers up one of her thighs.

Cali's back arched at the softness of his touch, and she hissed out a breath.

"Do you wish my fingers were hers?" He asked the question tentatively, his eyes watching his fingers dance across her skin.

She shook her head quickly. "Both." She hesitated and swallowed loudly. "I want your fingers *and* hers."

A ghost of a smile played on his lips.

She lifted onto the balls of her feet and leaned forward to whisper up at him, "Do you wish my pussy was hers?" She already knew the answer, but she wanted to hear him say it; needed to hear him admit how much he wanted Precious in that deep voice that made her entire body vibrate the day they met.

He raised his eyes to look at her; through her. But he didn't speak at first. He just watched her breaths grow ragged and her lips part in ecstasy as he dipped his fingers between her legs to slip across her folds. He waited until he'd worked two fingers inside of her, the soft squelch of her wet center giving away just how excited she was, before leaning forward to whisper "both" against her lips, followed by the delicious press of his tongue into her mouth.

# PROLOGUE

## Moving In

Precious had barely slept last night. She hadn't had much packing to do, since she'd never really gotten the chance to unpack, but that wasn't what kept her awake. It was her thoughts about them that kept her awake. Her imagination was running wild, remembering Cali's fingers lightly holding her hand, brushing her hair from her face, and Mike's silent presence watching her, watching them. She knew she shouldn't have been thinking about her new roommates in this way, but she was.

When the movers showed up at her old apartment, she was both delirious with exhaustion and buzzing with excitement. She was so grateful to be able to lose herself in watching them pack her belongings into the van and then rushing to Cali and Mike's place because at least it gave her a break from her erotic thoughts.

But that was before Mike opened the door shirtless. She'd stared at him, mouth agape, while he rushed around the apartment.

"Cali's at a shoot, but she'll be back this afternoon," he said, still shirtless, his abs rippling, muscles moving underneath his tanned skin.

Precious nodded, mouth still agape, stomach clenching in lust along with another body part.

"There's food in the fridge if you need something," he said, turning to her. His sharp jaw clenched and then released, and then he smiled at her.

It took Precious a few seconds to come out of the haze of desire and focus on what he'd said. "Oh, oh, that's okay," she stammered. "I can order something."

Mike shrugged. "If you want. But just in case. What's ours is yours," he said nonchalantly.

Precious swallowed and nodded silently again.

"Alright, I'm heading to the gym. Your keys are in that bowl by the door, and Cali left our names and numbers on the kitchen island. Call us if you need us," he said, and then pulled her into a hug.

Precious squeaked.

"Oh, sorry," Mike said, pulling back. "I'm a hugger. That okay?"

Precious nodded some more, faster this time, and then softly inhaled his warm spicy scent as his long, strong arms enveloped her. She was too nervous to hug him back or relax against him like she wanted to, but she did close her eyes and enjoy the fast-paced thrum of his beating heart.

All too soon, it was over, and he was smiling at her, waving and closing her new front door behind him.

She collapsed onto the couch and focused on just breathing while she waited for her movers to arrive.

It barely took her movers two hours to unload her belongings and take half of her savings, but when they were gone, Precious stood in the middle of her new room and felt herself relax. Her bed was shoved into the far corner and she was thankful that her movers had put it back together. Her desk was pushed in front of the window, piled high with boxes of books.

She looked at her watch. It was just past one. If she hustled, she could get everything unpacked, order some food, and be in bed with plenty of time to get her regular six to seven hours of sleep and then up for the first day of classes. This was the fastest and most efficient move of her life, and she hoped so much that it was the harbinger of good things to come.

"Want some help?" Cali's voice startled Precious.

She hadn't heard Cali come home but when she turned around, she was most shocked by how beautiful and elegant she was. She was just in a pair of tight yoga pants and a loose cropped tank top, but Cali looked like exactly what she was, a gorgeous model, and Precious felt insecure as she looked down at her own baggy harem pants and muscle tee. She wondered if this was what it would be like to live with Mike and Cali; if every day in their presence would make her feel plain in comparison.

"No, no, I'm okay. I've got it," Precious said, running her hand down the front of her shirt, unable to keep her hands still.

Cali smiled and cast her eyes around Precious's cluttered room. "You sure? This is a lot. And this is what roommates are for, right?"

Precious chewed her bottom lip and considered. She didn't have much experience with roommates. As an undergrad, she'd frustrated her mother's anticipated empty nest and commuted thirty minutes to the local state university, saving on room and board. She'd spent the previous academic year sharing a room in the graduate dorms with a third-year biology student who was completely nocturnal and hummed all night. She'd decided before the fall semester had ended to never do that again. But maybe this roommate relationship would be different, she thought to herself.

Cali looked at her expectantly, her offer sitting between them, like a heavy weight Precious could feel all over her skin. She let her bottom lip plop out of her mouth and smiled. "Yeah, okay," she whispered.

"Great," Cali squeaked, and tiptoed into Precious's room, weaving through the boxes until she was right in front of her. She smiled. "Can I hug you? I'm a hugger. You can say no."

Precious couldn't help the smile that spread across her face. "That's what Mike said to me this morning. You two must really like to hug."

Cali shrugged and batted her long curly eyelashes.

"Alright," Precious said, the word barely out of her mouth before Cali's arms were wrapping around her waist, pulling her in.

With Precious's limited roommate knowledge, she rationalized that maybe hugging was a normal roommate thing, and helping her unpack was nice. But she felt sure that she wasn't supposed to like the way Cali's arms felt wrapped around her, her fingers just barely under the hem of her t-shirt, ghosting over her skin. And she probably wasn't supposed to notice the way their breasts felt pressed together. Or the way Cali's perfume made her mouth water. Or the fact that wisps of Cali's hair tickled her nose and made butterflies settle in her stomach. That wasn't something that would have happened with Laura if they'd moved in together.

But Precious didn't have long to consider that before Cali pulled away and buried her face in the directions for Precious's new bookshelf.

Precious busied herself hanging up her clothes and tried not to think about Cali and Mike's hugs, but every time she and Cali accidentally brushed past one another, Cali turned to her with a smile and Precious couldn't help remembering what her body felt like, and it was confusing, but not disconcerting.

They both turned at the sound of the front door opening.

"Anybody home?" Mike called out.

"We're in Precious's room," Cali yelled.

Precious thought she heard Mike's soft laughter, but when he appeared in her doorway, his face was relaxed, neutral.

"Unpacking," Cali said, not bothering to turn to know he was there.

For reasons she couldn't quite identify, Precious found that bit of familiarity and ease comforting.

"Need some help?"

"Nah, we've got it," Cali said, concentrating on organizing the books onto Precious's bookshelf.

Precious turned her head to smile. Cali was organizing the books by color, which wasn't useful for Precious to work, but it was adorable to watch her sort them so diligently.

"Alright, I'm going to shower," Mike said, and turned down the hall toward his and Cali's bedroom.

Cali turned to her, rolled her eyes and smiled. "He hates unpacking. He would have whined the whole time."

"I can hear you," Mike called from the other room.

"Good," Cali yelled back.

Precious giggled and then gulped loudly when Mike reappeared in her doorway, naked but for the towel wrapped loose and low on his hips.

"Don't try and poison Precious against me," Mike

said. "Or I'll have to tell her all the ways you're a terrible roommate."

Cali rolled her eyes at Mike and turned back to Precious. "He's just lashing out. I'm a great roommate."

"Liar," Mike said. "I've got an extra pair of earplugs whenever you need 'em, Precious." He winked at her and then continued down the hall to the bathroom.

Precious tried to smile, not fully understanding their playful fight, but enjoying being included in their adorable banter, nonetheless. Also, her brain was in a fog at seeing Mike's broad chest and the indent of his well-toned hips on display again. She licked her lips. She wasn't sure if she'd ever get used to that sight, but she was very interested in trying.

When she turned away from the empty door frame, her eyes crashed with Cali's. She was watching her with a small smile on her delicate mouth, just barely lifting the corners of her lips.

"We're both really happy you're here," Cali whispered, and Precious felt every one of those quiet words in her throbbing pussy.

---

Precious had been living with them for three weeks, and Cali had spent each day in a haze of arousal that made it hard to concentrate on anything outside of their apartment. She'd always been a homebody, but she lost all desire to leave the house or let Mike and Precious leave either, and she forced herself to tamp down on those impulses. She had shoots and auditions booked, and they had bills to pay. Besides, she couldn't imagine asking Precious or Mike to stay at home with her and cuddle with her on the couch. Could she?

Still, whenever she was home, she imagined that this was what heaven felt like. There was something about Precious's presence that made her feel lighter than ever, even as she was frustrated that she couldn't touch her, at least not the way she wanted to. She felt as if she'd somehow willed her fantasies into almost being, and each day the desire for her almost fantasies to turn into reality grew just a little bit more.

Cali had always loved physical affection, craved it even, but she'd also worried about hanging all over Mike, worried that he would find her too needy. Somehow, Precious's presence undercut that anxiety. She happily leaned into Cali and Mike's daily embraces. And when they worried that they might hold on to her too long or too tight, they turned to one another. Mike let her lean into his side and clutch at his arms, or threw his arm around her as they crowded into the doorway of Precious's room and talked to her, oddly charmed by the way she looked with her hair pulled into a messy bun on top of her head and her dark-framed glasses teetering on the tip of her nose. And at night, when Cali felt as if she was nearly overcome with emotions — some she recognized, others she didn't know what to do with — he held her tight in his embrace and fucked her as slow or as hard as she needed.

Precious hadn't been with them for long, but Cali had already stopped worrying as much about clinging onto them. She stopped being afraid that if she cuddled Mike too long after sex, he wouldn't want her hanging off him throughout the day. She let herself enjoy walking into the kitchen every morning and wrapping her arms around Precious while she stood at the kitchen island eating her cereal. And she happily crawled into Mike's lap as the three of them ate dinner together — accidentally at first, and then it became a ritual — and talked and laughed.

She'd even managed to be okay, or as okay as possible, when Mike turned her music down so they didn't have to shout across the room at each other. She stopped worrying that their apartment would be too quiet as it filled with the sounds of the three of them learning to live with one another. It was unexpected, but somehow Precious took the pressure off of Cali's fear of being alone. Cali didn't worry that she was too much for Mike, and she imagined that he got a reprieve from the burden of filling all the silences that terrified Cali, even if he didn't understand exactly why she was afraid. She woke up this morning in Mike's arms feeling energized that her relationship had turned some kind of corner.

It was still dark outside.

The speaker by their bed was turned down low, playing a mix of Cali's all-time favorite slow jams. She could just barely hear the beats mixing with Mike's soft snores in her ear. She pressed her head closer to his and lost herself in his rhythmic breathing.

But then she heard Precious's bedroom door open and her quiet steps to the bathroom and that door closing. Cali's body moved from relaxed to tense against Mike's. He unconsciously pulled her closer.

He was on his side, his large body wrapped around hers. She lay on her back, their heads sharing the same pillow. He mumbled into her hair.

"What?" She didn't know why she whispered.

"What's wrong?" His voice was thick with sleep.

Cali turned her head, rubbing her cheek against his five o'clock shadow affectionately. "She's up."

He barely moved, but Cali knew Mike was more awake now with just those two words. They listened to the sounds of the bathroom door opening and the old wood floors creaking under Precious's feet.

"Tell me," he mumbled.

The floorboards went quiet. Cali licked her lips. Had she heard him? Did she know? But then Precious's door squeaked closed. She and Mike listened for the metallic sound Precious's bed made when she crawled back into it.

"I dreamt about her again," Cali began. "She was wearing that yellow dress she wore the first day of classes."

Mike groaned and Cali smiled.

They'd both watched, dumbfounded, as she flitted around the kitchen, grabbing a banana, pouring juice, and triple-checking her backpack before she left. Their eyes had been trained on the contrast of her sunshine yellow dress and her beautiful, rich, dark skin. They watched the hem of the dress play along her thighs as she ran barefoot around the apartment, one of her cheeks distended with a bite of banana. It was mesmerizing. She was mesmerizing, and Cali could tell she didn't even know it.

When Cali pulled Precious into an impromptu goodbye and good luck hug, the scent of Precious's perfume enveloped her and then mixed with Mike's when he playfully threw his arms around them both. Cali was overcome with their bodies pressed against so much of her own. The way Precious's mouth parted in something that looked a lot like arousal, Cali hoped, but was probably just shock, Cali assumed. And as soon as their front door closed, Cali's senses were thrown into a frenzy at the hard pressure of the back of the couch pressing against her stomach, and Mike's dick easing inside of her as she told him how badly she'd wanted to slip her hand underneath the skirt of Precious's dress.

That innocuous yellow dress had come to represent all of Cali's feelings about the need coursing through her body at having Precious and Mike under the same roof. Just mentioning it made Cali's thighs clench together. She moaned as Mike ran his hand roughly over her breast, down her stomach, and then settled the weight of it over her sex, heavy and promising.

"Keep going," he huffed.

"You were on the couch. She was sitting on your lap," Cali said.

Mike gulped loudly in her ear.

"You were touching her. Her breasts. Pinching her nipples." Mike's hand slipped inside Cali's panties. She opened her legs for him and gasped as his fingers grazed her wet lips. "You were touching her everywhere, but only where I told you. Only when I told you." He easily moved two fingers inside of her.

"You didn't touch her?" She could hear the incredulity in Mike's voice and she laughed.

"Not at first. That's how I knew it was a dream," she whispered, and then let out a reedy laugh.

Mike's laughter was much louder, a sharp bark that made her jump and caused her heart to speed up.

But Cali shushed him. They didn't want Precious to hear. Or maybe they did. It was confusing and exciting.

He pumped his fingers in and out of her as they both fought to quiet down. They shifted under their covers and waited, listening for any sign that Precious had heard them. Her bed squeaked, but only a bit. Besides that, her room was quiet on the other side of the wall separating them.

Mike curled his fingers inside of her and she shivered.

She turned to him and whispered. "Be quiet," she directed him, but also herself.

He pressed his lips together and nodded seriously at her. She smiled.

Mike was always beautiful. It was the first thing she'd thought the day they met. The other models were good-looking in the way lots of models can be, awkward, or a bit strange, sometimes buff, but always — allegedly — universally attractive. But Mike took Cali's breath away. Her eyes had widened, her heart sped up, and she had to press her lips together to stop from blurting that out and embarrassing herself.

But he was even more beautiful first thing in the morning. The shadow of his beard darkened his jaw, his eyes were bright and his hair disheveled. And he looked at her like she was the entire world, mirroring what she felt in the deepest recesses of her heart.

She placed a kiss on the corner of his mouth before she continued. "I watched you both. I watched her come completely apart in your lap. She was a beautiful mess in your arms."

Mike unconsciously pumped his hips into Cali's side at the word "mess."

Cali smiled and ran her fingernails along the arm across her body, loving how heavy even that limb felt over her.

"I wouldn't let you touch her like this," she said,

clenching around his fingers. He buried his head back inside her hair and moaned. "I wanted to torture you both. But I tortured myself, too, and I couldn't take it for as long as I wanted. Eventually, I sat on the couch next to you both and kissed you. You whispered her name into my mouth. And then I kissed her, sucking on her tongue the way you like."

Her voice gave out on that last word, coming out of her mouth in a breathy moan. Cali's legs widened, and Mike rewarded her by grinding the heel of his hand against her clit. She whimpered and ground her hips upward. She was always so desperate for him to touch her any and everywhere.

She started panting, and her words came out slowly. She had to stop every now and then, just to moan as quietly as she could. "I told you to hold her close to you, and then I got on my knees in front of you two."

Mike added a third finger.

The wet squelch of her pussy sounded so loud Cali actually worried that Precious might hear, but she didn't care, she was too far gone to pretend that she *didn't* want Precious to know what she did to them.

"I moved that pretty skirt up her thighs so slowly while you both watched. And then I licked her slowly over her underwear, teasing her some more. When I pulled her panties down her legs, I let you slip a finger into her pussy, but just for a little bit. And then I had you move that finger to her mouth. And then I told her to suck it at the same pace I sucked her clit."

"Jesus, Cali," Mike breathed, pressing his groin into her hip.

Cali clasped one hand around his wrist and slipped her other into his boxers, wrapping her hand around the soft steel of his erection. Mike groaned in relief.

Neither of them cared about how loud they were being now, but they'd completely stopped speaking. Their quiet room filled with their ragged breaths, and they stroked each other to intense releases that made Cali's thighs shake as Mike buried his face into their pillow to muffle his deep scream. He wrapped his arms tightly, almost painfully, around her as he came messily in her hand. Cali wished she could spend every moment of every day in a hold so tight.

Vaguely, they heard the incessant squeaking of Precious's bed, but they were too wrapped up in their fantasy to notice.

---

Their air conditioning was on the fritz. They'd called the landlord, but apparently the entire HVAC system was fucking up.

Cali was distressed, terrified that all her plants would suffer in the heat.

Mike tried to be there for her, but he didn't know anything about plants, and he'd never told her, but all those damn plants terrified him. He liked looking at them, but he was scared that if he got too close to one of them, he'd kill it. Whatever the opposite of a green thumb was, he had that, but worse.

So, he decided to stay out of her way as she ran back and forth from their bay window garden to the kitchen to fill up her watering can and mister and globes.

Besides, he was worried about Precious. She'd barely been in the apartment a month and their modern, newly renovated building was nearly as hot as a sauna. Maybe that would have been fine under normal circumstances, but with the last vestiges of summer descended on the city like a heavy, humid blanket, he'd become terrified that she would start to rethink her decision to move in with them.

It had only been three days — three obnoxiously hot days — but that was enough time for the fear to begin to consume him. Well, it was part fear and part lust, because with the temperature in their apartment well above one hundred degrees, they were all wearing much less than they might normally.

Well, maybe not Cali; she didn't like to wear much around the house year-round. But Mike and Precious had been forced to strip off more clothing, as the days dragged on and their box fans did nothing more than circulate hot air.

And if he'd thought she was adorable and alluring in her cute summer dresses and her baggy sweats, she was fucking hot in the loose tank tops she seemed to have in abundance and wore like dresses. That might have been okay under normal circumstances; normal circumstances being when she wore pants and a bra. But this heat wave was anything but normal, and Precious had taken to wearing those tank tops without a bra, and in the smallest pair of boy shorts he'd ever seen. Even Cali didn't have any that small. And they were driving him absolutely wild.

Mike only had a few recourses for working off pent-up sexual energy, and Cali was too preoccupied with her plants to fuck him *every time* Precious walked through the living room to refill her water bottle, and he'd taken more than his fair share of ice-cold showers since their AC stopped working. The only avenue he had left to blow off some steam was to work out. Technically, that would have been a great idea. It was almost certainly cooler outside than in their apartment, and the gym would have air conditioning. But he still hadn't made his way there yet, because as much as he needed to work out the sexual energy building up in his system, he didn't have any desire to be away from Precious and her tiny underwear any longer than necessary.

"Oh my god," Precious groaned as she walked into the living room.

Cali was spraying her hanging plants, and Mike was watching her while holding a bag of ice against his neck and chest and, when his eyes caught on Precious, his aching dick. After three days of prancing around the house in a long tank top that at least almost covered her hips, she'd decided to change into a shorter tank — much shorter — and this one barely covered her small breasts.

"It's so hoooot," Precious whined, and shook her head vigorously.

Mike pressed the bag of ice harder into his lap and swallowed a groan. "Yeah, sorry about that."

Precious stopped on her way to the refrigerator and looked at him. Her smooth ebony skin had a light sheen of sweat that accentuated the evenness of her skin tone. And since he was looking her in the face, he noticed how cute she was when she pouted, and how long her eyelashes were, and how much he wanted to kiss her. Torture.

"Why are you sorry? You didn't break the building's HVAC." She smiled mischievously at him. "Or did you? Was this just an elaborate plan to get Cali to wear as little as possible around the house?" she asked, and then winked at him and threw back her head with laughter.

Mike wanted to lick the sweat from the column of her neck.

"Mike doesn't have to do much to get me nearly naked," Cali said from right next to him.

Mike jumped. He hadn't even heard her walk into the kitchen. When he turned to her, she had a small, knowing smile on her face.

She sucked her bottom lip into her mouth and let it out slowly. "I love being naked. Mike knows that."

"Oh," Precious said.

They turned to her. She was clutching her now-filled water bottle against her chest. "Are you wearing more clothes because of me? You don't have to do that. You can just pretend I'm not here. I mean... if you want."

Mike's body was overheating everywhere except his dick. He shivered at her words and the thoughts they inspired.

Cali leaned forward to place her elbows on the kitchen island. She smiled at Precious. "That sounds fun. We should just be naked at home."

"Oh no, I..." Precious shook her head and swallowed. "I couldn't."

Mike's eyes raked up and down her body, too far gone with lust to care if she noticed. "You're nearly there," he said before he could think not to. He wasn't certain, but he could have sworn that he saw her shiver. He wondered if it was having his eyes on her, or maybe his vision just shimmered because of the heat and arousal.

But what he knew he hadn't imagined were the hard points of her nipples through her shirt. Those hadn't been there before, he was certain. He lifted his eyes to her face and found her staring at him with wide eyes and parted lips. He wanted to taste her.

"You two want popsicles?" Cali asked.

Mike tore his eyes from Precious and had to blink a few times to make sense of the world again. "We have popsicles?" His voice sounded strange, deeper. He knew it was the lust.

"I had some delivered when I ordered groceries yesterday," she said happily.

He watched as she walked around the island, bumping Precious playfully out of the way with her hip. She pulled open the freezer and then turned around with a box of popsicles. "What flavors do you want? There's grape, watermelon and strawberry," she said, reading from the box.

"Grape," Precious said quickly.

Cali smiled at her. "Me too."

"St-strawberry," Mike said.

Cali dished out their treats and threw the box back in the freezer.

Mike immediately wished he'd left before this conversation started and just gone to the gym. This torture was too much. It was one thing to watch Cali suck and lick at... well, anything, but to watch Cali *and* Precious caress their popsicles the same way he'd dreamt they'd suck and lick at his dick...

Mike couldn't stop the groan from escaping from his lips this time.

Cali turned to him with a devilish smile on her face. "You okay, Mike?"

He pressed the ice against his groin again and shook his head. "So hot," he mumbled. Who knew if he was talking about their apartment, his body, or them?

Cali knew. And Mike knew that she knew what he meant, because she winked at him again and pushed her popsicle back into her mouth.

"Your popsicle's melting," Precious said.

Her voice sounded hoarse to Mike's ears, but he was so horny that he couldn't trust his own perception anymore.

And then Cali walked back around the island and turned him in his seat. Her eyes flickered to his lap, and her smile widened when she saw the bag of ice there.

He was begging her with his eyes to be kind to him. If she recognized the pleading in his eyes, she decided to ignore him. Instead, she kept her eyes on his face and lowered her mouth onto his popsicle. And then, because Cali could be relentless when she teased him, she moved her mouth from his popsicle to his hand.

Mike groaned loudly as Cali began to lick the melted juice from his hand. He heard Precious's sharp intake of breath, and that fear he'd been living with that she would come to regret moving in with them tried to resurface. Tried, but failed; it was no match for Cali's tongue on him.

Besides, if Precious was beginning to question them as roommates, it didn't show on her face. When Mike turned to look at her, her eyes were riveted to

Cali's tongue as she licked at her own popsicle. After a few licks, Mike realized that she was licking her popsicle when Cali licked him.

He groaned again and Cali's eyes flew to his.

She didn't look scared or appalled or nervous; Precious looked horny as she pushed her popsicle into her mouth and then hollowed her cheeks as she pulled it slowly out.

"Oh, fuck," Mike said, and threw his head back. He grit his teeth as he came in his pants with Cali's tongue bathing his knuckles and Precious's eyes taking it all in.

# 1

## Eight Months Later

It was still dark out. The cast-off rays from a streetlight outside illuminated the corner of the room where Precious had shoved her desk. But it was nearly pitch black in the corner where she lay on her bed, snuggled under her covers.

Some people hated waking up before their alarm clock, angry that they were missing out on just a few more minutes of sleep, but Precious didn't mind. She listened to her body and set the pace of her day based on that. If she woke up fifteen minutes, an hour, or even two hours before her alarm clock, she didn't fret; she just laid back and mentally ran through her schedule, preparing for her day, enjoying the brief moments of peace before the insanity of her life.

She also loved this time when the light was a kind of fuzzy black, still dark, but just light enough to see the suggestion of shapes in her room. She loved that it wasn't yet warm enough to keep her windows open, so she could just barely hear the sounds of the city below her in the probably chilly early spring morning.

Her schedule wasn't packed today, she thought to herself.

She needed to get an hour, maybe two, of reading in, and then she had a response paper to write, a discussion board comment to post for her own class, and then another board to close and grade before Professor Min's Intro to Sociology this afternoon. She had to be out of the house by nine to make it to campus on time and then school would become, as it always was, her entire world. Precious probably wouldn't even make it home until the early evening, maybe later if she decided to study in the grad student offices for a few hours to get a head start on tomorrow.

She was weighing the pros and cons of working in her office later than normal when she heard it; the real reason she didn't mind waking up before her alarm clock, and didn't want to stay on campus any longer than was absolutely necessary.

She should feel ashamed, and maybe at some point, today, she would. Maybe in the shower, or as she rode the train two stops to campus, or in the too quiet library on the twelfth floor where no one besides tired graduate students liked to work. At some point, the memory of this moment would come back to her to make her skin tingle and her core heat, and make her face warm as the somehow complementary emotions of arousal and shame mingled.

But that distinct tangle of feelings was for later.

For now, she shifted on her bed, cringing at the metallic squeak of her cheap bedframe, and raised the t-shirt she slept in out of the way. She lightly traced her fingertips up and down her abdomen, shivering because her skin was already so sensitive with growing arousal.

She heard Cali's choked groan and wondered if Mike was just touching her, the way Precious was touching herself, with his hands. Or was he using his mouth on her? One of Precious's hands played at the edge of her underwear; she wished it was Cali's. She added the other and wished it was Mike's.

Cali giggled, and then there was the low hum of their voices as they spoke to one another. Precious couldn't make out their words, and she both hated and loved that. Mike moaned, louder than normal. Precious pressed her thighs together, clenched her vaginal muscles, and then released.

Her hand slid into her panties. She was wet. She always was.

Precious knew the minute they switched from foreplay to sex.

They always tried not to wake her, whispering to one another and moaning in hushed tones that teased and infuriated her. But eventually, whatever leash they had on their voices would snap, and it was usually when Mike was finally inside Cali. Precious didn't know how she knew that's what it was, but she did; she could feel it deep in her bones. As Mike fucked Cali, her moans and Mike's pants incrementally became loud, and then louder, because waking Precious was no longer their concern.

Or maybe it was. She often hoped that waking her was one of those soft things they whispered to each other during foreplay. But that was indulgent and foolish.

Besides, she wasn't sleeping. How could she have slept when listening to them was the best part of every morning?

Sometimes, they were so loud and reckless, Precious could bury her fingers so deep inside and fuck herself, to the sound of Mike's body slapping into Cali's. Today was one of those days, and she was beyond grateful as she kicked her covers to the bottom of her mattress. She needed this orgasm.

Precious's hands were soaked with her own arousal. She strummed her clit with one hand and sawed her fingers in and out of herself with the other. And all the while, she tried to conjure a mental image of what Mike and Cali were doing on the other side of the room to match their grunts and groans and the sound of skin against skin.

She was close. Her body was shaking, her legs bent, with her knees spread wide. She could hear her own wetness and she loved it. The only thing that could have made this moment better was if Cali and Mike could have heard it, too.

As her orgasm neared, she pulled one of her pillows over her face and pressed it close. She started moving her thumb in hard circles against her clit and stroked her fingers in and out of herself with increasing speed. When Cali screamed out her orgasm, the muscles in Precious's legs tensed and the sound of her own climax joined her, muffled by her pillow. Mike let out a sharp, hoarse yell.

All too soon, their apartment was quiet again.

The sun was coming up.

Precious's room was now a soft gray.

Mike and Cali were talking again, and she still couldn't hear what they said. Suddenly, the wall between their bedrooms felt thicker, and her isolation in her own small room that much more complete. She listened to the muffled sounds of their voices as she licked her orgasm from her fingers. She pulled her covers back over her body and turned on her side toward the wall.

This had become such a part of Precious's daily routine that she'd adjusted her alarm clock to make sure she never missed a morning with Mike and Cali, even though it wasn't quite a morning *with* them. It was pathetic, she knew, but she couldn't help herself. She didn't know how to stop wanting them as desperately as she did, but she didn't know how to ask them if there was any chance for... something more, either.

She considered herself smart and pretty good at making new friends, but this situation wasn't one she had any idea how to navigate. Was there a way to get your roommates to invite you into a threesome? Was a threesome what she wanted? She didn't have any answers for her questions, even after months of trying to work through them. Even this post-orgasmic confusion had become all too familiar.

Eventually, the sound of Mike and Cali's voices drifted off to quiet, and all too soon, Precious fell back to sleep, sexually sated but alone.

# 2

The apartment was quiet.

Cali hated the quiet.

She'd fallen back to sleep, only vaguely registering the shuffle of Mike crawling from the bed, but when she woke up, he was gone. She shivered, even though she was wrapped in their warm blankets. They still smelled like his cologne, her lotion, and sex, which made her feel comforted and sad at the same time. Dr. Toussaint had been helping Cali become comfortable with the rush of conflicting emotions instead of focusing only on the negative, but she was a work in progress, and she muttered that to herself as she crawled out of bed and threw one of Mike's old t-shirts over her head.

She tiptoed past Precious's closed door and sighed. She was either still asleep because they hadn't woken her up while having sex, or she was working and didn't want to be disturbed. Either option made Cali sad. She made her way into the kitchen, frowning to herself.

Mike had left a note on the fridge that he had gone to the gym. She ran her fingers across the small slip of paper as if it was his body and felt her frown deepen.

Cali hated being alone.

She closed her eyes and took a few deep breaths. She tried to remind herself that Mike would be back. That Precious was just in her bedroom. That alone wasn't the end of the world. This was a familiar check-in that Dr. Toussaint often practiced with her, teaching her how to work through the lies her brain often told her; someone else's voice masquerading as her own thoughts. It didn't often work, and this morning was one of those failures. Maybe because she was tired, hungry, and a little dehydrated. Or maybe it was because she'd had to postpone her weekly therapy session when a shoot ran longer than expected. She wasn't sure, but she could feel her heart beating faster than normal, a sure sign of her impending panic, but she couldn't remember any of Dr. Toussaint's strategies for heading off a spiral, which only threatened to send her spinning faster. This was why she hated being alone.

But then she heard the creak of Precious's bedroom door opening.

She swiped at the single tear falling down her cheek and called out, her voice almost normal, "Hey."

The groggy croak of Precious's reply made Cali smile. "Morning."

"You want breakfast?" Cali turned toward the living room at the center of their apartment just in time to see Precious walk through the hallway toward the bathroom.

Precious turned her head and Cali's smile widened; she was adorable first thing in the morning. "Eggs," she croaked, and then walked into the bathroom.

Cali nodded and then called out, "Sure thing. Coming up."

Mike was the chef of the house. He could make almost anything, and if he couldn't, he always enjoyed learning how to master a new recipe for Cali and Precious to enjoy.

Precious was the cook. She could make most things, and made them well enough to satisfy her own hunger. She also realized Cali's insecurities, in a way Mike never had, about what she could and couldn't eat regularly, and she enjoyed figuring out quick and fast things to eat that wouldn't trigger Cali's anxieties about her body any more than normal.

But Cali could make eggs. That's it.

It was a cute inside roommate joke. Mike was the chef, Precious was the cook and Cali could make eggs. Technically, she also made some damn good lemon bar edibles, but that was their inside *inside* roommate joke, for their ears and mouths only.

While Precious was in the bathroom, Cali ran back

to her bedroom to grab her phone, looking for music to blast through the Bluetooth speaker in the kitchen. Why hadn't she thought about that before? When she'd navigated to her favorite album of the moment, something melancholy with heavy bass, she set her phone down and began pulling ingredients from the fridge and cupboards. She was whisking the eggs, almond milk and seasonings together when Precious emerged from the bathroom.

Her eyes were big and round behind the lenses of her glasses. Her hair was pulled up in a ponytail, and Cali tried to ignore the way the swish of Precious's hair when she walked always made her want to reach out and twist the end of that ponytail around her finger; how much she always wanted to touch her. It was too early in the morning for that.

"This song again," Precious said with a playful roll of her eyes.

"I like this album," Cali whined.

"You must. You've been playing it nonstop for a week." Precious moved to the speaker and turned down the volume from "you'll be hard of hearing by forty" to "yay, I don't have to yell across the room," as Mike liked to categorize her preferred volume choices.

Cali normally hated to be teased and used to bristle when he said this, no matter how warm his smile. Her pride was brittle and deadly sharp in places after years of feeling like the butt of everyone's jokes. But that was one more way that Precious had seemed to dull those pinpricks, and helped her follow Dr. Toussaint's advice and focus on the good: Mike's warm smile, amplified by Precious's matching grin. Cali also loved the way Precious always seemed to touch her when they talked, as if she knew how much Cali craved physical contact. Mike had been like that once, but the harder it became to communicate with Cali about the small things in their relationship they needed to work on, the more he pulled back. Until Precious.

She moved behind Cali to pull the fridge open and their butts bumped. Precious giggled and Cali smiled.

"You can put on something else if you want," she said timidly over her shoulder to Precious.

Precious shut the fridge and turned back around. She placed a carton of juice on the kitchen island and wrapped her arms around Cali's waist, resting her adorable chin on Cali's bare shoulder.

Cali pursed her lips shut and breathed deeply through her nose. She tried to regulate her breathing and slow the frantic beating of her heart, not wanting to let on how much she loved the way Precious's body felt pressed tight against hers.

"I won't change it," Precious said into the crook of Cali's neck. She smelled minty, and Cali swallowed a groan. She couldn't stop the shiver at Precious's breath on her skin, however, and she wondered if Precious noticed.

"I love how you love an album to death," Precious

giggled. "You go ahead and listen to this until the wheels fall off."

"And based on prior experience, that'll be in about two more days." Precious jumped at the sound of Mike's voice.

They both turned to the front door to see him. He had a huge smile on his face as he turned the locks.

"Jesus, Mike, you scared me. How do you move so quietly?" Precious took one arm from Cali's waist to clutch her chest.

Cali tried not to frown at the loss.

"Well, first of all, I'm magic," he said, tossing his keys into the bowl by their front door and toeing off his shoes, before stalking toward them. When he was close, he reached out to put an arm around Precious's shoulders. "And second of all, Cali has the music turned up so high I could have tap danced in here."

"Technically, I just turned it down," Precious offered helpfully.

Cali inhaled the pleasant musk of Mike's sweat and relaxed. It made her remember how he'd felt on top of her this morning, but that also made the intimacy of Precious's arm around her waist that much more arousing.

She lifted her eyes to Mike's and knew instantly that he'd recognized the lust in her eyes.

"Well, what have we here?" he asked, mischief in his eyes.

Cali's eyes widened in shock and she sucked her bottom lip into her mouth.

Precious giggled, oblivious. "Cali's making her specialty." Precious moved to clutch Cali closer just as Mike leaned down to kiss her cheek. Cali forgot about the eggs she was overbeating with both of their bodies bracketing hers; like all of her fantasies. And she was reminded, at that moment, that she was naked underneath Mike's shirt, at the same time she realized that she was very wet.

"Is there enough for me? Or is this just for you two ladies?" Mike asked, watching her like a hungry hawk.

Precious moved away from them and mercifully, Mike replaced her arms around Cali's waist.

She walked around the island, opened a cabinet and snatched a glass from the middle shelf. "It's just eggs," Precious said, shaking her head.

Cali cleared her throat. "There's enough for all of us." Her face felt hot. Her entire body was on fire.

Mike laughed and nodded toward Precious, "Can you pour me a glass?"

"Yep. You want some too?" she asked Cali.

Cali smiled and nodded, but couldn't speak.

When Precious turned away, Mike leaned down to whisper, "Behave," in her ear at the same time as he lifted the back of her shirt. Cali shook her head quickly, begging him not to touch her. She wouldn't be able to temper her response right now; she was too excited.

Mike smiled and let the hem of her shirt fall. "You gonna throw those eggs in a pan or are we on a raw diet again?" he asked, loud enough for Precious to hear. His joke broke the tension between them, and Cali let out a reedy laugh that joined with Precious's tinkling giggles.

Cali turned toward the stove and busied herself with cooking their eggs. She snuck peeks over her shoulder, every now and then, at Mike and Precious sitting at the island, drinking juice and talking basketball scores, stuff Cali didn't know or care about. When she dished out the eggs onto their plates, Mike pulled her into his lap and they changed the topic of conversation to their favorite tv show about zombie space aliens. They watched it religiously each week; one of so many things they did together as roommates and friends.

This wasn't the roommate situation Cali and Mike had been expecting when they'd put that ad on Craigslist. They'd actually had very few expectations besides one third of the rent. In all the ways Cali could imagine, living with Precious was everything she'd ever dreamed and more. Sitting down to breakfast together was a sacred thing to Cali; it represented the kind of warm comfort of home she'd prayed for as a little girl but never experienced, and to have that with Mike *and Precious* sometimes made her want to cry. She and Dr. Toussaint had been working through the idea that sometimes tears were a good thing.

But then there was the other part. The part where Mike's hands rested on her legs, just barely under the hem of her shirt; his calloused hand caressing her thigh while they talked to Precious about where to get dinner for their roommate date tomorrow. Cali knew his hand would move higher eventually, and she'd part her legs to let him. They were waiting for the right opportunity, for Precious to run to the bathroom to get ready for work or — in Cali's fantasies — for their roommate to ask Mike to fingerfuck her while they enjoyed their breakfast together.

Almost as soon as Precious was done with her eggs, the alarm on her phone started to blare and she ran to her bedroom to shut it off. She was barely out of the kitchen before Mike's hand was between Cali's legs, stroking her bare pussy teasingly.

Cali moaned and ground her ass into his crotch, begging him with her body to use a firmer touch.

"You're wet. Typical." He didn't put his fingers inside of her, just let them glide up and down her slit.

"You're hard. Typical," she said in a husky purr.

"You're lucky I'm not inside of you right now after coming home to you two all over each other."

"She was just hugging me. You know how she is in the morning."

"And I know how you are in the morning," he whispered into her ear, just slipping his index finger inside of her.

She smiled and moaned in relief. She loved when

he teased her, especially when Precious was elsewhere in the apartment, or on the other side of their bedroom wall; whenever Precious was around.

"More," she breathed airily.

They could hear Precious coming back down the hall. Mike pulled his hand from between Cali's legs, and she watched him lick her essence from his fingers. She gulped loudly as Precious entered her peripheral vision.

"Asshole," Precious muttered as she tapped at her phone.

"Your brother?" Cali asked, leaning back onto Mike's chest, even more turned on, but also much calmer now that the three of them were together.

Precious frowned. "Nope. The chair of my department. Or I guess, now the former chair." Precious waved her phone in the air and waved it around. "The asshole sent an email resigning his position so he can, and I fucking quote," she yelled, reading from her phone, "'fight these *baseless* accusations against me.' Can you believe this shit? He cheats on his wife, strings my friend along for a year and then dumps her when he realizes he could lose his tenure. And now he's slandering her in our inboxes. What the fuck?"

Cali was not the nurturing type. But in the same way that Precious allowed her to put aside her armor and be teased, she also inspired protective instincts Cali hadn't even known she possessed. She slid from Mike's lap, crossed the kitchen and reached out to embrace her roommate. Precious clutched her around the middle, and then giggled when Mike pressed himself against her back. They stood like that, Precious sandwiched between Cali and Mike, all their bodies locked tight to one another.

Cali's grandmother had always said she was a greedy, spoiled child. And in this moment, her front pressed to Precious's front, Mike's scent enveloping them as she murmured soothing words to Precious, it was hard not to wonder if maybe she hadn't been right. And maybe because she felt so safe, she thought about something Dr. Toussaint had suggested once: maybe the fact that she loved to love didn't have to be a bad thing. Her grandmother had always told her that loving love was a bad thing to suggest that she didn't deserve love, but maybe she'd been wrong. Maybe Cali could want more and more love from the people who loved her and be happy with that, instead of letting a woman who didn't love her — and was long dead anyway — define how she saw herself.

"Thank you," Precious whispered, her breath tickling Cali's jaw.

"Anytime," she responded, and locked eyes with Mike. "We'll always be here for you."

He smiled softly back at her and tightened his arms around them both.

# 3

Precious's commute to school was twenty minutes, door-to-door, but today she wished it was longer. She was dreading walking into the teaching assistant offices in her department, not so much for herself, but for Laura. Precious knew her friend would be sitting proudly at her desk pretending not to hear the other grad students whispering behind her back; Precious was already angry on Laura's behalf, and that anger would take away from her concentration.

She was already struggling to get her brain to settle today. It seemed as if the moment she left the house — after another long, fortifying, and oddly intimate group hug with Cali and Mike — her anxiety had spiked. The walk to the train station didn't calm her as it normally did, and she stood on the platform stressed and fidgety.

When she jogged up the stairs from the subway station, her phone vibrated with a new text message.

Drinks. Tonight. Lots.

Precious could feel Laura's stress in those three words. She was normally chatty and sent blocks of text, but not today. Precious responded quickly and affirmatively. She forced herself to smile, as if it would make her message seem happier, and would in turn lift Laura's mood.

She crossed the street onto campus with a heavy sigh. She used to love this place, but ever since Laura and Dr. Friedlander's relationship had been exposed, the university had been transformed from the space where she felt most safe to the place she couldn't wait to run away from.

Precious pushed into Brown Hall and waved at the department secretary, Mrs. Johnson. She pushed the elevator button and rode up to the fifth floor, or the Grad Hovel, as the undergrads called the TA offices. The floor was separated into two large rooms: one bare space with basic tables and chairs that almost passed for desks for master's students; and a larger, better decorated room, with cubicles, posters on the wall, an ancient copy machine and a microwave for the doctoral students. Precious wished she could hang out with the MA students, but she headed to the doctoral office where she knew Laura would be suffering in silence.

Just before Precious opened the office door, her phone beeped with another text message.

She smiled down at the picture Mike had sent to their roommate group chat. It was a selfie. Cali was sitting on Mike's lap, her tongue out as if about to lick Mike's cheek, and Mike's eyes were shut with laughter. As she was staring at the picture, Cali sent a text:

Good luck, babes. Let us know if we need to beat anyone up for you! xx

It was such a small thing, but their picture reminded Precious that her life didn't revolve around the university anymore; this place wasn't her entire life. And even though she wanted to be there for Laura, when it all got to be too much, Precious could go home, fall onto the couch, lay her head in Cali's lap and drift to sleep while Mike massaged her feet and calves. It made her feel stronger and calmer than she'd felt during her commute.

Precious looked through the half window into the doctoral student office and spotted Laura's red, angry face. She took another deep breath, reached out to turn the knob and thought of Cali and Mike.

---

"I can't believe him! Can you believe this shit?"

Laura's voice filtered through the haze clouding Precious's brain from two glasses of wine, a shot of Jack, and boredom. Precious didn't have any idea what exactly Laura was talking about, but she shook her head and tried to contort her face into a look that was incredulous and a little bit annoyed, with a touch of empathy. She wasn't sure what she actually looked like, but Laura kept talking, so Precious assumed it worked.

"I held him while he *cried* about giving up his 'art' for her," Laura spat.

Precious cringed at the venom in her voice. More than once since they'd power walked to Little Brother's, their favorite campus dive bar, Precious opened her mouth to point out that maybe Laura's ire was misplaced on Dr. Friedlander's wife, a woman neither of them knew, but each time, Laura barreled through her attempts to talk.

"He told me," she hiccupped. "He told me that I was the love of his life. Can. You. Believe. That?" Laura paused, waiting for an answer.

Precious knew what Laura expected her to say. No. No, she couldn't believe that their fifty-year-old professor who hadn't published so much as a book review in almost five years and was swiftly going bald had lied to his gorgeous, twenty-three-year-old grad student about his marriage being over. Of course, she couldn't believe that he'd said he was in love with

Laura just to fuck her. She knew what Laura wanted to hear, but she couldn't say it.

Maybe it was the booze. Maybe it was a day spent frying her brain grading student essays. Or maybe it was the fact that Cali had sent her two texts seeing if Precious was okay in the past half hour, while Laura hadn't bothered to ask how she was doing in the past six months. Either way, when she opened her mouth, she shocked Laura and herself.

"Of course, I can."

Laura's red face was splotchy. Precious couldn't tell if it was from anger or the alcohol.

"What?" Laura hissed.

Precious hadn't meant to say that, but she decided to answer Laura's question head on.

"He's old and washed up. Of course, I can believe he lied to have sex with you. Didn't you even consider that possibility?"

It felt wonderful and terrible to say those words. It was one of the thousand things she'd been thinking ever since Laura had bailed on living with her. She'd wanted to say these words when Laura went MIA while Precious frantically tried to find a roommate. She'd wanted to say them when Laura had popped up, after hearing from Mrs. Jones that Precious was renting a room near campus, as if nothing had ever happened. But Precious hated confrontation, and had buried all the anger she felt toward her friend instead. And then Dr. Friedlander had dumped Laura, and

Precious had been forced to bury all those emotions even deeper inside herself to be a better friend to Laura than Laura had been to her. But she couldn't hold her tongue anymore.

"Of course, I didn't. He was so romantic. I thought..." Laura spluttered before giving up on whatever she was going to say, and Precious was happy about that. Nothing Laura could have said would have convinced Precious that she was that naïve.

"I know," Precious said, reaching out to grab Laura's hand. "This fucking sucks. He never deserved you."

There was a beat of silence between them, broken by a group playing pool on the other side of the bar.

Precious watched the first tear fall down Laura's face, charting a path through her mascara, and it made her heart ache. Laura always took such care with her makeup, and Precious counted this public ruination of her work as yet one more thing Dr. Friedlander didn't deserve.

"It's okay, sweetheart. Let's get you home," she whispered.

Laura nodded and swiped at her face. They stood, grabbed their bags and coats and headed toward the door.

Out on the street, Precious was shocked to find that it was still light out. The bar had been dark and hazy, but outside the sky was the light gray of early evening. The street was still crowded with cars and buses, and there were still students littering the campus lawn across the street.

Precious reached out to steer Laura toward the graduate student dorms at the end of the block. In the shabby dorm lobby, Laura veered to the left to check her mail and Precious walked to the elevator. She pressed the call button and slipped her phone from her pocket. She angled her body away from the mailboxes and typed a quick message to Cali and Mike.

Dropping L off. Home in 20.

Cali's response was immediate.

Drinks? Action movie?

Mike replied before Precious could.

I'll put some wine in the freezer.

Precious smiled immediately as she typed her reply.

Yes, please to alladis! Best roommates!

"Who are you texting?"

Precious jumped at the sound of Laura's voice. Her smile dimmed when she saw the scrutiny in Laura's gaze.

"Roommates," Precious said simply, slipping her phone into her back pocket.

The elevator dinged and the doors opened. They rode up to Laura's floor in silence. When they reached her door, Laura turned to Precious.

"Come in?" Laura's voice was small; broken. Precious wanted to say yes, but she also didn't. Maybe eight months ago, she would have prioritized Laura's needs over her own, but she felt like an entirely different person today.

"Sorry, I told Cali and Mike I'd be home in a bit."

Precious watched the hurt distort Laura's features and then morph quickly to anger.

"What's going on with you and them?"

Precious froze. She wasn't expecting that. Well, that wasn't actually true. For months, she'd been worried someone would ask this exact question. She just hadn't expected it would be Laura, because Laura hadn't been that interested in Precious's life for a while.

"What do you mean?" she responded pathetically.

"I mean, every time I ask you to get together, you tell me you're hanging out with your roommates. They're just..."

Precious held her breath wondering at, and dreading, the end of that sentence.

"They're just your roommates, P. They're, like, way out of your friend league."

Precious could feel her skin heating. "What the fuck does that mean?"

Laura knew she'd fucked up. Precious watched the realization of what she'd said fight through the drunken haze.

"I didn't mean it in a bad way. I just... well, I just meant they're *models*."

Precious could feel her heart pounding in her chest. Laura said "models" with equal parts disdain and reverence.

"They're not like us," Laura added, as if that clarified anything.

Precious's hand moved to her back pocket, clutching at her phone as if it could connect her to Cali and Mike.

There were so many things she wanted to say to Laura, but she didn't. They were both tipsy and stressed, and Precious wasn't sure she could defend her relationship with her roommates without betraying her feelings for them. And since she wasn't certain what those feelings meant and didn't want to explore them in the dim dormitory hallway, she swallowed her emotions.

"You don't know shit about them," Precious said meekly, before turning to run back to the elevator. Laura yelled after her, but Precious refused to turn back. She fidgeted the entire elevator ride back to the lobby, blood rushing in her ears.

As she walked quickly to the subway station, she

pulled her phone from her pocket and opened her roommate chat again. When she saw the new messages from Cali and Mike, her heartbeat began to slow and her breathing returned to normal.

Let's get drunk and watch some muscly men blow some shit up!

Mike texted.

Precious could practically see Cali's eyes roll in her head. She was probably sitting next to him on the couch, filing her nails.

Calm down, Rambo.
Hurry home for roommate cuddles!

Precious scrolled to the top of their texts. Eight months of messages that started off formal and polite became warmer, friendlier, and sometimes bordered on flirty and inappropriate. She kept her eyes on their words and the occasional selfie as she navigated the familiar route home.

Not for the first time, she wondered why she ever left when she had Mike and Cali at home.

---

Mike's day had gone immediately to shit. He'd almost immediately followed Precious from their apartment, heading to a fitness shoot with one of his regular clients, a small athletic brand that had given him his big break. In the middle of the shoot, his phone rang. When he had time to check his messages, he heard his agent's voice, tight with tension, telling him to call her as soon as he left the studio.

His former agent.

It wasn't about him. Sarah had told him that a million times. She'd just gotten a better position at another agency, and since Mike's contract was with the Kenneth Waters Agency and not her directly, this was the end of their professional partnership. "At least for now," she'd promised, trying to sound optimistic. He didn't feel optimistic, though. As soon as he'd hung up the phone, the panic set in.

He'd spent three years as one of his agency's top earning commercial models, but in the aftermath of that phone call, his brain kept running through the lowlights of his first six months in New York.

Every agency he went to passed on him — most times without even looking up from his headshots — and he went to hundreds of open castings without booking a single job.

He was too tall.

Too short.

Too Asian.

Too skinny.

Too fat.

Those were the absolute worst months of his life.

Every other day, he'd given serious consideration to quitting modeling and applying to law school like his parents wanted. But then he'd met Sarah at an open call. She'd seen something in him that he'd almost been convinced didn't exist. She'd fought to sign him, and he'd booked his first campaign in less than a month. He couldn't imagine doing this without her, but he had to.

As he was wallowing, he got an urgent email from his agency and instead of heading home, he hopped on a train to Midtown where he'd been quickly ushered into a conference room. He'd then had to pretend that he was okay — that everything was fine — while some of the other junior agents tried to reassure him that nothing had to change at Sarah's departure. He didn't believe them, because he hardly recognized them. They'd looked over and through him for years, never seeing what Sarah saw in the Asian kid from Ohio who'd walked through the doors ten pounds "overweight."

He knew that everything would change. He just didn't know how, and that unknown haunted him as he met with a couple of agents seriously interested in taking him on. It followed him back downtown to his gym, and weighed heavy on his shoulders through his workout. And it trailed behind him all the way to his apartment like a depressing puppy.

The only thing that stopped him from breaking down in tears on the subway was the thought of home.

He kept imagining himself unlocking his front door and hearing Cali's music blaring at ear-splitting levels. He wanted to sit at the kitchen island and watch her make lemon bars for their roommate date tomorrow. And he wanted to forget the mess of this day while Precious's hands kneaded the knots of tension from his shoulders. He just wanted to go home and feel safe.

But when he actually arrived home, it wasn't quite as warm as he'd hoped. Cali was watering her succulents and listening to some European singer-songwriter emo shit that made Mike want to jump out from a window or curl up into a ball. She was in a bad mood; sad, and that made his own mood darken. He thought to ask her to play something less depressing, but when their eyes met, hers were watery and red. She'd been crying. He wanted to go to her and hug her. He wanted to ask what was wrong and tell her that everything would be okay, but he thought she would hate that and he didn't want to make her feel worse. So, he smiled, weakly, and yelled that he was going to take a shower, hoping they would both feel better once he was done.

But half an hour later, he stepped out of the shower and still felt as terrible as he had most of the day. He could hear Cali's downer music from the Bluetooth speaker in the kitchen. He wrapped his towel around his waist in the steamy bathroom and decided to give Cali more alone time. Mike swiped at the fogged mirror and began to smear a clay face mask on his cheeks when Precious texted that she'd be home in twenty minutes.

He didn't know how she did it, but the minute Mike saw Precious's message, his heart began to race and that heavy weight of his own fears finally started to lift.

He sprayed cologne on his bare chest and pulled open the bathroom door, feeling reenergized. He rushed down the hallway to his and Cali's bedroom and found her there already, rifling through their closet. She pulled his favorite gray Cleveland Cavaliers shirt from a hanger and threw it on the bed with his favorite gray sweats. She turned to him and her gaze immediately went to his bare chest and down his stomach. Her eyes stopped on the edge of the towel and she licked her lips.

Mike felt himself harden under her gaze.

"Wear these," she said in a husky voice. "I'm going to shower."

"You could have showered with me," he said, his own voice deeper than normal.

"You didn't ask me to," she whispered. Mike wasn't certain if she sounded hurt or if that was his mind playing tricks on him.

Cali walked to him and lifted on her toes to press her lips lightly against his. When she pulled away, there was a little smear of his face mask on her nose. She was adorable. He loved her.

He wondered if she would have said yes if he'd

asked her to shower with him; if it could have been that easy to just ask her for what he needed; to be with her; closer to her.

Always.

She pushed past him and was halfway down the hall before the words began to form on his lips. He frowned at yet another missed opportunity between them.

---

Cali was trying to calm herself. She wasn't normally the kind of person who fidgeted because she'd always had to be in terrifying control of herself, but this day had taxed her self-control and seeing Mike walk through their front door with a sadness in his eyes he probably thought she didn't notice only made her feel worse. Cali had wanted to rush to him and wrap her entire body around his, but she didn't, because wanting to do a thing was always easier than doing that thing. Her entire relationship with Mike had exposed how little she knew how to be in a relationship, even with someone she loved desperately. So, she'd watched him run away, and her own sadness had only grown.

Today had been a day. That's how Precious would have described it. Nothing negative had happened, not really. Her first stop of the day was a fitting for an upcoming fashion showcase, then she'd gone to an audition, and finally, a high fashion shoot that her agent was certain would catapult her to supermodel status. Cali loved days like this, when she could jump from one work thing to another and another with no time for the melancholy she never quite managed to escape overtaking her.

But once her day was done and she was in her hired car heading home, the sadness started to set in. She'd tapped at her phone screen, navigating between her text messages and social media, searching for a lifeline. Mike hadn't texted or called. Neither had Precious.

Cali tried to remind herself that Precious was at school and Mike was at a shoot or the gym; they had lives that didn't revolve around her, but without other distractions the hurt of their silence felt like a fog descending on her. By the time she walked into their building's elevator, tears had begun to run down the thick, editorial makeup on her face. It was irrational, she knew that, but she couldn't stop her brain.

She ran straight from their front door into the bathroom. She wiped off the layers of makeup, cleaned her face and put on a sheet mask, letting her skincare routine calm her. She started watering her plants, which never failed to center her, primarily because she needed to do something with her hands.

She'd wanted to be her regular self when Mike or Precious walked through the door, but she wasn't. But neither were they, and realizing that made Cali feel closer to them. Somehow, they'd all had bad days and had scurried home to safety.

Cali hugged Precious as soon as she walked through the door, finding it easier to go to her than Mike, even if she didn't understand why. Precious sagged into Cali's embrace, a soft sob escaping her lips, just as Mike walked into the living room, with a worried look on his face.

Cali steered Precious to the bathroom.

For someone who loved noise, she didn't try to talk to Precious. Sometimes in her therapy sessions, Dr. Toussaint tried to dissect Cali's fear of silence, while Cali tried to figure out why she could tolerate it only with them, Mike *and* Precious.

They all crowded into the bathroom. Mike pulled Precious from Cali's hold and pressed her against his body while Cali turned on the shower for her. Cali couldn't remember how skincare routines had become a group activity, but it had, and they'd become comfortable — if not excited — huddling in their bathroom while they brushed their teeth, swapped face masks and serums, and one time, they'd even shaved Mike's head when he lost a bet.

But this time was different, and if they were being honest with themselves, they could all admit that this moment had been coming for a while.

Precious didn't register when the mood changed, maybe because it felt natural, comfortable, and more than anything, inevitable.

Mike held her against his hard chest while Cali ran her hands over Precious's shoulders and down her arms. She pressed her body against Precious's back and whispered into her ear, "Can I undress you?"

Normally, Precious would have rationalized all of this to herself, too afraid to hope that Cali meant the words in the way Precious wanted. She would have told herself this was just regular roommate behavior. Given enough time and denial, Precious would have been able to convince herself that all of the touching and heated looks and sometimes the subtle presence of Mike's erection were figures of her overheated imagination and not real at all, but she didn't have the energy for that level of self-delusion tonight.

She shivered as Cali's fingertips moved her clothing aside. Everywhere she touched left a trail of fire along Precious's skin. Her breath made Precious's sex clench, and the feeling of Cali's small breasts pressing into her back made her want to scream in ecstasy.

"Yes," Precious breathed into Mike's t-shirt. "Please," she moaned.

Cali pulled Precious's body away from Mike's, and Precious lifted her eyes to see that his warm brown eyes were dark with desire. He watched Cali's hands start to caress Precious again, beginning at her shoulders, moving down her arms. Her fingers jumped to Precious's stomach, ran up her abdomen, and then over the curve of her breasts.

Precious and Cali moaned together at that first touch they'd both been wanting for so long.

Cali's hands traveled the path again, but when they reached her stomach this time, her fingers hooked under the hem of Precious's shirt and lifted the fabric to bare her skin. Cali's fingers skimmed lightly along Precious's stomach and up her rib cage.

Precious's brain overloaded and then shut off completely when Mike's fingers followed in Cali's wake.

Cali pulled the shirt over Precious's head, and one of Mike's hands skimmed along Precious's neck and back down to her cleavage while the other twisted and pinched her nipple through her bra.

Precious groaned.

Cali moved her hands down Precious's arms. She leaned forward to press her lips to Precious's ear. She hooked her fingers under Precious's bra straps and Mike helped her move them down her arms.

Precious moved backwards slightly to press her body more firmly into Cali's, even as she reached forward to wrap her arms around Mike's waist to pull him closer, and he stepped forward immediately. There was something so freeing to finally know that she hadn't been alone in her need; that Cali and Mike had been right there with her.

She turned to Cali and saw that her eyelids were drooping, her lips parted, her face flushed. She saw there a cousin of the look on Mike's face, and probably her own: lust. So much lust. Eight months of pent-up lust.

She moved to unclasp her bra.

Precious watched as Cali's eyes followed the movement, widening at the sight of Precious's naked breasts, and she licked her lips. Cali reached out to lightly brush the pads of her fingers across Precious's left nipple. The sound Precious made was somewhere between a gasp and a scream, and she jumped at the sound of Mike's groaning response.

"Calm down," Cali said, although Precious wasn't sure if the words were meant for her, or Mike, or Cali herself. Cali's voice was oddly calm, even though Precious thought her eyes had gone wild with desire. She loved the contrast.

Precious turned to look over her shoulder and moaned at the sight of Mike biting his bottom lip in concentration. She let her gaze scan down his body and sighed at his large hand wrapped tight around his erection through his sweatpants. She'd spent so many nights trying to map the contours of his dick through those exact sweats, and finally getting a better image of it now felt like a triumph and made her arousal spike.

And then Cali pressed her body to Precious's front. Precious breathed a soft moan as Cali kissed her tenderly on the jaw. "Take a shower. Relax." Cali's words ghosted along Precious's skin. Mike groaned again. "We're not going anywhere. I promise," she said, and Precious knew those words were as much for Mike as for her.

Precious wasn't a greedy woman. In fact, most people would likely go on and on about how selfless she was, and she didn't usually mind that, but in this moment, with every one of her fantasies at her feet, she didn't want to be selfless. She wanted Cali and Mike; she wanted everything.

She turned back to Cali. "Kiss me." It was a demand when Precious never demanded anything.

Cali smiled instantly and leaned forward, torturously slow. It was just a soft press of lips until Mike leaned down, rubbing his cheek along Precious's.

"More," he whispered against their mouths.

And then their lips were moving, and Cali's tongue was tentatively encroaching into Precious's mouth. But Mike was right, Precious wanted more. She thrust her tongue into Cali's mouth and felt triumphant when Cali moaned and gripped Precious's slender hips in response.

Mike's hands ghosted up and down their sides and backs, making their kiss even more intense.

Cali pulled back abruptly, gasping, but Precious only got a glimpse of her before Mike's hand nudged Precious's jaw toward his face. And then he was kissing her, his tongue probing and urgent. Precious moaned into his mouth, certain that she'd never felt so turned on or safe than in this moment.

Cali kissed Precious's jaw again, but this time her tongue darted out to taste her.

Precious lost track of time as she moved back and forth between Mike and Cali's mouths, never getting her fill. Their hands roamed over her breasts and pinched her nipples. Their fingernails scraped her skin, making her shiver between them. When they kissed each other, Precious took the chance to explore their bodies, nibbling Cali's ear lobe, pressing her butt back against Mike's dick. But they always turned back to Precious, wanting her and needing her just as much as she wanted and needed them.

It was a heady feeling. It was everything she'd been dreaming about for months, but far too soon for Precious's liking, Cali clucked her tongue and hummed against Precious's pulse.

"Shower," she said, and pulled away. Precious felt her absence immediately.

It took a while for Mike to pull his mouth away and move his hard penis from pressing into the small of her back. His fingertips clutched at her hips one more time before letting go.

Without their bodies bracketing her and their hands holding her close, Precious felt exposed, even though she was only half-naked. She also felt alone, and she hated it. She hadn't felt alone in eight months, not really, just kissing the edge of Cali and Mike's relationship and wanting them. But now that she'd had a literal taste of what it felt like to be in between them, she wanted more, and without them kissing and touching her, she felt incomplete in a way she'd never experienced before.

"Take a shower, Precious," Cali whispered again, as she and Mike walked out of the bathroom. "We'll be here when you're done."

# 4

Mike felt the way he normally did after an intense workout; his heart was pounding, his skin was warm and his muscles were clenching all over his body. The big, heavy difference was the fact that his dick was so hard it was aching between his legs and tenting his sweatpants. It was hard for him to focus on anything besides the sound of the shower behind the closed bathroom door, the mental image of Precious's half-naked body in the steamy bathroom, and the sway of Cali's ass as she walked on shaky legs into the living room.

He reached out to Cali in desperation, digging his fingers into her hips to pull her back to him.

Her breathy gasp turned to a moan as he pressed his erection into the small of her back. They walked together into the living room and trapped her between his body and the back of the couch. When he pressed his mouth to her ear, he had to take a few deep breaths to calm himself enough to speak.

"Do you want to do this?" he asked, afraid she might say no, and of what this might do to their relationship if she didn't.

"Do you?"

She always did that. Answered a question with a question, as if she was afraid he might swat whatever she said aside; as if he didn't care what she thought. He knew it was a pretty good sign that someone in her past had dismissed her frequently enough that she expected it, but he could never bring himself to ask her who, or get her to understand that he would never do that to her.

"I want you. I've always wanted to make you happy. Will this make you happy?" It was the wrong thing to say, he felt that as soon as he stopped speaking; he never could figure out the right words to say.

Cali's body went stiff in his arms.

He exhaled loudly and stepped away from her, wanting to give her room. She turned to face him, but he kept his hands resting lightly on her waist.

He'd begun to steel himself for a fight when she reached up to press a warm, shaky hand against his cheek.

"I thought..." She pressed her lips together and took a deep breath through her nose, and her eyes refused to meet his.

Mike realized that Cali couldn't figure out how to

say what she wanted, and that made him hopeful because Cali was rarely at a loss for words; she always seemed so completely in control of herself, especially when they were arguing. It was yet another of those things he loved about her, even as it frustrated him.

"You thought what, sweetheart?" He turned his head in her hand to place a kiss in her palm, reassuring her that he was a safe place for her; that he wanted to be her safest place.

She chewed on her bottom lip for a few seconds before lifting her head to finally look at him. "I thought we both wanted her," she said in a tiny voice. "But if this is all because I want her, not because you do too, then maybe we should stop."

Mike felt the pressure of tears at the back of his eyes. He didn't think Cali had ever been so straightforward about her emotions; at least not with him. His shock mixed with a long exhale of relief. The past eight months had never been just about Cali wanting Precious. From the moment she'd shown up at their door, he'd lived with a burning desire for Precious and a small knot of fear that Cali *only* wanted her.

There was so much that he and Cali should have said to one another before tonight, and it was probably a bad idea to even consider adding Precious into the mix before they did, but hearing Cali offer to give up being with Precious — something they wanted desperately — for him, made him happier than he could have imagined. Their relationship wasn't perfect, but through it all, he loved her, and he'd been able to love her even more for the past eight months as they'd bonded over their desire for Precious. They'd unexpectedly opened a door to a relationship that he had always worried was just out of their reach.

Mike moved his hands to cup Cali's small, heart-shaped face, and reminded her of their confessions the night they'd met Precious. "I want you both," he whispered.

She smiled a big, toothy grin that made him wonder what she'd looked like as a child. "I want you both, too."

"So, I guess the only question left is, does she want us both," he said, running his thumbs along her cheeks.

"Oh," Precious gasped.

Mike and Cali turned, and their eyes widened in shock when they saw Precious standing in the hallway, naked.

"S-sorry," she stammered. "I thought I made that clear in the bathroom. I want you both *very. much.*" Precious said those last two words slowly and deliberately, with a serious scowl on her face. Mike imagined that she looked at her students like that when she had to relay a very serious or important piece of information.

The words were music to his ears. Or at least, they would have been, if his pulse wasn't drumming out all other sounds and his brain weren't completely preoccupied by the sight of her naked flesh; beautiful dark brown skin, hard nipples, and the sharp pain of Cali's nails digging into his forearm. It was a sensory buffet that he'd only ever been able to dream about and whisper into Cali's ear while he fucked her into their mattress.

"Fuck," he whispered, just before everything about the life they'd lived in their small apartment permanently tilted.

---

Cali had an active imagination. It was one of her favorite things about herself, but also the thing she kept closest to her chest, and on a very tight leash. Her grandmother had always insisted on it.

*No one wants to hear the half-mad ravings of a colored girl.*

But ever since that first night they'd met Precious, her imagination had been running wild, and no matter what she did, she couldn't stop it; she didn't want to stop it. But the vivid erotic images in her head had nothing on what it felt like to finally have those fantasies kissing at her fingertips the way she wanted to kiss at Precious's. Her body was thrumming with a kind of energy she couldn't contain, and it felt amazing. Better than amazing.

Mike took Cali's hand and pulled her toward Precious, but Cali was so eager that she bumped into his back. It made them all chuckle lightly, nervously, excitedly.

He held out his free hand to Precious and tilted his head toward the end of the hallway to his and Cali's bedroom. There was a small smile on Precious's face that exposed the blink-and-you'll-miss-it indentation in her left cheek, which Cali always thought was more like a suggestion of a dimple than the real thing. She'd spent a lot of time staring at that would-be dimple, searing its position on her cheek in her brain. She'd always wanted to kiss it, and it dawned on her, as Mike crossed the threshold into their bedroom, that she finally could.

Cali leaned into Precious's side and pressed her mouth against Precious's adorable face. Precious giggled and leaned into Cali's touch. Cali slowly dipped just the tip of her tongue into that soft indentation, just barely tasting her as Mike let go of their hands.

Cali pulled away from Precious reluctantly and smiled nervously at her. "I've always wanted to do that." Precious's shy smile made Cali's heart warm.

"Can I do something I've always wanted to do?" Precious asked innocently.

Cali smiled, nodding her head quickly, and chewed her bottom lip in anxious anticipation.

Precious reached for the hem of Cali's tank top, slowly at first, her fingers curving tentatively under the fabric and her knuckles brushing against Cali's stomach. She lifted it up Cali's body slowly, the backs of her hands grazing Cali here and there, on her ribs, under her left breast, across her nipples, at her collarbone, until finally it was over her head. She tossed it aside triumphantly.

"That's it?" Cali asked in a hoarse voice that indicated that there was nothing "just" about it.

Precious nodded slowly. "You don't know how many times I've dreamt about undressing both of you," she whispered.

Mike groaned. "We can imagine."

Cali's body shuddered with laughter and lust as the cool air in the bedroom made her nipples harden painfully.

Precious's eyes were wide with excitement as she reached out to brush her fingertips over Cali's left nipple, almost as if she couldn't help herself.

Cali's mouth opened in a gentle squeak of a gasp.

Precious's smile sharpened, and she watched Cali's face as she pinched her nipple, not hard enough to hurt, just a soft pressure.

"She likes it harder," Mike said from his seat on the bed behind them, his own voice deep with a lust that had become as natural as the oxygen circulating in their apartment for months.

Precious pinched Cali's nipple harder and Cali moaned, rubbing her thighs together in frustration.

"Like this?" Precious asked with her eyes trained on Cali, but they all knew the question was for Mike.

"Yes, but turn your hand as you pinch, and she'll be so wet, she'll start dripping down her thighs," Mike replied helpfully.

Cali wanted to tell them that listening to them talk about her like this already had her dripping, but they were on a roll, so she pressed her lips together and let them continue. Her moans became an insistent hum in the back of her throat as she waited for Precious to implement Mike's directions. She didn't disappoint. She pinched Cali's nipple and twisted her wrist with just the right amount of pressure. Cali's head fell back and her mouth burst open on a delicious scream that filled the quiet room. She felt her own moisture beginning to wet her inner thighs.

"Was he right? Are you dripping wet?" Precious asked innocently, and was met immediately with Mike's choked laughter.

Mike and Cali had had a conversation about this once. He'd been adamant that Precious would be as timid in bed as she was around the apartment, nervous and a little shy. But Cali had suspected — hoped — that the opposite would be true. She tried to make a mental note to remind Mike that he'd lost yet another erotic bet, but she couldn't quite hold onto the thought because Precious was leaning down to swipe her tongue over Cali's nipple, soothing the pain from her rough touch.

Over Precious's bent head, Cali made eye contact with Mike. He'd taken off his shirt and sweats while they weren't looking. He was sitting on their bed, lightly stroking his dick and watching them with hungry eyes.

"Was I right?" he asked.

Cali let out a choked moan as Precious sucked the hard bud into her mouth at the same time as she reached over to pinch and tweak her other nipple. She whimpered and made eye contact with Mike again as Precious's mouth moved to her other breast. She licked and sucked and soothed the reverberating sting of pain in that bundle of nerves as well. Cali cradled the back of Precious's head in her hands and smoothed the end of her ponytail with her fingers.

Her voice was barely a whisper of an invitation to Mike. "Why don't you come find out?"

To his credit, he didn't run to her. She could tell he wanted to, but that he was doing his best to rein in his enthusiasm. They all were. They wanted to be gentle with one another. No quick movements. Not yet.

Cali's eyes started to water. She wasn't sure if it was the swell of her emotions or the feeling of Precious's fingers and mouth and tongue playing with her nipples, but it was an overwhelming rush of so many feelings she didn't know how to name, but that filled her with so much joy that she thought she would burst.

When Mike reached them, he trailed a hand up Precious's back, his fingers walking across her spine. Cali felt her shiver and moan against her breast. His other hand cupped Cali's head and she closed her eyes, leaning into his touch. Mike kissed each of her closed lids, and the tears she'd been holding in fell down her face. He kissed a wet trail down her cheek and then pressed his mouth to hers. She tasted the salt on his lips and opened to let his tongue slide against hers.

Precious moved, kissing and licking her way up Cali's collarbone, over the tip of her chin, and then pecked at the seam of Mike and Cali's mouths joined together.

Mike's hand snaked in between Precious and Cali's bodies and slipped into Cali's underwear. She broke the kiss to moan but Precious's mouth covered her, sucking Cali's moan into her own mouth along with her tongue. The kiss was perfect but far too short.

Precious leaned just enough away to breath her words into Cali's panting mouth. "Is she wet?" she asked Mike with a devilish grin on her face.

Cali spread her legs to give Mike more access to her pussy.

He easily slipped his index finger into her sex. Cali shivered. And Precious pressed her body closer to Cali's, trapping Mike's hand more firmly between them and their soft naked skin.

"Dripping," Mike groaned. He shifted his head to whisper in Precious's ear, loud enough for Cali to hear. "She was this wet the night we met you."

Cali bucked against Mike's hand.

He pushed another finger inside her and strummed his thumb lightly across her clit.

"Really?" Precious breathed the question into Cali's mouth.

"Really," Mike said, and then kissed the corner of Precious's mouth so gently that it made Cali's heart ache in the best way.

The smile on Precious's face was innocent, but feral. She moved her hands from Cali's breasts down her sides and around to her back. One hand landed on the small of Cali's back and pulled her closer, while the other slipped into the back of her panties. Precious massaged first one and then the other cheek before moving her fingers between Cali's legs.

Mike grunted when his fingers collided with Precious's. He dropped his head to kiss and suck on her neck. She smiled and huffed out a shocked and pleased breath. Cali had always thought she'd enjoy watching them, but she was wrong; she loved it.

"I want to taste," Precious said, her eyes boring into Cali's. Cali and Mike groaned in response.

Mike pulled his hand from Cali's underwear and brought his fingers to Precious's mouth. She kept her eyes on Cali as she opened her mouth and he slipped his fingers inside. Cali didn't know where to look; on Mike's eyes, half-lidded in lust as he watched Precious; on Precious's eyes, challenging and seductive; or on Precious's lips, sucking Cali's wetness from Mike's fingers with the occasional peek of her pink tongue.

She couldn't decide, so her gaze darted back and forth while Precious's fingers grazed the folds of her sex.

When Precious's fingers pushed inside of her and began to pump into her in earnest, Precious released Mike's fingers from her mouth with a gentle pop. And as if they had rehearsed it, he pushed his hand back into Cali's panties, using his wet digits to rub hard circles on her clit.

Cali's desperate panting became insistent moans. Precious tipped her head back, offering her mouth to Mike, and he took advantage with a big smile on his lips.

Cali watched them, refusing to look away. She didn't want to miss a second of their lips and tongues swirling together, Precious's teeth sometimes nibbling on Mike's lips.

It was the most beautiful sight in Cali's world, she thought to herself, and then she came, hard and wet, on their fingers.

---

For the past eight months, Precious had spent almost every morning fucking herself, with her fingers and every sex toy she could afford, to the sound of Mike and Cali fucking each other through the wall, dreaming of what it would be like to be in their bed with them. And now that she was here, she didn't want to forget even a millisecond of it.

Cali was sprawled on the bed, her body hot and flushed, still shaking from the aftershocks of her orgasm.

Mike was lying next to her, whispering softly that everything was alright. "We have you."

Precious tried to concentrate. She was a planner by nature, and all those months of fantasies had really been preparation for what she'd do if she ever got this chance, even though she'd convinced herself that she never would. Her brain had worked overtime to tell her that the flirty tone of her relationship with Mike and Cali was just an unintentional byproduct of their friendship. She'd reasoned that if she sometimes thought she saw them staring at her with a lustful gleam in their eyes, it was just a manifestation of her own desire; pure projection. But here she was, kneeling at the foot of their bed, their naked bodies laid out for her perusal, and she was grasping at straws trying to figure out which one of her fantasies she wanted to reenact first.

But she couldn't get her brain to focus, because she kept getting stuck on Mike's words.

*We have you.*

*We.*

She wanted that *we* to be more than temporary. She wanted them for more than just tonight. Now that she was finally in this bed, she knew she'd never get enough.

Cali's weary voice cut through Precious's mental overload. "Calm down, Precious. We have all night."

There was that "we" again. Precious locked eyes with Cali and exhaled with a soft smile. "I was thinking. Planning."

"We know," Mike said with a soft chuckle.

Precious turned to him with interest. Whereas Cali was still drifting in that soft haze of her orgasm, Mike's eyes were burning. Precious smiled, a plan forming.

"Come lie in between us," Cali said.

Precious's pulse began to race. She crawled up the bed, but it took longer than it should have. She kept stopping to explore her body. She kissed Cali's knee, making her giggle. She ran a hand up Mike's inner thigh and made his dick jump. She looked up the angular planes of his flat stomach and chest.

His pupils were dilated, his nostrils were flared, and his lips were pressed together, as if he was too afraid to speak just in case she stopped; but she had no plans to ever stop touching them.

She held his gaze and dipped her head to lick the head of his dick. She swirled her tongue around the tip and sucked it into her mouth.

Mike grabbed at the sheets and groaned.

Cali smoothed her hand along his chest and rubbed his nipples. Precious could feel the way his body tensed.

Precious leaned back to suckle gently on the head

for a few beats before letting his dick pop from her mouth.

"Beautiful," Cali whispered softly into his skin.

Mike moved quickly to grab Precious's hands. He pulled her up his body and their mouths crashed together.

Precious compared his kiss to Cali's. Hers was soft and gentle, but Mike's mouth was harder, more teeth, and this time playful. She loved them both.

She and Mike giggled around the crush of their lips and tongues as Mike shifted to his side, depositing Precious between his and Cali's bodies where she nestled comfortably between them.

Cali draped herself across Precious's side and snuggled against her. "You owe me a new dress," Cali said to Mike, as she licked softly at Precious's nipple.

Mike's dick was resting heavy and wet on Precious's right hip. She wrapped her hand around it and began stroking him.

"What bet did I lose this time?" he asked, understandably distracted.

Cali's mouth was wide, sucking on the tender flesh of Precious's breasts. She giggled, and Precious moaned at the vibration.

"You said she'd be shy as a dormouse in bed, but she hasn't stopped playing us like pianos since this whole thing started."

Precious gasped in mock outrage, "You two made a bet about what I would be like in bed?"

Mike snorted. "We've made lots of bets about you? Thanks for always walking around the house in a towel that barely covers your ass, by the way. I mean, thank you for letting me win that bet, but also just thank you for doing it."

"Best bet I ever lost," Cali whispered against the space between Precious's breasts, her words followed by her tongue.

Precious's face was warm with embarrassment, but not shame. "I couldn't help myself," she said.

Cali reached up to grab just the end of Precious's ponytail. She wrapped her hair around and around her finger.

"I wanted you both so much, I just... I think I got a little carried away wanting you to notice me," Precious admitted.

"We definitely noticed you," Mike said.

"Always," Cali whispered.

"I feel like my alarm clock is going to go off any second and this is going to all be a dream," Precious admitted, her hand stilling on Mike's cock.

Cali ghosted her hand down the center of Precious's body in a kind of response.

They all turned their attention to watch her delicate digits glance over Precious's skin. At Precious's core, Cali slipped her index finger along Precious's clit and between the folds of her sex. Precious and Mike groaned.

"Does this feel like a dream?" she asked.

Precious let out a huff of laughter, "Yeah, actually. It does."

They all laughed. And then Mike's hand was covering Precious's, helping her to start jacking him off again. When he'd reestablished her rhythm, his hand joined Cali's between Precious's legs.

Precious watched as Mike and Cali played with her pussy the way that he and Precious had played with Cali. It was glorious. She bent her knees, offering herself to them without any restrictions.

Cali was fingerfucking her with increasingly fast strokes, and she had begun to grind her wet pussy onto Precious's thigh.

Mike was stroking tight circles on her clit, and he leaned over Precious's body to pull Cali into a sloppy kiss. Precious was squirming between their bodies, watching them, fisting Mike's dick and falling apart on their fingers.

"Fuck, I've had a dream just like this," she yelled as she came.

---

Mike's body was in sensory overload.

Between Cali and Precious, there was just too much bare skin that he wanted to feel and taste, even as he just wanted to watch them feel and taste each other. But he decided to let the girls set the pace. He was really just immeasurably happy to even be in the room. Besides, he knew that they'd all eventually get everything they needed.

Mike had been hard for what felt like hours without any release, and his balls ached, but he really couldn't complain. How could he? Cali was leaning over Precious's body, sucking his dick gently while Precious's hand moved between Cali's legs. He could tell by the movement of Precious's arm and the wet sound of Cali's pussy what she was doing, and it made his abs tense. He clutched the covers beneath them, trying desperately to stave off the orgasm threatening to rip through him.

Mike decided that if he died like this, it would be more than worth it.

But all too soon, Cali's mouth abandoned him. He wanted to whimper, but then he heard the sound of a foil wrapper ripping. Cali smiled down at him with a wicked smile on her face, and then she bent forward to roll the condom onto his dick. Once it was in place, she gripped him at the base, shut her eyes and moaned through another orgasm at Precious's fingers.

Mike covered her hand to squeeze his dick harder, shuddering at the sensation.

Mike felt as if every muscle in his body would give up in exhaustion, but he still wanted to wait for Cali's orgasm to subside. Then Precious pressed her fingers into Mike's mouth and kissed him around them. She smiled as they shared the taste of Cali's pussy, their tongues swirling together over her digits.

That was the end of Mike's restraint. He groaned and pushed Precious's hand out of the way, needing to kiss her properly. Vaguely, he registered Cali's body moving, but he couldn't process it until she pulled Precious's mouth from his.

He moaned in frustration. Cali laughed softly as she turned Precious's head so that she could kiss her.

Mike considered whining, but in their new position he realized that Precious's body was open to him. He happily lifted her leg and angled himself at her entrance.

He eased his dick inside her. "Fuck," he whispered into her hair, wrapping an arm around her and holding her close. He wanted to fuck her hard and fast, but held himself still for a few seconds. He'd dreamt of this moment for so long that he wanted to allow himself the pleasure of enjoying the warmth of her body.

But then Precious clenched her internal muscles around him. He shuddered and his back bowed.

When he looked up, he wasn't surprised to see that Cali was the culprit. She'd repositioned herself at the foot of the bed with her head between Precious's legs. It was an intensely dirty sight in an evening of intensely dirty play, and it was perfect.

Mike finally started to move in and out of Precious's body with long, slow strokes. He buried his face in her hair and whispered against her strands how long he'd been waiting for this moment, how good she felt, and how he never wanted this moment to end.

Precious answered him, not so much in words, but in loud moans that got louder as Mike fucked her harder and Cali sucked her way up Precious's body, eventually latching onto her breast.

Mike hadn't thought he could last long after so much denial of release. But each time Precious came all over him, screaming his and Cali's names, he forced himself to make it last just a little bit longer.

But eventually he couldn't hold off anymore. He pushed Precious's chest into the bed, spread her legs wider and pumped into her faster while Cali massaged Precious's back and his chest. When he was close, wild and grunting with each thrust, he bent over to kiss Cali, pumping his hips into Precious.

Wanting to be connected to them both.

Needing them.

Both.

# 5

The sky was still dark when Precious woke up the first time. She blinked back into consciousness as the middle spoon in the bed, with Mike and Cali's bodies pressed firmly against her back and front. It should have been too much in their perpetually warm apartment; too hot and too close. But waking up this way was the stuff of so many dreams, and she'd snuggled deeper into the mattress and Mike's hold, tightened the arm thrown over Cali's waist to pull her closer, and then drifted back to sleep.

The next time she woke up, Mike was planting soft kisses on her neck and still holding onto her. It was so safe and warm, she thought she might fall back to sleep again. But then she heard Cali's giggle, and the same curiosity that used to wake her up in her bedroom at that sound just to listen to them have sex pulled Precious's eyes open into small slits. She could see a figure hovering over her, which was probably Cali since Mike — and his erection — were at her back.

"Are you awake yet?" Cali's voice was soft yet urgent. Precious offered a groggy moan in response. "Wake up so we can go shower?"

Precious fully opened one eye and then the other. "I'm listening," she croaked.

Mike laughed softly in her ear.

The three of them stumbled down their dark hallway together, crowded into their bathroom and brushed their teeth. It all felt so normal for them to crowd around the bathroom vanity with one too few sinks and laugh about nothing and everything while waiting for the shower to heat up. This was how it had always been between them. Almost from the minute Precious had moved in, they'd built a friendship that was easy, intimate and shockingly uncomplicated, even when it should have been.

The only real difference now was that they were naked, but that was freeing. Precious thought it was amazing not to have to throw on a t-shirt, just barely hiding her nakedness from them when what she wanted desperately was to rub up against them and beg them to touch her. Not having to hide her desire and their desire for each other was the best feeling in the world.

When Mike and Cali climbed into the shower, their hands gliding over wet skin, Precious hung back.

She hopped onto the bathroom counter and watched them while waiting for her clay mask to dry, yet another thing she'd always wanted to do.

Mike turned toward the spray of the showerhead and Cali slid her loofah over his wide back. Cali smiled over her shoulder at Precious as her hands moved down Mike's body. Precious couldn't see exactly what Cali's hands were doing but after a while, Mike's head fell back and he groaned loud enough for Precious to hear over the shower. Cali winked at her and turned back to Mike's body.

Precious smiled at them, mesmerized by how beautiful they looked together. Cali turned Mike around and squatted in front of him, her head level with his groin. His dick was hard; it hadn't been a few minutes ago. Cali dropped her loofah, giving up the pretense of cleaning him, sort of. Precious watched with hungry eyes as Cali used her soapy hands to slowly clean his dick, stroking him up and down with intense concentration. Mike's entire body was red from the hot water and his hands spanned the sides of the shower, holding onto the wall and the glass door to keep himself stable as Cali brought him to orgasm for Precious to see. When Precious lifted her eyes to his face, she sucked in a shocked breath to find his eyes on her. He was moaning and cursing and eventually coming in Cali's hands, but his eyes were focused on Precious's face and it made the experience beautifully surreal.

She wanted to join them. Her mask had dried, and

was softening again from the humid bathroom and the sweat of arousal at her hairline. But she held back. She wasn't in a rush, because this was only the beginning, she desperately wanted to believe.

When his body stopped quaking, Mike finally tore his eyes from Precious. He bent over to drag Cali into his arms. Precious heard Cali's soft laughter as she wrapped her legs around his waist, which turned to a moan as he lowered her onto his dick.

Precious smiled and leaned back on the counter. She planted one foot in the bowl of a sink and spread her legs apart, touching herself as she enjoyed the show. She slid her fingers softly along the folds of her sex. She avoided her clit so she wouldn't be distracted. This wasn't about getting off, not yet, at least. She just wanted to watch now that she finally could.

Mike's strong arms moved Cali up and down his dick at a leisurely pace. Cali's arms were wrapped around his shoulders, holding on tight. Their mouths were moving together sensually; they weren't in any rush either, and Precious loved that.

Precious wondered if they were as happy to be watched as she was to watch. She hoped so.

When Mike began to move Cali's body faster, Precious became greedy. The sound of the water was hiding the thing she'd always loved the most. She called out for Mike to turn off the water; she wanted to hear them; their bodies joining and Cali's soft mewling and Mike's gentle groans.

"Shut the water off," she called again as her fingers moved to tease her entrance.

Cali turned to look at her with a devilish grin on her face. "You could get in here and help Mike make me scream."

Mike placed a gentle kiss on Cali's cheek, still fucking her as he turned to smile at Precious as well.

Now that their eyes were on her, Precious slipped two fingers inside of her pussy and moaned. Mike's body turned, and Cali scrambled to turn the knob to shut off the water. Precious watched as Mike lifted Cali from his dick and set her on her feet. Cali turned to face Precious, swiping at the fogged shower door, and pushed her upper body against the glass.

Precious licked her lips at Cali's beautiful breasts pressed against the partition. Mike moved behind her and entered her slow. They watched her while she watched them and they all got off like that, their eyes devouring each other in sexually charged glee.

Eventually, Precious's thighs began to shake and the need she felt was too much. She jumped from the counter and walked on shaky legs to the shower. She picked up Cali's discarded loofah and washed their legs and backs while Mike fucked Cali faster and faster until they were both screaming out their orgasms. And then they turned the shower back on and really cleaned their bodies this time.

They used up all their hot water and then tumbled back into bed to fall happily back to sleep. This time

Cali was the middle spoon, and Mike threw his long arm over them both.

Precious fell asleep with a smile on her face, even as some traitorous part of her brain whispered into the almost unconsciousness of sleep with a question.

*How long can this last?*

# 6

This relationship should have been strange. Shouldn't it? That's at least what Mike was wondering all day; at his shoot for an up-and-coming menswear brand, during a particularly grueling session at the gym, in line at his favorite juice bar, and definitely on the train home. All he could think about was being inside; getting back to their apartment — which was getting too warm with the change of seasons and their landlord procrastinating on turning the heat off — and crawling between Cali and Precious's even warmer bodies. He wanted to be home, but he couldn't shake the feeling that it should be weird.

Their relationship should have fundamentally changed. All their relationships, certainly, but especially his and Cali's. Right? Except they hadn't, and Mike had no idea what to make of that. The only real change was that after eight months of him and Cali being desperate to be as close to Precious as possible, now they were even closer than they let themselves believe possible. They could touch and taste her as much as they wanted and she could do the same.

Besides that, oddly enough, very little had changed in their day-to-day lives. Cali still made them eggs most mornings, he made coffee for everyone, and Precious flitted around the apartment running late for class. Cali still rummaged around in his closet, preferring to wear his clothes whenever possible. Mike still complained that he never had enough clean clothes, pretending that he didn't love the sight of her drowning in his shirts. And Precious still snuggled up next to them on the couch while they watched tv at night. Mike still played video games whenever he had a few errant hours. Precious still followed Cali around the living room to water her plants. And he still fell asleep comforted by the sensation of Cali's nails scraping over his arms or scratching at his scalp. Except now the sound of Cali and Precious's voices followed him into his dreams. It was the same, but better.

When he made it to their apartment, he checked the mail before taking the stairs to the sixth floor, his legs burning and his mind still puzzling over their new arrangement.

When he reached their front door, he knew immediately that no one was home. It took a few seconds, while he locked the door behind him and dropped his keys in their bowl. Finally, he figured it out. Cali wasn't playing her music loud enough to fill the hall. He listened for the telltale signs of Precious's presence, her fingers tapping the keys of her laptop or her snores after falling asleep reading a book, and couldn't hear that either.

He toed off his shoes and walked directly into the bathroom to shower. He washed his hair with Cali's shampoo, and his body with the vanilla body wash Precious liked. He was almost embarrassed at how their combined scents made him hard as a rock, but not embarrassed enough to stop himself from masturbating at the memory of their combined tastes on his tongue. The pounding water and the force of his orgasm did what even his workout couldn't do: it cleared all the confusion and doubt from his brain, and he relaxed against the shower stall happily.

By the time Cali pushed through the front door, Mike was sitting on the couch playing a video game in his favorite sweatpants and no shirt. She was all made up from a shoot, and she looked as relieved as he'd felt to be home. She kissed him on his cheek while he killed some weird zombie hybrids in his game. She swiped her lipstick from his skin before heading to the bathroom.

Cali was still in the shower when Precious came home, and Mike had just beaten the level and was saving his progress.

He turned to her with a smile. "How was your day?"

Her eyes were tired. She tossed her keys on the table and missed the bowl completely. She dropped her backpack and kicked off her shoes before she answered him. "Long. Over." She threw her arms around his shoulders and placed soft kisses along his jaw.

Mike felt her body go stiff when she finally heard the shower running.

"Is Cali in the shower?" she asked, breathing against his cheek.

He smiled and nodded.

Precious brushed her lips across his cheek bones and her tongue darted out to taste his earlobe.

"Coming?" she whispered into his ear.

He laughed and moved his hand to cup the crown of her head. "I already showered."

"Fuck the shower," she said, and sucked his earlobe into her mouth. "You can help me clean her," she whispered in that way he loved, where every word sounded like a moan.

Mike's body was tense again, but in the best way. His cock was hardening in his sweats and his chest was tightening with desire as Precious licked and sucked at him. It took every ounce of restraint he had to turn her down. "It's okay," he said in a harsh voice. "You two have fun."

She licked and kissed him over his pulse and Mike

shivered. "Don't touch that until we're out of the shower," she whispered.

Mike didn't have to see her face to know where she was looking. His own eyes dropped to his lap, where his dick was now a prominent bulge inside his sweats. He gulped.

Precious giggled and then let him go.

She was halfway to the hallway when he turned around. She stopped and turned to look at him over her shoulder with a wicked gleam in her eyes. And then she was gone. Mike started the next level of his game.

Eventually, Mike heard the bathroom door open. He turned to see Cali walking naked toward their bedroom. The ends of her hair were wet, and when she looked at him, she had a distant, satisfied smile on her face. Mike had paused the game to get a glass of water and he stopped to watch her. She blew a kiss at him, and his dick stirred back to life as he pressed play.

Soon enough, Precious and Cali were on the couch next to him. Precious was sitting sideways on the couch in one of Mike's tank tops and a thong, her legs drawn up as she graded a stack of essays. Cali was wearing another pair of Mike's sweats and a sports bra, flipping through a magazine. It was all so leisurely. So normal; their new normal.

They could have stayed like that all night. It wouldn't have been the first time they'd enjoyed just being near one another, and hopefully, it wouldn't be the last. But then the mood shifted from companionable silence to scorching tension.

He hadn't noticed when Precious put her grading away, or when Cali had left the couch. He only registered those two things when the sound of Precious's soft sigh pulled him from his game. He recognized that sound; it was the one Precious always made when he or Cali slipped a finger inside her slowly. It was relaxed, as if she'd been waiting for one of them to enter her all day; as if their soft finger strokes made her whole.

Mike's eyes widened to saucers when he saw Cali on the floor in front of the couch, between Precious's legs. Precious's thong was pushed to the side and Cali's fingers were lazily stroking her sex. Her legs were spread wide enough for Mike to see everything Cali was doing, and Precious's hips were canted to the side to make sure that he could. He was mesmerized. And then Cali's hand was rubbing his dick through his sweatpants.

She smiled up at him, her fingers still working inside Precious. "Are you done?" she asked, and then dipped her head to swipe her tongue over Precious's clit.

Precious's strangled moan was music to Mike's ears.

"With what?" he whispered, distracted.

They both laughed, although Cali's laugh was tight

with need and Precious's sounded more like a breathy moan.

Cali pulled his controller from his hand and set it down gently on the coffee table. She stood in front of him and pulled his pants down over his hips just enough to get his dick out. Mike groaned as Cali bent over to roll a condom down his shaft.

Cali gripped his chin, turning his head so that he could watch Precious touch herself now, and then she lowered herself onto his shaft, nice and slow. Precious turned to face them, her legs spread obscenely wide. She pushed two fingers into her pussy and grinned as she watched them.

Mike gripped Cali's waist and helped her keep a steady rhythm as she rode his dick. But his eyes were trained on Precious. Cali fucked him as she whispered into his ear how beautiful Precious was, how happy she felt, how she'd been longing to feel him inside her all day.

It was a surreal moment. And yet, it was all so devastatingly normal. Cali began to ride him faster and harder, and Precious moved her bra aside to pinch at her nipples, her eyes drinking them in and her beautiful lips whispering encouraging words to them as if there was a chance they might stop fucking. Not in this lifetime, Mike thought, reaching out a hand to caress Precious's breasts and roll her nipple between his fingers.

When Mike came, clenching Cali's body to his,

their mouths joined, he wondered if it would always be like this between the three of them. He hoped it would, especially when Cali crawled from his lap across the couch and between Precious's legs.

Mike tore the condom from his shaft and watched as Cali moved Precious's hand aside to replace it with her mouth. He stroked himself to another release, as Cali fingered herself to orgasm and sucked Precious's pussy to a shaking climax.

It was dirty and not what he'd expected, but this normal night on the couch made him accept that maybe normal was relative.

# 7

In hindsight, Precious could see that this day had started badly and only gotten worse.

Her phone was ringing at barely six in the morning, waking her and Cali up. Mike had already slipped out of the house to go to the gym, otherwise he would have shut the noise off immediately, and that made her miss him even more; that, and the coldness at her back where his body had been.

She scowled at the picture of her brother's smiling face on her cellphone screen. "Time difference," she whispered harshly as she tiptoed out of their bedroom.

"What time is it there?" Andre asked.

"You have a PhD in astrophysics, and you can't calculate the time difference between New York and Vienna? You're shitting me, right?"

To his credit, Andre actually sounded apologetic

when he replied. "Okay, I deserve that. I just haven't talked to you in a while, and I just wanted to check on my favorite baby sister."

Precious slipped into her largely abandoned bedroom to grab the robe from behind the door, wrapping it around her naked body as she walked into the kitchen. She smiled vaguely and her feelings at her brother softened. She never could stay mad at him for long.

"Also, mom told me your friend Laura pulled a Jerry Springer. She told me to call you. I don't really understand what she's talking about, but she knows I'm nosy, so she did the right thing because here I am, calling you. So, what's the tea?"

Precious could feel the scowl settling back onto her face and she rolled her eyes. "Nosy asshole," she muttered under her breath. "Of course you just want the dirt," she said, trying not to yell. She didn't want to wake up Cali.

"Don't act brand new. I should be mad at you for holding out on me."

Precious sucked her teeth but gave her brother the Cliff's Notes version of Laura's current predicament.

"Oh. That's not juicy," Andre whispered, "that's just sad."

"Yep." Precious poured herself a glass of juice.

"So, what's happening with the investigation?"

Precious downed her juicer and walked over to the

window looking out on the street below. "Human Resources should be releasing their report today."

"Oh, shit."

"Yeah," Precious breathed.

She'd been dreading this day for months. Laura's relationship with Dr. Friedlander had been one sordid thing, she guessed, when Laura had been convinced they were in love. It was improbable and naïve, but at least it allowed Precious to believe Laura was happy. But once he'd dumped her, Laura had had to come to grips with the fact that she'd been used by a man twice her age, who then turned around and painted her as a home-wrecking seductress. They'd all had to accept that he was nothing more than an aging snake, perfectly willing to trash her reputation to save his own. And Precious, as Laura's only friend left in the department, had borne the brunt of supporting her friend through it all. It was a lot; too much, as far as Precious was concerned. And even though they'd moved past that spat from a few weeks ago, their relationship wasn't the same; it hadn't been for months.

But somehow, the worst of it all for Precious was knowing deep down in her gut that Dr. Friedlander probably wouldn't receive anything more than a slap on the wrist. Precious had seen the writing on the wall. As the HR decision loomed, Laura had abandoned the TA offices and taken to working in the library, hiding away from everyone. Meanwhile, Precious felt like Dr. Friedlander was everywhere: in the main office at the coffee machine, at the campus cafeteria laughing with half the faculty and a few of the advanced PhD students, and at the department's end-of-year awards ceremony. If he was persona non grata last semester, once he'd dumped Laura and gone back to his wife, the department seemed ready to welcome him back into the fold with open arms, with Laura as the sacrificial lamb that bought his passage back.

Precious was so angry that she'd practically exiled herself as well.

She still went to her classes, Professor Min's large lecture and her office hours. And she made sure to meet up with Laura a few times a week for lunch, or study sessions in the library, or a couple of drinks at Little Brother's so she didn't feel isolated. But with each passing day, Precious had spent as much time at home as possible and, even better, she practically glued herself to Mike and Cali's bodies, losing herself in sex and cuddling so she didn't have to think about anything happening outside of their front door.

She found solace in their apartment even more now than before. Precious followed Cali around the living room, listening to her talk to the dozen or so plants on their windowsills or hanging from the ceilings, charmed at the way the plants comforted her. When Mike stayed home to work out, she'd happily crawl onto his back, locking her legs and arms around his torso, providing resistance during his pushups and whispering her dirtiest fantasies into his ear until he gave up. Then she'd let him throw her over his shoulder, grab Cali and they'd all retreat to bed, their laughter and moans filling the apartment, feeling safer than she ever had before.

But now that the HR report was due to be released, her safe space was closing in on her.

"Precious?" Cali's voice sounded sleepy, but she also sounded scared.

Precious turned and found Cali in one of Mike's too big tank tops. It was slightly askew and her left breast was bared, her dark nipple contrasting with her light brown skin. She was so beautiful first thing in the morning, in the middle of the day, in the dead of night, and Precious knew she'd never get tired of looking at her.

"I've got to go, Andre. I need to get some more sleep before school." She sounded distracted to her own ears.

"Okay," he said casually. "Text me and let me know what happens, okay?"

"Will do. Love you," she said, hanging up the phone. She dropped it onto the couch and walked into Cali's embrace, pressing her face into the crook of her neck and breathing her in. Cali smelled like Mike's cologne.

"Let's go back to bed," she whispered into Cali's skin.

"Mike'll be home soon," Cali whispered into Precious's ear, kissing her ear sweetly.

They both shivered.

---

Mike had planned an easy leg day; nothing too strenuous, and nothing that would keep him from home any longer than necessary. But just before he'd walked into the gym, his phone beeped with a new email from his management. He opened it, skimmed it, and then sat down on a bench in the men's locker room to read it once again and more closely, trying to understand what he was seeing. His eyes kept sticking on a single word: "restructuring."

There wasn't anything in the email that should have worried him; not really. Even without Sarah or a new agent, he was still one of the agency's highest earners. But he was fast realizing that earning potential and bookings weren't enough. He didn't want to compare everyone to Sarah, but he couldn't stop himself. She'd seen his potential and treated him like a person, and had valued his health and wellbeing more than how many campaigns he booked each season. He'd suspected that she was special, but now he knew for sure. He still hadn't felt comfortable signing with another agent and without one, he'd booked fewer new jobs in the last month than since he'd joined. Soon enough, he knew that he wouldn't be the highest paid commercial model in the agency, and then what? He didn't know. And there was something about the word "restructuring" that seemed to reignite all the anxiety he'd been avoiding while hiding out in the comfort of their apartment.

That word made him feel vulnerable, and he hated it. That word chased him onto the gym floor and it made him work harder than he'd planned. He practically limped home. Every part of his body hurt, but walking across the threshold into their apartment somehow made a tiny fraction of his worries fall away. Another fraction disappeared when he heard Precious's moan. He walked gingerly to their bedroom and stopped at the threshold.

What restructuring? What agent? What worries? Mike's troubles just seemed to disappear when he saw who was waiting for him.

Precious and Cali were naked, the covers and all their clothes littering the floor. Precious was on her back, her hands massaging her breasts, her legs spread wide, Cali's head between her thighs. One of Cali's hands was gripping Precious's thigh while the other moved at her opening, fucking Precious with her fingers. They were a beautiful tangle of sweaty brown skin and soft flesh. And moans. The room was full of so many moans and pants, and even soft feminine grunts as Cali buried her face between Precious's legs and devoured her.

Mike couldn't help the smile that spread across his

face, or the way his dick had become heavy in his gym shorts. He cleared his throat.

Precious opened her eyes only a bit, her fingers still pinching her nipples. She smiled at him, excited and relieved.

Cali lifted her head and turned to him. Her face was wet from Precious's sex. She licked her lips and smiled, her hand still moving between Precious's legs.

"Morning, sweetheart," Cali breathed. Mike's eyes widened. It was the first time she'd ever called him by a term of endearment instead of just Mike, or Michael when she was mad at him. She even called Precious by her first name only; sweet nicknames weren't her thing. To be fair, sometimes in the midst of their passion, Mike thought they said each other's names like terms of endearment, but this was different.

He smiled back at them both. "Good morning."

"We've been waiting for you," Cali breathed. Precious moaned loudly, her back arching from the bed.

"I can tell."

Cali raised the lower half of her body and pushed her ass into the air. She spread her legs to show him her wet sex; the invitation clear as the sky outside. "Come to bed, babe," she said lazily, before she turned to lower her head back between Precious's legs.

Mike's overworked muscles suddenly felt light and loose. His brain cleared as he pulled his shirt over his head. He walked to the bedside table and pulled open the nightstand drawer to fish out a condom. He rolled the soft latex down his shaft and was able to let all of his worries float into the ether. He'd have to deal with it all eventually, but not right now. Everything that wasn't in this apartment — in this bed — could wait, he thought as he slowly inched his dick into Cali's warm pussy.

# 8

Cali never really loved being on set. She showed up, did her job like a professional, and then left as soon as she could. Her job wasn't good or bad, it just was. But ever since she'd stepped on set for a luxury jeweler's holiday ad campaign today, all she'd been able to think about was how much she couldn't wait to go home.

She'd sat anxiously in the makeup chair, watching the hairdresser — who clearly had no idea how to do Black hair — set out her tools. Normally, Cali could endure most things on set, but not today. Not when the hairdresser had picked up a hard bristle brush and turned to Cali's head, her hair dry and no leave-in conditioner in sight. Her heart had begun to pound in her chest at what it would sound, look and feel like to have that brush ruin her curls.

She'd had to call to mind the image of Mike sitting

on their couch, his gaming headset on as he cursed out whoever he was playing halfway around the world to calm her nerves. She'd jumped from the hairdresser's chair and told her in a firm voice — that was steady, even though her body was shaking — that she needed to get someone who knew how to do her hair or she was going to walk. She was terrified but she wouldn't compromise on this.

Cali was at an awkward stage in her career. She wasn't a new model anymore, and she refused to let any hairdressers or makeup artists pull and tug and rip and poke at her as if she was a pincushion. She'd done that enough in her early career to never do it again. But she also wasn't of the stature of supermodel who could stand up for herself without fear of repercussion. If even one person on set labeled her as a problem, there was a very real chance that her bookings would dry up in an instant.

Her arms were locked over her chest in frustration while the hairdresser just stared at her as if she were speaking a different language. Cali was freaking out internally, but she tried her hardest not to show it. She didn't let herself relax until the hairdresser had stormed out of the trailer. She didn't move even when she was alone. She knew she couldn't let herself relax, so she focused on memories from just this morning; her head between Precious's legs, Mike moving inside of her, Precious's soft giggles against Cali's mouth followed by her tongue, she and Precious sitting at the kitchen island, sharing their morning smoothie. She tried to recapture the calming intimacy of the two of them sipping from the same straw — passing the cup back and forth between them — while Precious read before her class and Cali flipped through the latest issue of *Vogue*, dog-earing pages with poses she wanted to practice, their sides pressed tight to one another.

When the hairdresser returned with a Black makeup artist, Cali tried to suppress the hope she felt; she wasn't out of the woods yet. The makeup artist smiled reassuringly at Cali and waited for her to sink back into her seat. The new hairdresser's hands were gentle as she sprayed some water into Cali's hair, squeezed some leave-in conditioner into her palm and began to style her soft curls.

But that unexpected battle was more energy than Cali had to spare and even as she relaxed, she still just wanted to go home.

As soon as the shoot wrapped, Cali took an Uber to her agency offices. She sat in a meeting about her upcoming schedule, only half-listening. Her stomach was rumbling because she'd forgotten to eat lunch, which made her mood plummet, and she couldn't stop the negative thoughts about herself — in her grandmother's voice — from resurfacing. Mike and Precious would be mad at her for being irresponsible and refusing to take care of herself, she thought.

But still, she couldn't wait to go home, and the longing was palpable.

She called to mind the memory of Precious climbing on top of Mike last night. Cali remembered watching her pussy stretch and engulf him, a small moan escaping from her lips; the small hum that always made Cali want to kiss her. Cali had drifted to sleep with her head resting on Mike's shoulder as they both watched Precious ride him slowly, gently, lovingly. She used it to get her through the rest of the meeting, and to her favorite sandwich spot downtown, and then to Dr. Toussaint's office.

She checked the clock on her phone, and was shocked to find that it was barely five o'clock. This day had felt like the longest day ever, and it wasn't over yet. When Dr. Toussaint, who always reminded Cali that she could call her Mary even though Cali never did or would, opened her office door, Cali felt a sense of relief that enveloped the longing. She still wanted to go home, but she also needed to talk to her therapist.

When she greeted Cali, Dr. Toussaint's face bore the same smile she always greeted Cali with. It was comforting and set Cali at ease. Not for the first time, Cali wondered if they taught therapists how to do that smile or if it was innate; either way, as soon as she stepped into Dr. Toussaint's office, she felt calm as they eased into the regular routine of their sessions.

There was that first minute or so where Dr. Toussaint offered Cali tea, coffee, or water. Cali said water — always water — and Dr. Toussaint made a cup of tea for herself. Cali wondered, again, how much tea the woman drank in a day as she downed half the glass of water before their session even began.

From there, the appointment started the way that it always did. Dr. Toussaint's friendly smile faded into a neutral look that invited Cali to tell her everything or nothing at her leisure. Her therapist tilted her head to the right and asked the first of a series of seemingly innocuous questions. "How are you today?"

Cali usually hated this question. She'd been seeing Dr. Toussaint for almost four years, and no one in the city knew as much about Cali's past. The woman could probably tell how Cali was doing as soon as she opened her door, but still she asked the same question every week, giving Cali something she'd rarely had as a child: control. It was at the root of all Cali's issues and Dr. Toussaint knew that.

Sometimes, Cali wanted to yell at Dr. Toussaint to just take the lead and fix her. For once, she wanted the woman to tell her what she was feeling and what she needed to do to not be broken. But she knew Dr. Toussaint's reply would be that Cali wasn't broken; there was nothing to fix.

But this week, Cali didn't chew her bottom lip anxiously as she tried to figure out a way to vocalize her feelings; the mistakes she thought she'd made, her bouts of anxiety, or the days she woke up sad for no particular reason. This week, she knew exactly what she wanted to talk about.

"I've told you about my roommate," she hedged,

not quite a question or a statement. She'd mentioned Precious every now and then, never outright telling her therapist that she was sexually attracted to her, or that she and Mike had spent so many months lusting after her. She didn't know how to tell her therapist that she and her boyfriend had regularly fucked each other senseless while whispering their fantasies about their roommate into one another's ears.

But Dr. Toussaint wasn't stupid. Cali only spoke about the people who had made an indelible imprint on her life; the good (Mike and Precious) and the bad (her grandmother); she didn't have the mental or emotional space for anything in between.

"Yes," Dr. Toussaint replied neutrally.

"Well, over the last few weeks there's been some developments on that front."

"What kind of developments?"

Cali had been preparing herself for this question ever since the first night she and Mike had sex with Precious. She took a deep breath. "Mike and I have... Well, I don't know if we're in a relationship with her, we haven't labeled it or anything. But the three of us are... together. I mean, we've been together. A lot."

Cali took a sip of water. She remembered the feeling of Precious's lips on hers, their tongues wet and forceful in each other's mouths, the sound of a basketball game on the television and Mike's angry muttering as his team lost. She grabbed onto the memory of Precious breaking their kiss as the crowd screamed and Mike cursed. Her team had beaten his. Cali had laughed. Precious had jumped around their living room before crawling into Mike's lap, gloating right up until she slipped her hand into his sweatpants and her tongue into his mouth. Cali had laughed harder.

She couldn't wait to go home.

"And how do you feel about all of you being together?" Dr. Toussaint asked with that same neutral look on her face.

"Happy," she replied without hesitation.

Dr. Toussaint's neutral mask slipped briefly. Her mouth lifted into the bright smile she always used to greet Cali. "Then I'm happy for you." But then her face became that passive mask once again. "Have you told them about your grandmother?"

---

Mike was in the middle of an open casting call when the Kenneth Waters Agency contact showed up on his phone screen. His stomach dropped as he answered. The voice on the other line was Toby, Kenneth's personal assistant.

"Kenneth would like to speak with you today," Toby had said in the bored tone that Mike used to imitate to make Sarah laugh.

Mike agreed to the meeting, because what other choice did he have? They agreed on a time and Toby hung up with barely a goodbye, then Mike received a calendar notification that sat on the lock screen of his phone as he waited to give his portfolio to the photographer and posed for test shoots. It glared at him as he went to a fitting for a show he was walking in the summer. And it haunted him back uptown to the agency's main offices. He felt Sarah's loss keenly all day. She would have sent him a heads up and prepped him for whatever was coming. But most crucially, she would have made sure to schedule the meeting days in advance and during business hours.

But Mike had been too terrified to put this meeting off. Without an agent, he had no idea where he stood in the agency day-to-day, and Toby had exploited all of his insecurities. He made a big deal of Kenneth's busy schedule and all but said that Mike should feel special that Kenneth wanted to meet with him personally at all; so much so that he was fitting him in before he headed out of town for a month. Toby had said it in that haughty tone that Mike had noticed he only used when talking to the models.

The sun was still in the sky when he pushed into the building. He tried to slow his breathing as the elevator ascended to the tenth floor, which Kenneth had taken entirely for his office, a studio and a small bedroom, just in case. Mike had always avoided asking what the "just in case" could mean, and Sarah had always gotten a look on her face that was part revulsion, part annoyance when someone brought it up. When the elevator doors opened onto the large cement studio with tall ceilings, Mike's stomach lurched. He wished he hadn't come. He wished he was home.

He walked slowly through the studio, his hands clutching the shoulder straps of his backpack. Kenneth's office was just a section at the back of the studio, separated from the rest of the room by tall windowed partitions. Next to it, with false walls — that some models gossiped were soundproof — was the bedroom. Mike avoided looking that way.

He sighed in something like relief when he could see into Kenneth's office. He wasn't alone.

The three men were facing away from Mike toward a large corkboard at the far wall. Toby stood just to Kenneth's left, his iPad in his hands as usual. The other man in the room was the agency's in-house photographer, Jared. As Mike closed in on the door, he realized what the men were looking at; tacked onto the board were rows of headshots from all the agency's models.

He walked through the open door and cleared his throat.

Jared turned and smiled at Mike over his shoulder. But that was the only recognition of his presence he received. It took agonizingly long seconds before Toby finally turned to Mike and said, in his most superior voice, "Kenneth will be with you soon."

By the way he said "soon," Mike knew that he meant whenever Kenneth felt like it. He sighed and sat down on the black leather couch in the corner of the office and waited. His eyes darted to the windows. They faced east, so he couldn't see the sunset, but the sky was a brilliant orange, and he knew that soon enough, it would darken. Once again, he missed Sarah, but mostly he missed Cali and Precious and their tiny apartment.

The longer he sat, though, the longing turned to boredom. He hated sitting still unless he was sitting on his couch with his gaming headphones on.

Mike pulled his phone from his backpack and unlocked it to see a text from his mother. He smiled down at the picture she'd sent of her and Mike's dad — a selfie definitely taken with her selfie stick, her favorite travel accessory. The two of them were standing in front of the Eiffel Tower. They were on a second honeymoon and adorable. He reminded himself to set up a Skype call with them when they got back to home. He typed a quick message to his mother and then checked his Instagram notifications, but quickly lost interest.

He opened the roommate group text and frowned. He didn't have any messages from Cali or Precious, and they rarely went more than a few hours from texting each other. This was the worst day for them to go quiet, because he needed them. He hadn't told them that he was coming here tonight because that would have meant telling them about Sarah leaving the agency, and that strange feeling in his gut that his career was circling the drain. He'd been telling himself that it was because he didn't want to worry them, but really, he just didn't want to burst the bubble they were living in; he didn't want to taint the happiness he felt in their apartment with the anxiety that consumed him whenever he left. But now, as he sat staring at their quiet group message, he wished he had told them so they might have checked in, and he considered texting it all to them now, but then Kenneth cleared his throat.

When Mike raised his eyes, Jared was packing up to leave and Toby was straightening a pile of papers on Kenneth's desk.

Mike's eyes drifted to the corkboard. He felt a pang of narcissism when he easily found his headshot. It was old, but still great in his opinion. It took a minute of staring before he realized that all the models surrounding him were Black, Asian and Arab. His eyes flitted to the other side of the board. All the models on that side were white. Mike's stomach dropped.

"Mike," Kenneth said, his voice ringing with false excitement. He raised his arms in greeting as if Mike hadn't been sitting there for nearly half an hour. Kenneth clapped his hands together sharply. The sound echoed around the barely insulated loft. "I want to talk to you about finding a new agent. We're restructuring, as you know, and it matters to us that you feel taken care of."

*Taken care of.*

Those words shouldn't have sounded like a warning bell, but they did because he could remember that when Sarah lobbied for the agency to sign him all those years ago, Kenneth had seemed... annoyed by it; annoyed by him. And before she'd left, Kenneth hadn't bothered to speak to him, not even after he signed his first big contract with the biggest client the agency had at the time, and not any of the times they'd ridden the elevator up together. Before Sarah left, Mike was completely invisible to Kenneth, but here he was, treating Mike as if he cared about him; as if he cared about his career. But he didn't, and Mike knew it.

Sarah always said that Kenneth only cared about one thing, but it wasn't his models, his agents, or even the money. The only thing Kenneth cared about was aesthetics. Mike's eyes moved back to the corkboard and it made sense now, even if he didn't know all the details.

Mike stood from the couch, slipping his phone into his back pocket. "I want to talk about the clause in my contract that allows me to terminate our business relationship when my manager leaves: clause 3A, paragraph three."

Mike didn't miss the tiny gasp that escaped Toby's lips, or the frown and simmering rage in Kenneth's eyes.

Sarah had always told him to trust his gut, and right now, his gut was screaming at him that whatever

Kenneth was planning in the restructuring, and whatever that corkboard was meant to convey, wasn't anything he wanted to be a part of.

What followed was a lot of yelling that Mike ignored and threats he tried to forget. But in the end, he walked out of the Kenneth Waters Agency with a copy of his contract, signed and dated to indicate that he was now a model without an agency and with no idea what the future held.

His phone rang. He looked down, saw a picture of Cali's smiling face and promptly shoved the phone deep into his backpack. And then he walked into the first bar he passed and ordered a shot of whiskey, and then another. He downed each one with a cringe and tried to figure out what he was going to tell Cali and Precious. He wondered if Sarah would be willing to sign him at her new agency, if she even could. He tried to calculate how many paychecks for completed jobs he had coming, how much money was in his checking and savings accounts, and how long he'd be able to survive on that just in case Kenneth followed through on his threats to have Mike blackballed.

He was terrified.

---

They were grading final exams in one of the library's study rooms when the HR memo hit Laura's email inbox. The decision was exactly what Precious expected. Even though Dr. Friedlander had clearly violated the University's fraternization policy, because it was a consensual relationship the committee had decided to sanction him with a three-month paid suspension. But then Precious received the email, this time as a forwarded message from Dr. Jones, the Sociology Department's acting chair.

Laura gasped when she saw he'd sent the message to the entire department, not just the "interested parties."

Precious rushed to close the door to the study room. Laura read Dr. Jones's letter aloud in a tiny voice. Her face turned a violent shade of red, and her eyes filled with tears.

Colleagues and students

Per the Office of Human Resources (see attached), Dr. Friedlander has been cleared of the allegation of gross misconduct. He will take the summer to reset, after that I'm happy to report he will resume the reins of department chair again in the fall. As the semester ends, I want to congratulate everyone for a wonderful year. May we all take the summer to consider what kind of professionals we would like to be. For our graduate students, you should be striving to emulate your advisors, maintain professional boundaries and not let yourself get carried away by fantasies that might severely harm those who ultimately hold your futures in their hands.

Happy grading!

Dr. Jones

Precious and Laura closed their laptops, stuffed their papers in their bags and walked across the street to Little Brother's. They drank tequila shots and complained about how garbage their department was and started plotting Laura's escape.

It was too late for Laura to transfer to another school. And even if she could, she was terrified that every department she applied to would call Dr. Jones or Dr. Friedlander for an unofficial reference and she'd be stuck. They tried to approach the issue from every angle. But eventually, Laura just decided to leave the program even if she couldn't get into another program. And then they started crying.

"I think we're really fucking drunk, P," Laura slurred eventually.

"Pizza," Precious said, not quite in reply to Laura so much as her rumbling stomach.

"God, yes," Laura said.

They grabbed their bags and stumbled onto the street. It was dark out. Precious pulled her phone from her shoulder bag. She squinted at the screen, shocked to see that it was almost nine in the evening and she'd missed three calls from Cali and one from Mike. How long had they been in Little Brother's?

"Is it your roommates?" Laura asked, gently.

"Yeah," Precious whispered. "But I don't want them to see me like this. We're really fucked up. I'll call them after we eat."

They started walking away from the bar toward their favorite hole-in-the-wall pizza joint, Get A Slice O' You. About halfway there Laura started to speak carefully, only the smallest slur to her words. "So, I really don't mean this in a bad way, but what's going on with you and them?"

"Them?" Precious was maybe slightly less drunk now that they were walking, and the cool night air was slapping her in the face and making her eyes water. But she still wasn't sober enough to track the path of the last few minutes of silence.

"Your roommates," Laura said, rolling her eyes.

"Oh." Precious could feel the smile blossoming on her face. She licked her dry lips. She'd been practicing how she would answer this question for a while. When someone finally asked. "It's... complicated," she said, even though it wasn't. She shook her head. "No, sorry, it's not. They're together. And I'm... with them. Together. Too," she spluttered.

She felt lightheaded, and not because she was drunk. Now that she'd finally admitted to someone what was going on with her roommates, she felt like she was floating. She made a mental note to practice saying it again and again until she could put all the right words in the right order. She'd said it once, she couldn't wait to say it again.

She turned to Laura, a bit of fear creeping in at the edges of her happiness at how her friend would respond to her admission. Laura had a strange look on her face when she turned to Precious.

That strange look turned into a smile. "Oh my god, P. Just say you're fucking them and be done with it."

Precious and Laura laughed. A real, loud, secret laugh that reminded Precious of what their relationship had been like before Dr. Friedlander.

"We're not just fucking," Precious said, maybe a little too loud. "It's not just fucking," she repeated in a more normal voice. "It's so much more than that. I've never been in a relationship so real and intense. Everything is just so much more with Cali and Mike."

Laura giggled. Precious rolled her eyes.

"Not just because there's two of them," Precious said. "I just feel like I've found where I belong. The people I belong with. It sounds crazy, especially because of everything happening... right now. But I just—" She shrugged. "I'm happy."

Laura took a minute to think about what Precious had said.

Precious soaked up the feeling of finally having her friend back, even under these circumstances.

After a few minutes, Laura finally responded. "I think I get it," she said. "And I'm happy for you. I know I've been not the best friend to you recently, and I'm sorry."

Precious stopped walking and turned to Laura. "Excuse me, what now? Can I hear that again?"

"Absolutely not," Laura said, laughing. "I can only apologize once every five years."

Precious laughed and reached out to hug the friend she'd so desperately missed.

When Laura pulled back though, her face was serious. Precious knew she wasn't going to like what she said.

"I'm happy you're happy, but I have to ask the thing you would ask me if I were in your shoes. The thing you probably would have asked me if I'd told you about... him earlier." Laura took a deep breath. "What if they decide they don't want you anymore? What if this was all an experiment with you and they go back to only wanting each other?"

Precious wanted to tell Laura that wouldn't happen because the three of them were perfect together, but she didn't say that, because that had been her biggest fear ever since that first night together. She'd been too afraid to bring it up to Cali and Mike because she didn't know what they'd say. So Precious didn't answer Laura's very reasonable question.

They walked to the pizza parlor in silence and got a table near the window.

"Oh my god, I've got it," Laura said with wide eyes after they'd ordered.

"Got what?" Precious asked.

Laura rolled her eyes. "I know what to do."

By the time their food arrived, they'd already started plotting Laura's escape from the Sociology

Department with minimal damage to her reputation. With a belly full of bread and cheese, they both realized that Laura could just transfer to another unit on campus. Laura had been admitted to the History Department at the same time as Sociology, and still had a professor there interested in working with her. It would all be so easy, they realized, and left the restaurant with a solid foundation of a plan they decided to hash out when they were both sober.

Laura offered Precious the spare bed in her dorm room, but more as a formality than anything. She was clearly surprised when Precious accepted. Precious told her it was because she was too drunk to take the subway home and she didn't want to waste the money on an Uber. But really, it was because Precious had been thinking about Laura's question the entire time they'd been eating.

Finally hearing her biggest fear out loud made the knot of anxiety Precious had been resolutely ignoring grow. It was a feeling that she'd been able to pretend didn't exist whenever Mike and Cali's bodies were rubbing against hers. But without them, Precious felt as if there was nothing left besides that knot, and the thought of going home scared her because she wanted to be with them forever, and she knew she wouldn't be able to bear it if they didn't want the same.

She didn't want to leave the sanctuary of their apartment. She didn't want to wake up without Cali's loud music, following her around while she watered her plants. She didn't want to grade her papers without the soundtrack of Mike's grunting workouts or shouts at his first-person shooter games.

She wanted meals around the kitchen island and weed-laced lemon bars on Wednesday nights while they watched their favorite tv show together. She wanted the taste of Cali on her tongue and Mike's dick inside her. She wanted the comfort and safety of being Cali and Mike's middle spoon.

But what if all the things she wanted had an expiration date?

---

Cali hated the subway, and she was willing to do nearly anything to avoid it.

She'd learned to accept Mike and Precious's teasing about all the money she wasted on Ubers because they liked to tease her and, now that she didn't feel the need to have skin quite so thick, she found that she liked to be teased by them. Especially when she was sitting cross-legged on their bed and Mike leaned forward to gently bite her nipple, and suck it into his mouth in between verbal jabs. Or if Precious was gently stroking her pussy, teasing her body with her fingers just as much as her words.

When she walked down to the subway station after her session with Dr. Toussaint, she smiled to herself thinking about the big production they'd make of this very rare occasion. Trying to imagine some of their jokes helped to ease her mind as she thought about how to tell them about her grandmother, her parents and all the secrets she'd been keeping. She didn't have a full plan when she walked through their front door, so the fact that their apartment was quiet and dark was an unexpected blessing. Cali even marveled that the quiet didn't terrify her for once. She decided to take it as a sign that Dr. Toussaint was right; she was growing, she had the capacity to change.

She turned on all the lights in the living room and kitchen and connected her phone to the Bluetooth speaker. She put on something fast and catchy, but not as loud as she normally would have. She filled her water pail and began to check on her plants as she thought, figuring that by the time Precious or Mike walked through the door, she'd have a solid plan.

But then all her plants were watered. She'd taken a shower and done an exfoliating treatment on her face. Her playlist was starting over and her stomach was growling.

She called Mike. He didn't pick up.

She called Precious. Her phone went straight to voicemail.

It shouldn't have been so easy for her to spiral; she had coping mechanisms for this. She blamed Dr. Toussaint for making her talk about her grandmother. She blamed Mike and Precious for slithering under her defenses. And in the end, she blamed herself, because her grandmother had been right. She always was.

When Cali fell asleep that night, she was still alone, her music turned up loud enough to just barely chase the loneliness away. The lights in the bedroom were still on, and her pillow was wet with tears. The last thought in her head told her that she was just too difficult to love, and the voice sounded exactly like her grandmother.

# 9

Precious felt gross, and taking the subway hungover in yesterday's clothing only made her feel worse. She'd downed two bottles of water and brushed her teeth with her finger before leaving Laura's dorm room.

She could have stayed, showered, borrowed some clean clothing and maybe even had brunch the way they used to, but Precious and Laura weren't the same people they'd been a year ago. They'd grown up and apart. And even though they'd started to mend their friendship, this was the first morning she'd woken up without Cali and Mike in a month and a half, and she didn't like it.

So, she'd slipped out of Laura's dorm. She'd stopped to get another water and a fried egg sandwich at a bodega on the way to the train. She blamed the greasy sandwich for the roiling in her gut. She clutched her stomach as the elevator lurched up to the sixth floor and ran to her front door.

As soon as she put her key in the door, though, she knew something was wrong.

---

When Mike told his parents he wasn't going to law school and wanted to move to New York to be a model, his mother stopped speaking to him for a week. She still did all the same mom things she normally did, but her disappointment filled their house like a sad, angry fog.

He'd realized then how silence could be the worst punishment of all.

When he stumbled into the apartment at two in the morning and found all the lights on and their bedroom door closed and locked, all the whiskey he'd drunk suddenly came up.

He'd hoped Precious and Cali would hear him getting sick and take care of him, but they didn't. He was kneeling beside the toilet for so long he passed out for a bit. He woke up in the middle of the night feeling disgusting and sad. He crawled into the shower alone, trying not to remember every time Cali and Precious had crowded in with him.

He threw a towel around his waist and knocked on the bedroom door, softly at first. When no one answered, he knocked again, but louder. Still no answer. He took out his phone and called Cali. He heard her phone ringing behind the door because the music on her Bluetooth speaker shut off, but she didn't pick up, and then the music started again. He called Precious but couldn't hear her phone ringing. She didn't pick up.

Mike walked into the kitchen, angry and hurt. He drank some water, made a piece of toast to coat his stomach and then walked to Precious's room. He angled his too tall body onto her normal-sized twin bed and wrapped himself in her blankets, the towel still around his waist.

He left the door open, just in case.

---

The apartment was too quiet.

Normally, Precious could feel Cali's music on a Friday morning. Precious liked to sleep in on Fridays since she didn't have class or office hours, and she could hang out at home all day in sweats with her head in a book, or between Cali and Mike's legs. But Cali never slept in. Once she was up, she was up. And if Cali was up, her music was on, and then the entire apartment was awake.

As soon as Precious stepped into the apartment, the silence was deafening. Sunlight streamed in through the living room windows. She kicked off her shoes and walked to the hallway. Her stomach was doing flips with each step. She needed to shower, but she just wanted to see Cali and Mike first. Their bedroom door was open, and she walked toward it, but stopped when she saw someone in her bed in her peripheral vision.

Mike's long body was sprawled diagonally on her bed, wrapped inside her comforter. Precious turned to the other bedroom — their bedroom — and walked inside. The room was empty. The bed was made. Cali never made the bed.

Precious turned back to her bedroom. Mike was fast asleep, snoring lightly. She reached down to shake him. "Mike," she whispered. "Mike, wake up."

He shoved his face into her pillow and mumbled, "Oh, now you want to see me?"

Precious's brow furrowed. "Mike, wake up. Where's Cali?"

Mike's eyes shot open, and he sat up so quickly, Precious had to jump back before she got mowed down by one of his impossibly long limbs. His eyes were unfocused, but Precious couldn't help but admire how beautiful he was. It made her self-conscious because she felt like day-old leftovers forgotten on the kitchen counter.

She took another unconscious step back.

"What's happening?" Mike said, less a question than general confusion.

"Where's Cali?" Precious asked again. "I just got home and it's so quiet."

Mike squinted up at her. "Just got home? Where have you been?"

"I got drunk with Laura last night and stayed with her," Precious whispered, feeling sad and ashamed.

"You mean you weren't here when I came in this morning?"

"This morning!?" Precious didn't mean to yell. A headache bloomed in her temple. "Where were you?"

"I was—" His eyebrows pinched together, and he looked down. "Something happened at work. I went out for a drink and got back at like two this morning."

"What happened at work?" Precious asked, the worry and confusion making her headache worse.

"It's complicated," he said, and changed the subject. "Cali called me a few times last night, but I didn't pick up."

Precious frowned. "I didn't pick up when she called me, either."

Even though they'd spent the last few weeks becoming very intimate physically, and before that she'd become as close to Mike and Cali as she was to Laura, Precious accepted there was still so much about her roommates she didn't know. She knew Cali loved eggs, took her hair and skincare routines very seriously, hated to be alone in their apartment and could not tolerate the quiet, but she didn't know why.

When Mike raised his head his eyes full of worry, Precious felt like the floor had dropped from underneath her. She ran to the bathroom and threw up.

---

Mike pulled his phone from the nightstand charger. He called Cali while he walked into their bedroom, needing to see for himself that she wasn't there. She didn't pick up, so he called her again. He walked to the kitchen. He could hear Precious throwing up in the bathroom and it broke his heart. He filled a cup with water and left a message. "Call us. Where are you? I'm sorry I wasn't here last night."

He walked to the bathroom and sat next to the toilet. He rubbed Precious's back with one hand and texted Cali with the other.

Cali pick up your phone. Please.
I love you.
We love you.

When Precious stopped throwing up, he flushed the toilet and handed her the water. He watched her drink while checking Cali's social media.

Nothing.

"She's not picking up," he told Precious. He was trying to keep his voice calm, even though his heart felt like it was beating out of his chest.

Precious wiped her mouth with her sleeve. She kept her arm in front of her mouth while she spoke. "What happened at work?"

He smiled. She was adorable; still as adorable as

the night they met. He wanted to hug her and pull her into the shower. He wanted to wash her back, sliding his hands over her skin until she felt better. He wanted to fall into bed with her and sleep off their hangovers together.

He wanted Cali to be there with them.

"I left my agency," he said softly.

"What?" she yelled, although the sound was muffled by her sweater sleeve.

"It's complicated."

"You already said that," she screeched.

He smiled. "And that's all I'm going to say until we find Cali."

Mentioning Cali made tears spring to Precious's eyes. "I would have picked up," she said in a small voice. "I just... thought you were with her."

His smile faltered. "And I thought *you* were with her." There was a sad beat of silence between them, and then he laughed. It wasn't so much mirthful as rueful. "There are too many people in this relationship. We need to get trackers for each other."

Precious laughed, and one tear rolled down her cheek. "Ah, yes. Just some light electronic stalking. That's exactly how we'll convince people that this is a healthy relationship."

Mike laughed in earnest this time.

Precious dropped her hand from her face.

Mike frowned.

"This is a... relationship, right? The three of us? It's not just you two and me?" she asked nervously.

She sounded so sad, and it made Mike feel terrible. It was naïve to only just now realize that she might feel insecure in their relationship, but he'd been so worried he was the third wheel — that he was expendable to Cali — that he hadn't even considered how Precious might feel being with a couple. He'd assumed they'd made it clear how much they wanted her, but he only just realized that they'd never said it aloud.

He opened his mouth just as his phone beeped.

"It's Cali," he said, finally exhaling in a brief moment of relief.

Omw home. We all need to talk.

Mike gulped. Whatever happiness he felt at finally hearing from Cali was washed away with foreboding, and he saw the same fear on Precious's face.

He reached out to rub her shoulder.

"Come on," he said, leaning over to kiss her forehead, "let's get you in the shower."

He tried to busy himself by throwing on some clothes and making coffee, but he felt like he was waiting for his execution. The cell phone in his basketball shorts felt like an anchor weighing him down. He put on a brave face when Precious walked out of the bathroom, her too short towel clutched tightly around her body. She threw on a pair of boy shorts and a tight tank top and joined him in the kitchen. His eyes drank her body in appreciatively; it was second nature by this point. He couldn't stop the wave of lust he felt, especially not when, once again, he saw his feelings mirrored in her face.

But without Cali, neither of their hearts were in it.

# 10

Cali was wrapped in their blankets all alone. They smelled like Mike's cologne. She turned her head into her pillow. It smelled like Precious's leave-in conditioner. Her eyes were already wet with tears.

She felt like she was suffocating, and it scared her.

She sat up in bed and immediately reached for her phone.

She ignored her social media notifications. Her thumb stumbled over Mike's missed call. She turned her head toward the door, knowing he was out there. She wanted to go to him, but she couldn't. She never could, and all the progress she'd made felt like a distant memory. There were no missed calls or texts from Precious.

She took a deep breath and called the only person

who could help her sort through the mess of her feelings.

"Hello," Dr. Toussaint said.

Cali felt terrible calling this early, but Dr. Toussaint had always encouraged her to reach out when she needed help. Cali had never taken her up on the offer and she hoped she could forgive her this once, because she needed all the help she could get.

"Hi, Dr. Toussaint. It's Cali."

"Hello, dear. Is everything alright?"

"Yes. No," she said quickly. "I need... Do you have time to talk today? I can come anytime you're free."

Cali wasn't sure if she sounded as lost and desperate as she felt or if Dr. Toussaint was a saint, but when she said she could fit her in before her first scheduled appointment, Cali thought she might faint in relief. She was like a whirlwind, grabbing whatever clothes were closest. She'd pulled on an old pair of jeans, one of Precious's tank tops and Mike's favorite sweatshirt without thinking.

She unlocked their bedroom door and eased it open. The quiet made her skin tingle in a not great way, but she pushed herself to step into the hallway.

She heard Mike's snores from Precious's bedroom. She stopped in the doorway and smiled at the sight of his long body on her short bed. She stepped unconsciously into the bedroom; the urge to crawl on top of him and listen to him sleep was so strong it brought tears to her eyes, but she stopped herself.

She looked at him for a few seconds more before going to the bathroom. She brushed her teeth and washed her face as quickly and as quietly as possible. She scanned the living room and kitchen, surprised not to see Precious anywhere, and she realized what she hadn't been able to comprehend in last night's sadness; Precious was probably with Laura.

And then she slipped out of the apartment.

---

They went through the same old routine, just like yesterday and every week before it, going back four years.

Cali's nervous, jumping leg.

Dr. Toussaint's smile.

Coffee, tea, water?

Water.

Tea.

Neutral face.

Head tilt.

"How are you today?"

Cali felt like a balloon ready to pop, and when Dr. Toussaint asked that familiar question, she gave herself permission to split herself open.

"Terrible," she said in a relieved breath. She continued before Dr. Toussaint could interject with a follow-up question. Cali had plenty of follow up on her own. "I went home last night ready to tell Mike and

Precious about my grandmother and they never came home!"

Dr. Toussaint's neutral mask shifted into a look of confusion. "Never came home?"

"Well," Cali hedged, "Mike came home early this morning, but Precious wasn't there when I left."

"Where is she?"

"I think with her friend Laura. She's been going through some stuff—"

"Precious?"

"No. Laura." Cali jumped up and started pacing around. There was so much backstory to tell and the movement helped her focus. "She was dating their married professor and he left his wife. That's how Precious became our roommate; Laura bailed on her. Which I think is shitty, but she's Precious's friend and I don't want to rag on her."

"Except you do," Dr. Toussaint offered.

"Oh, I totally do. What the fuck kind of friend does that? But I haven't met her, and I haven't wanted to pry for more info than Precious wants to give, so I've just kept my mouth shut. But honestly, she sounds like a dick."

"And you think Precious was with Laura last night?"

"Yeah, because Precious is way too good of a friend to her."

"And that makes you angry?"

Cali stopped pacing. She looked at Dr. Toussaint. "I do sound angry, don't I?"

"Yes, you do. But are you?"

Cali began pacing again, chewing on her bottom lip as she considered the question. "Maybe. I'm starting to realize that I might be a little territorial in my relationships."

"Is that why you said no to Mike's friend being your roommate?"

"Rick?" Cali had to think about that. "Yeah, I guess. They would have just sat around the house all day playing video games without me."

"Without you?"

"Yeah. They're Mike's thing."

"Does Mike not play video games now?"

"No, he plays them all the time."

"By himself?"

"No, he has a headset thing and he plays with his friends back home and Rick and randoms from all over the world. He mostly just yells at them to 'watch his six', whatever the hell that means." Cali rolled her eyes.

Dr. Toussaint chuckled lightly. "And what do you and Precious do while he's playing?"

Cali shrugged. "Whatever. Bake, read magazines, paint our nails. Whatever." It was a conscious effort to stop herself from listing some of the other things they got up to while Mike played his video games. Dr. Toussaint didn't need to know all that.

"And why couldn't you have done that if Rick had moved in?"

Cali sat back down in her chair and leaned over with her elbows on her knees. "Ok, I might be very territorial," she said in response.

"But you didn't veto Precious," Dr. Toussaint said.

Cali couldn't stop the grin from spreading over her lips. "There's no need to be territorial when it's just the three of us."

"And why is that?"

"That's the thing, I don't know. That's why I'm here. Last night I went into a spiral. I was emotional and crying and all I could think about was the way my grandmother used to tell me that no one would ever love me."

"Your grandmother was a terrible person, as you've pointed out many times. And I agree, by the way."

Cali smiled weakly. "I know. But every time I'm feeling insecure, her voice is the only one I can hear. And last night all I could think is that after a month and a half with me, they both just ran away. Because it was too much. I was too much."

"Well, that's not true," Dr. Toussaint replied.

"I know, I know, I'm not supposed to let myself think like that—"

"No, I mean, that's just factually untrue."

Cali's eyebrows bunched together as she stared at Dr. Toussaint.

"You've been with Mike almost three years, and from what you've told me, artful omissions aside," Dr. Toussaint continued with a sly grin and a raised eyebrow, "it sounds like the three of you have been building this relationship since the moment Precious moved in. Just without the sex, until recently."

Cali sat back, a brief flash of that voice in her head screaming about her posture. "You really do know everything going on with me, don't you?"

Dr. Toussaint let loose a loud guffaw that made Cali smile. "Well, technically that *is* my job. But no, I actually don't know everything. And feel free to continue the artful omissions. But I will say that I knew something had changed with you weeks before you ever mentioned Precious."

"How?" Cali asked, reaching over to grab her glass of water.

Dr. Toussaint sat up straighter, and Cali realized that whatever she was about to say was something she'd been longing to say for months, maybe even years.

"You've spent every minute of your relationship with Mike agonizing about how to tell him what you want and need and wondering if and when you should tell him about your grandmother. We had to discuss your offer to move in together for almost four months before you felt comfortable even saying the words. You've kept that man at arm's length, while wishing you could pull him closer. You try so hard to not let your past touch your present. But then one day, you swan in here—"

"I don't swan," Cali laughed.

Dr. Toussaint ignored her. "You swan in here and tell me that you told your sister about Mike. It wasn't a question. You didn't want to discuss it. It already was. You made the decision to tell your sister about your boyfriend on your own and then you did it. I knew then that something must have changed. And apparently, it had."

Cali sat with that thought, taking small sips of her water. Dr. Toussaint sipped her tea, allowing Cali the space to consider.

"Something did change," Cali whispered to herself.

"Precious," Dr. Toussaint breathed.

Cali nodded.

"So, here's the question I've been mulling over with regards to this unconventional relationship."

Cali rolled her eyes and smiled.

"Are you in a relationship with Mike, and you both invite Precious to be with you sometimes?" Cali had already started shaking her head, but Dr. Toussaint finished, "Or is it really the three of you together, all the time?"

"It's all the time. Mike and I might have been together for three years before Precious, but like you said, I never could let myself just be with him. I was too nervous about opening up?"

"Because of your grandmother?"

"Yeah," Cali breathed. "And I guess that was the problem last night. My grandmother always said that I was spoiled, nothing like my perfect sister. I was too dark, too loud, too greedy, everything I shouldn't be. Even wanting Mike like I'd never wanted anyone before made me self-conscious. I kept wondering if I was too clingy, and then I'd pull away.

And adding Precious to all of that should have made me feel worse. How could my grandmother have been wrong about me if I'm here wanting these *two* people? But I ignored that voice in my head for the longest time because I couldn't get enough of them. I don't think I'll ever get enough of them. But last night, when they didn't come home, I was just consumed with the thought that she was right."

"You know she wasn't right, don't you, Cali?" Dr. Toussaint was using the soft, gentle voice she reserved for the times they had to tread lightly over all her trauma.

Cali licked her lips and was silent as she considered — really considered — the question. She made eye contact with Dr. Toussaint. "I do," she said, smiling so wide her cheeks made her eyes squint closed.

Dr. Toussaint smiled back.

"Good. So, how about you go home and talk to your boyfriend... and girlfriend. You don't have to carry the burden of your past alone if you don't want to."

It wasn't a new piece of advice. Dr. Toussaint had been telling her some version of this message since their very first appointment. Only Cali had never been able to hear her. But now Cali was ready to hear Dr. Toussaint loud and clear.

# 11

After her shower, Precious felt clean but raw.

Mike kept refilling her glass of water and made her some toast, even though she'd only been able to eat half of it. She could see that he wanted her to eat more, but he was too distracted by worry and his own hangover to needle her about it. They were sitting at the kitchen island across from one another, not talking. Precious couldn't remember their apartment being quiet for so long, and she didn't like it. She pulled her sweatshirt sleeves over her hands and willed the queasy feeling in her stomach to stop and her heartbeat to slow.

Their heads turned at the sound of keys unlocking their door, but neither of them moved. They watched the door open and Cali breezed into their apartment with a white bakery box in one hand. She dropped her purse and keys on the coffee table and made her way to the kitchen.

Precious studied her face, trying to decipher her mood, but Cali's face was blank.

When she walked into the kitchen, she stopped, clutching the bakery box in both hands nervously. Precious could smell sweet dough and peeked at the logo and knew the box would be full of Mike's favorite donuts. When her eyes lifted to Cali's face, the neutral mask slipped away and Cali smiled. Precious saw the play of emotions in her face. She was nervous, which made Precious nervous. Precious turned to look at Mike and saw relief mixing with confusion on his face.

"Where have you been?" he asked. Precious could hear fear and simmering rage in his voice.

"I brought donuts," Cali said, dodging his question. She put the box in the center of the island and opened it. She turned to Precious. "I got the sweet potato ones you like."

Precious smiled weakly, but frowned again when Cali stayed at the head of the island. She usually found a way to crawl into Mike's lap in the morning or press herself against Precious's side because she loved to touch them and be touched. It was one of the things Precious loved about her immediately.

"Are we breaking up?" Precious blurted out. The insistent throbbing in her left temple had intensified.

Mike pushed to stand and lean against the kitchen sink. "I don't know. Are we?" He aimed the question at

Cali, which wasn't fair, but he didn't know who else to ask in this moment, and neither did Precious.

Precious watched Cali take a few deep breaths before she turned to Mike. "Do you remember what we were fighting about the night we met Precious?"

Mike's eyebrows knit together but he nodded. "I told you I wanted to meet your sister and you got angry at me for prying."

Precious turned to Cali, waiting on her answer. "Right, because it wasn't really about my sister. She's a florist in Boston, single, no kids, lots of pets, and she keeps racking up astronomical late fees at the library because she forgets to return the books after she reads them. Very normal."

Mike was incredulous. "Why are you just now telling me this? I was expecting something off-the-wall, like a spy or she'd disowned you or something." He laughed, but it wasn't a happy one.

"Because," Cali said, and turned to Precious so that it was clear that this was for both of them. "My sister used to be a Rhodes Scholar. She was like this insanely smart botanist who was going to start her own biotechnology firm or something. And then my grandmother died." Cali took a deep breath, and Precious could tell this was a painful story for her to tell. "When my grandmother died, my sister told me she finally felt free.

She dropped out of school. Used her inheritance to travel for a bit, trying to find herself, and then she settled in Boston. She forgets to return the books because she doesn't have our grandmother hounding her to be perfect anymore. She can just be herself. And apparently who she is doesn't give a shit about deadlines. It's sweet. And considering what our grandmother put us through, it could be much worse."

Precious heard her own intake of breath from far away. Mike's back had gone rigid. "What did she put you through, Cali?"

Cali smiled through her tears. Precious wanted to run to her and hold her, but she wasn't sure if that was what Cali needed.

"My sister's beautiful. Tall, naturally thin, really pale skin. Most people don't even realize she's Black when they meet her, especially if her hair is straight. And our grandmother made sure that it was always straight." Cali chewed her lip and swiped at her tears. "I was not so perfect or beautiful. Compared to Selene, I was too much like my mother. Eventually I realized that just meant I was too Black. And my grandmother had never approved of her only son — her only child — marrying a Black woman."

Precious and Mike moved at the same time, reaching for Cali. She stepped back and put her hands up to keep them at bay while she finished.

"She kept me on a restrictive diet, trying to keep me as thin as Selene. She never had a nice thing to say to or about me. I don't—" She hesitated, chewing on her lip and wringing her hands. "I don't really remember my parents, but I remember going from a home that felt full of love and laughter and noise to a house that was quiet and dark and lonely."

She turned to look at Mike again, her eyes wet and sad. "Your mom calls you every Sunday and sends you your favorite junk food from Ohio and Korea." She turned to Precious, "You and your mom write each other real letters, and your brother calls you from Vienna all the time. That's not my life. I'm really happy when my sister sends me a birthday card within four months of my actual birthday. Like honestly, that's the highlight of my year.

Selene is all I have left, but I don't really have her. Whatever my grandmother did to my spirit, neglect was better in some ways than all that pressure she put on Selene. And I guess," she closed her eyes to finish her sentence, "I didn't want to give my grandmother a chance to ruin this, too."

Mike pulled Cali to his chest and Cali pressed her face against his body. Precious knew Cali was crying and she wrapped her arms around Cali's waist, fitting herself behind her. Cali's soft cries turned to wails, but she relaxed between them.

---

They took the donuts to bed. Of all the things they'd done in this bed and this apartment, eating a box of still warm donuts was a fantasy Mike hadn't realized he'd had.

Cali was sandwiched between him and Precious. Normally, when they got donuts, she split a single donut with Precious but barely ate her half. But this time, Mike watched her lick sugar from her fingers after eating an entire donut by herself. Mike didn't want to spook her by commenting on it, but he smiled around a bite of his own donut.

He hadn't planned to blurt it out, but he had loose lips when he was happy, his mom always said.

"My agent quit almost two months ago and last night I got out of my contract with my agency."

Precious sat up coughing.

Mike patted her on the back and then nudged her to the nightstand and her glass of water. Cali was frozen in between them, her index finger still in her mouth.

When Precious finally stopped coughing, Cali seemed to come back to life. She moved the box of donuts off her lap. "Two months?"

"*About* two months," he corrected, trying to lighten the mood.

"Tell me everything," Cali said. Her mouth set into a fierce line. She wrapped an arm around Precious while the fingers of her other hand laced with his. Something about it reminded him of the day they met four years ago.

*They were shooting a holiday campaign for a new*

*athleisure brand. Mike's star was on the rise with Sarah's steady guidance. He'd become the new "ethnic" face of men's athletic wear, but he had his eye on an expansive commercial career. His mother had even called him after seeing one of his campaigns at their local mall. She'd gushed for a full five minutes about how good he looked, before telling him he wasn't allowed to do any underwear modeling. He'd been so happy that she was happy that he decided to hold off on telling her about the underwear shoot he'd already done.*

*All in all, things were looking up for the "fat" Asian kid from Cleveland.*

*He noticed her as soon as he walked on set. He'd never seen Cali before. If he had, he wouldn't have forgotten. She seemed even smaller than the other models from far away; more fragile. But up close, he realized that the thin wrists that he'd taken for frailty were actually the smooth musculature of a well-toned body. And her small waist masked beautiful, wide hips.*

*But she never smiled.*

*All the other models joked around with one another, but Cali kept her distance. She wasn't rude. She spoke to some of the other female models when they spoke to her, but she didn't seek out any attention and didn't seem to notice that she had all of Mike's.*

*It was a coincidence when the photographer put them together for couple shots. Mike had said a silent prayer of thanks for that.*

*They were facing one another, waiting for the photogra-*

*pher's direction. Mike smiled and opened his mouth to speak, but she cut him off.*

*"Don't talk."*

*He frowned.*

*Her eyes tracked that small movement of his lips, and then she made eye contact.*

*"Sorry," she said. "I didn't mean to be rude. I just need to concentrate."*

*"Concentrate on what?"*

*"My poses," she said, as if it was obvious. "I don't want them to seem too editorial."*

*Mike smiled. "You don't normally shoot commercial?"*

*She gave him a shy smile that made his heart warm. "No. But I want to diversify my portfolio."*

*Mike leaned down and whispered in her ear, "Step number one for commercial models: loosen up."*

*And then she laughed. Mike pulled back to see how the laughter changed her face; the flash of her bright white teeth and her bright pink tongue.*

*They heard a camera click.*

*The moment was gone. They went to work. It took Mike close to a year to get Cali to agree to go on a date with him.*

*It was worth the wait.*

*And when Precious blurted out that she'd seen their picture — that picture — of the two of them in Times Square, Mike had taken it as a sign.*

He told them about Sarah leaving and his agency's restructuring. He thought maybe in retelling it all, he might be able to figure out what to do next, but it didn't work. Mike reached for another donut, but Cali took it from him and started eating it herself. Precious giggled around a bite of her own donut.

Mike might not have found a solution yet, but he was happy not to have to share the weight of his burdens alone.

---

Precious wanted a nap. And more water. Also, she had to pee, and she wanted to talk about their relationship.

"You need to call Sarah," she said anxiously.

Mike's mouth was full of donut, and he finished chewing and swallowed before he answered. "I know. I am."

"No, now," she said, unsure why she felt such urgency, but also sure she was right.

"It can wait until tomorrow or later today," Cali said, running her hand through Mike's hair to soothe him.

"No, it can't," Precious replied.

"What's wrong, sweetheart?" Cali whispered.

Precious's brain was sluggish, and it took her a while to put together the threads that were nagging at her. Mike and Cali sat calmly and let her think, watching her. When she finally figured out why this felt so important, she sat up on her knees to face them. Cali had pulled off most of her clothes and crawled into bed in a pair of panties and Precious's tank top. Mike was in a pair of boxers and nothing else. Precious had to force her mind to focus on the topic at hand and not the lust she always felt when she was with them.

"Okay, so when Dr. Friedlander dumped Laura, everyone in the department was shitty, but mostly they left her alone. They thought the relationship had been a dumb decision on both of their parts. But then all of a sudden, Dr. Friedlander was everywhere, literally everywhere. At department events and in the main office, hanging around the faculty lounge, everywhere. But Laura felt like she had to move to the library, and it was like a flip switched, and everyone was talking about how she'd seduced him and was trying to break up his marriage.

And I just... Look, it's not a perfectly analogy," Precious said to the skeptical look on Mike's face. "But I just think you should reach out to Sarah before Kenneth does anything crazy. You have to take control of the narrative."

Mike was looking at her like she was growing a new head, but there was a smile on Cali's face when she spoke.

"I knew she'd be good for us," she said, burrowing deeper under their covers, her fingers still slipping through Mike's hair.

Precious blushed. "Was this another bet?"

Mike threw the covers from his waist and crawled

over Cali. He leaned down and pressed a quick kiss to Precious's lips. "Nope. I agreed with her." He winked at her and crawled from their bed. He grabbed his phone from the nightstand and sped out of the room.

Precious and Cali watched him with smiles on their faces.

Mike's voice drifted down the hallway. "Hey, Sarah..."

Cali moved the covers aside and patted the mattress next to her. Precious crawled under the covers and draped her body over Cali's side. She slipped her right leg between Cali's and rubbed the skin over Cali's stomach and ribs. So much had happened this morning, and Precious just wanted to touch her and be touched.

Cali smoothed a lock of Precious's hair between her fingers. Precious pressed her face into the crook of Cali's neck, breathing her in. They stayed like that, soft touches, their heartbeats beating together rhythmically.

When Mike returned, he crawled into bed and wrapped his arm around Cali's middle, his hand grazing the underside of Precious's breast.

"So, what'd she say?" Precious asked, breathing into Cali's skin. Cali shivered.

"She said she's been waiting two months to hear from me," Mike laughed. "She also said that Kenneth left her a voice message out of the blue last night, asking her to call him."

"I knew it," Precious said, leaning back to smile triumphantly.

Mike rolled his eyes. "Don't gloat."

Precious snuggled in closer to Cali and ran her hand up Mike's arm.

"Later," Cali breathed. "Let's take a nap. I just want to feel you both next to me."

"Same," Precious said, turning away from them. Cali turned and they pressed their bodies together back to front.

Mike threw an arm over them both.

"I was afraid this was all over this morning," Precious said, finding it easier to say those words now that she couldn't see them.

"So was I," Mike admitted in a quiet whisper.

"I cried myself to sleep last night," Cali said, her breath brushing the hair at the nape of Precious's neck.

"We need to get better at talking to each other," Mike said. "It's too easy to hurt each other with so many people in this relationship."

Precious could feel Cali nodding her head between them.

When she finally got the courage to say the thing that had been on her mind since last night, she swore she could feel her heart beating in her throat. "Are we —" She cleared her throat. "Are we *all* in this relationship, or am I... you know... you two plus me?"

Mike tightened his arm around them, and Cali pressed a kiss to the back of Precious's neck.

"Precious, you're ridiculously smart, but that was a very dumb question. We're literally all in this together. But if you need us to prove it to you," Cali yawned, and then continued, "I'm happy to show you just how much I want you, when I wake up from this nap."

"Ditto," Mike said. Precious could hear his smile in his voice. "Although, Cali can feel how much I want you poking into her back."

Precious laughed, big and loud. She drifted off to sleep, knowing that she was exactly where she belonged.

## 12

### Three Weeks Later

"Girl, you better remember to renew these books before you fly home," Precious said. She was looking at Laura's bookcase in her new office in the History Department in Leeward Hall, just across the street from the Sociology Department. It wasn't far from the Sociology Department, but the bright small office — that she only had to share with one other student — felt a million miles away.

"Ooh, good point. I really don't have the money for fines this year."

"You could just return them," Precious said, turning to make eye contact with Laura. They burst out laughing.

"I'll return these books if they're recalled, my fines exceed $100 or I actually find the time to read them," she said in a cocky voice. Precious thought she almost sounded like her old self.

"They'll definitely get recalled before you read them," Precious giggled. "I'm so jealous you have a window!"

They stepped in front of the window and looked down on the campus oval. It was the last week of regular classes, the sun was out, and students had poured out onto the grass wearing shorts and bikinis, barefooted to take advantage of the spring weather. Some of the students were pretending to study, their books open on picnic blankets in front of them, unread. Other people chatted to each other while they listened to music, dozed in hammocks or played Frisbee.

Precious almost wanted to join them. The end of the academic year was so close she could taste it on her tongue. "I'm gonna miss you," she whispered.

"I know. But I'm basically just next door," Laura said. "And we can still study together like normal."

Precious looked at Laura with sympathetic eyes.

It had been a shitty year, but the past few weeks had brightened Laura's mood and her pallor. After their drunken night of apologizing and scheming, it seemed like the stale air between them had finally begun to lift, and they'd both taken a turn for the better. Their relationship wasn't the same as it had been before Dr. Friedlander, but it would get there; Precious knew that for sure now.

"I'm really proud of you, you know that?" Precious said. She snatched her purse from the desk and walked to the door.

"Thanks, P," Laura said with teary eyes. "So, what are your summer plans, besides studying for comps?"

Precious couldn't help the smile that spread across her face, or the warmth in her cheeks.

Laura rolled her eyes. "So, your roommates?"

"Cali and Mike," Precious said. "You can use their names."

Laura chewed her bottom lip and thought about it. "If I use their names, it'll be like it's real. Like they're your boyfriend and girlfriend. Is that what it is?"

"That's exactly what it is," Precious said immediately.

"They make you happy?"

"Very."

"They treat you well?"

"Absolutely."

Laura looked at her seriously, taking her in from head to toe. Sometimes Precious could see the old Laura; confident, headstrong, and romantic to a fault. Other times — times like this — she could see the changes wrought by her relationship with Dr. Friedlander, and it made Precious mad. But if the new Laura was a little more protective of her heart, Precious hoped that was a good thing.

Finally, Laura took a deep breath in and smiled on the exhale. "Then I'm happy for you, P."

Precious rushed forward, pulling Laura into a tight hug.

---

Cali was sitting in Mike's lap on a bench outside of Leeward Hall while they waited for Precious to finish helping Laura move into her new office.

"Are you nervous?" Her hands were on either side of his head, her thumbs gently stroking his cheeks.

His eyes were closed in relaxation. His arms were loose around her waist. "A little," he replied.

"Why? Sarah loves you."

He opened his eyes to look at her. Cali's breath hitched.

"You never used to ask me how I felt," he breathed.

She leaned down and pressed a small kiss to the tip of his nose. He was smiling when she pulled back. "It wasn't because I didn't care. I was just—" She paused, trying to find the right word. She tried to imagine which word Dr. Toussaint would suggest, but all she could imagine was her therapist giving her a sympathetic smile, silently encouraging her to try out whatever word came to mind to see if it fit. Cali licked her lips. "I was just scared."

"Scared of what?"

"Scared that if I showed you how much I cared, you'd reject me, even though I knew you wouldn't. I just couldn't stop myself from thinking that everyone I loved would leave me."

Mike tightened his arms around her waist, knowing how much she liked the reassurance of that pressure. He closed his eyes again.

There was a moment of silence between them. Cali was working on accepting silence even when it was just the two of them. She wanted to give him time to think, like he always gave her. She focused on the way her skin felt rubbing against his, and his dark eyelashes, long and beautiful. He opened his eyes to look at her again and leaned up to press his mouth to hers.

"Tell me your middle name," he whispered.

The question threw her off, and she laughed.

"You always tell me it's too personal. Do you still think that?"

Cali shook her head. She felt like she could hardly recognize herself or her relationship with Mike, and for the first time in months, it surprised her and made her happy.

She smiled down at Mike. "It's Andromeda."

There was another moment of silence before Mike burst into laughter. Cali's face felt hot, but her smile didn't slip.

"Oh, you're kidding me," Mike said, wheezing. "Your parents named you Calliope Andromeda? Why? How?"

Cali hated talking about her parents. She missed

them in ways she and Dr. Toussaint had yet to fully uncover and work through. Their loss was like an open, festering wound that she'd tried to seal with tiny band-aids, but for the first time maybe ever, she didn't want to tiptoe around her own pain, or lash out at anyone who got too close.

"They met in a Classics course in college. They were huge nerds."

"Clearly," Mike said. He pressed his mouth to hers again. Cali sighed into his mouth and let her teeth graze along his tongue as it slipped from her mouth. He leaned back, that same loving smile on his face that made her feel safe and warm the day they met. "We've gotta tell Precious."

"Tell me what?"

They turned quickly and their breath caught at the sight of her. She was wearing a pair of Cali's jean shorts low on her hips, one of Mike's V-neck t-shirts loose and tucked in at the waist. Cali licked her lips as her eyes traveled up Precious's long legs.

Mike moved one arm from around Cali and motioned Precious to them. She walked into their crush of bodies without hesitation.

"My full name," Cali replied, before pressing a chaste kiss just behind Precious's ear.

"What?"

"Long story. Tell her," Mike said. His voice was so excited, but Cali could also hear that it was deeper now, full of lust.

Cali whispered her name directly into her ear. Precious shivered. Cali felt the soft girth of Mike's cock begin to harden underneath her.

"Beautiful," Precious whispered.

"Fitting," Mike said, his lips against Cali's shoulder.

"I love you two," Cali said, not needing to think at all before the words that best described her feelings in this moment came from her mouth.

She couldn't wait to tell Dr. Toussaint about her progress.

---

Mike's naked skin was flushed a dark red from the shower. He turned his torso side-to-side to look at his reflection from all angles in the full-length mirror. He had a shoot for new headshots and he wanted to look his best. When he'd signed his new contract, Sarah had reassured him that everyone was excited to work with him. But he was still nervous.

Precious and Cali stumbled into their bedroom naked and laughing, disrupting his close inspection of his body. Cali was holding Precious around her middle.

"Oh my god, stop singing," Precious giggled.

"What? You don't like my voice?" Cali laughed. She started to sing off-key, loudly, into Precious's ear.

"Stop," Precious yelled, wrenching out of Cali's grasp and running between Mike and the mirror.

"How do you listen to music all day and all night but can't sing?"

"She always plays the music so loud so she can't hear herself sing," Mike offered with a smile on his face.

"Bingo," Cali said, kissing him quickly on the lips before reaching around him to try to grab Precious.

They all laughed, and Mike watched as Cali pulled Precious toward their bed. Cali started to sing again so Precious took hold of her face and kissed her, finally shutting her up.

Mike smiled at them. "How did I never think to do that?"

Precious and Cali smiled around their kiss.

"She's the smart one," Cali said against Precious's mouth. "I'm beauty, and you're brawn."

"A perfect set," Precious said, kissing Cali again.

Mike shook his head and turned back to the mirror. He wondered if he could squeeze in a gym session before his shoot. But then Precious moaned, and the sound pulled his attention back to their bed.

Cali's hand was between Precious's legs. Precious's head was thrown back in ecstasy, and Cali was licking at her neck. She turned to look at Mike with the dirtiest smile on her face.

"Stop worrying yourself to death," she whispered against Precious's skin. "Come to bed." Precious squeaked out a moan as Cali's hand began to move faster.

"How did you know?" he asked.

"Because we know you," Precious groaned. She grabbed Cali's face and licked the seam of her lips before turning to Mike. "And we love you."

Cali sucked Precious's tongue into her mouth. Mike watched them, grabbing at his dick as he walked to the bed, thoughts of the gym completely forgotten.

When he reached them, he moved Cali's hair from her shoulder and placed butterfly kisses on her shoulder blade. Precious grabbed the back of his neck and slipped her fingers into the hair at his nape. He pressed his chest to Cali's back and ran his fingernails up and down her sides. He caressed her. They listened to Precious's soft gasps as Cali's fingers brought her to climax.

Mike and Cali lowered Precious to their bed. Her body was shaking. Mike ran his hands through her hair while Cali licked Precious's climax from her fingers.

The gym could definitely wait.

---

Precious had been working on how to explain their relationship to herself and other people — her mother, in particular. She'd concluded that eighty per cent of the time, being with Cali and Mike was like every other relationship she'd had; they hung out at home, watched tv while high, baked cookies at midnight, danced around their living room while watering their plants and stole each other's clothes. Having a third person didn't drastically alter the nature of their relationship at all, and it gave them more clothes to steal. But twenty per cent of the time, Precious was willing to admit that maybe there was something different about their arrangement. And she guessed that this was one of those moments.

Precious ran her tongue up and down Cali's slit slowly, reveling in the taste of her. Her thighs shivered around Precious's head every time Precious sucked her clit into her mouth. She gripped Cali's ass, a cheek in each hand, and angled her face to slip her tongue into Cali's pussy, her nose conveniently rubbing against her clit.

Cali moaned.

Precious assumed Mike's answering groan was from the vibrations of Cali's moan around his dick, and it excited her. She opened her eyes and shuddered at the sight of his dick disappearing into Cali's mouth. He was lovingly stroking her back while she took his shaft deeper into her mouth. Precious watched this while she moved to suckle lightly on Cali's clit. They all moaned again.

So maybe this wasn't the usual relationship — and she definitely wouldn't be telling her mother about the twenty per cent — but she'd never been happier or more satisfied in her life, and that was what mattered.

Cali pulled back on a gasp. Mike's dick fell out of

her mouth as she moaned loudly. Precious had just pushed two and then three fingers into her pussy.

"Fuck," Cali whispered, shivering violently on Precious's face.

Mike stroked her cheek and slipped his dick back into her mouth, moving his hips gently forward and back.

Precious rubbed her thighs together trying to stave off a climax. She wanted to touch herself. But she wanted Mike or Cali or both of them to touch her more. She needed them to touch her.

She was perfectly happy to wait for them, because she knew they'd never make her wait for long.

---

It wasn't that she and Mike needed Precious to make their relationship work. That had been Cali's fear once upon a time. But Dr. Toussaint had been helping her see that if their relationship wasn't going to work, it wouldn't; Precious's presence would only have expedited its demise. Now, they were working on how Cali could express this all to Selene. She didn't need Selene's approval, but she wanted her to understand how important this relationship was to her; what it felt like to be in a relationship where they were all essential; no third wheel. At some point, her relationship with Mike had ceased to be its own entity and this new thing between the three of them had blossomed in its place. It was stronger, healthier, and made Cali feel safe and not alone in a way she used to worry she didn't deserve. It sometimes made her cry just thinking about it.

This was one of those moments.

Cali had pressed herself against Precious's body as they both straddled Mike's lap. She had a hand at Precious's breast, rolling her nipple between her fingers, while the other held Precious at the hip, guiding her.

Mike was inside Precious, and she was shaking at being so full of him. Cali knew the feeling; she loved that feeling. She also knew how amazing it felt to be inside Precious and feel her wet and hot around her. She wondered if Precious was clenching her sex around Mike's cock. She kissed and licked at Precious's neck just thinking about it.

Mike's fingers were digging into Cali's thighs. She knew that feeling, too. He wanted Precious to move, but they were all waiting on Cali to set their pace.

She moved both of her hands to Precious's hips and pressed her body forward, encouraging her to move with her. They all sighed in relief. Cali moved Precious's body forward and back, slowly up Mike's shaft and then down again.

Precious ground her pelvis into Mike's. He moaned in response and gripped Cali's thighs tighter.

Cali sucked Precious's earlobe into her mouth. She and Mike locked eyes as Cali moved Precious faster.

Precious's moans grew louder, more unhinged. Cali could feel her own wetness dripping from her sex. There wasn't anything that turned her on more than when Precious's body was crushed between her and Mike and they fucked her together.

Cali moved one hand across Precious's torso to the apex of her legs. She kept her eyes on Mike as she slipped her fingers over Precious's mound to circle her clit.

Precious cried out.

Mike closed his eyes and grimaced.

Cali figured the wet grip of Precious's pussy was threatening to make him come and he was trying to fight it off. It was commendable, but he wouldn't last, not if Cali had anything to say about it. She kept Precious's hips forward. Cali fucked Precious onto Mike through one orgasm and another until Mike came apart.

He grabbed at them to hold them still and then started grinding his hips up into them. He was fucking them, harder and faster, until he clamped them all together and ground against Precious and Cali's body for his release. It was perfect. Cali had never felt anything like it. Maybe it did make her greedy, but she didn't care.

She couldn't find the words yet, but she would. She'd find a way to explain to her sister that Mike and Precious were her home. For the first time in the longest time, she was home.

# EPILOGUE

## Moving On

Precious checked her email against the address in front of her and buzzed apartment 4.

"Yes," a voice she didn't recognize said through the speaker.

"Hi, I'm Precious. I'm here to see the apartment."

The door buzzed and she pulled it open. She walked across the surprisingly clean lobby to the elevator and pressed the button to call it down. While she waited, she checked her phone.

No messages.

She tapped out a quick text to Laura.

Miss you!

The elevator doors opened and she stepped inside. She started composing a text message that she'd been working through in her head for weeks. It was time.

Her thumbs flew across her phone's screen as she typed. Her message to Andre was straight to the point:

Hey! I need to tell you something. I've been dating my roommates. Both of them. I like them a lot. They like me a lot. It's a thing. You have to be okay with this. Because you love me. And then you have to help me figure out how to tell mom. Because you love me.

She pressed send and exhaled loudly. And then she remembered to press the button to the fourth floor. She sent Andre one more text:

And I love you too.

It wasn't particularly late in the evening in Vienna, so she wasn't sure if she should expect his reply soon or not. Andre could be at the lab, or out with friends, or playing video games and avoiding his phone. He could also be staring at her text message in complete and utter shock. She tried not to think about it.

The elevator door opened and she stepped out into a hallway that was also clean and well lit. She walked to the door and knocked. When the apartment door opened, the realtor had a bright smile on her face. "Hello," she said, and stepped back to allow Precious to enter.

"Hi," Precious replied. She turned at the sound of Cali's voice.

"Okay, but I don't know if this is enough room for all of my plants."

Precious smiled at Mike's exasperated sigh. "This is more space than we have now. I promise you."

They were standing in the living room and Mike was right. This apartment was a real estate miracle. It was still in their same neighborhood, just one more subway stop away from the university. They had a larger kitchen, a half bath just off the living room, and a bathroom with a tub. Probably not big enough for all three of them, but they were creative. And all for just $200 more a month.

But the two things that had sold them on this place were the living room, with its big bay window for all of Cali's plants, and the two large bedrooms.

Precious walked into the living room. Her sandals slapped against the wood floor, and Mike and Cali turned at the sound with relief on both of their faces.

"Finally," Mike said. "Tell her this place is bigger than our current apartment."

Cali rolled her eyes. "No, tell *him* that our place is perfect and we don't have to move."

Precious just smiled. This was the easy part. This was where she felt most comfortable, stuck right in the middle of the two people she loved.

"Show me the bedroom?" Precious asked sweetly.

"There are two bedrooms, actually," the realtor called helpfully from behind her.

Mike smiled over Precious's head indulgently, but Cali skipped toward her, grabbing her hands and pulling her toward the bedroom they hoped would fit all of them and a much bigger bed comfortably.

---

Cali hated change, but she was working on it. She was working on herself.

She and Dr. Toussaint had been talking about this move for over a month, ever since Mike suggested it and Precious had jumped around the apartment in enthusiastic agreement.

She wanted to be like them, but she wasn't and that was okay. She was learning that it was okay for her to feel however she felt because Mike and Precious wouldn't judge her for it.

But still, the idea of moving to a new apartment hung between them for a couple of weeks until they could all agree that it was okay just to look. There wasn't any pressure to move. Only as soon as they'd started looking, Cali understood why Mike had suggested they find a new place. Their apartment was great when it was just the two of them, and it was even perfectly situated for a third roommate. But their bedroom was cramped, and Precious's old bedroom, now her office, was too small to be anything else. Mike wanted to buy some exercise equipment so he didn't have to trek to the gym every day, especially in the winter. Cali just wanted them to be happy.

This apartment had everything they were looking for, she knew that, but she couldn't help but nitpick.

"Is the living room smaller?" she'd suggested. It wasn't, but she had to ask.

"The kitchen doesn't have an island," she pointed out. Mike reminded her that they could buy one, or even a dining room table. There was plenty of room.

"The bathtub is too small for all three of us," she'd whispered while the realtor was in the hallway taking a call.

"We don't even have a bathtub in our current place and we manage just fine," he'd replied, rubbing his thumb over her right nipple. She gasped. He pressed his lips against the corner of her mouth. "You can always say no," he reminded her.

She turned her head to press her mouth to his. She wasn't sure how to tell him that even though she didn't want to say no, saying yes was hard — she was working on that as well — but she hoped the kiss would communicate some of what she was feeling.

In the bedroom with Precious, she made sure to focus on her breathing. This would be their bedroom if they chose this place, and it would be amazing. There were floor-to-ceiling windows on one wall. The room was big enough for the California king-sized bed they'd been saving for. They even had a deep walk-in closet that might fit most of their clothes.

Cali realized that the move was inevitable, but she was struggling to come to grips with it.

Precious pulled her into the middle of the room. They were holding hands. Cali was mesmerized by Precious's bright smile.

Mike was in the doorway, watching them.

The realtor's cellphone rang, and she called to them that she would be just outside if they needed her.

Mike moved into the room and closed the door partway. Precious pulled Cali's body to hers and gently kissed her. She slipped her tongue into Cali's mouth. Mike's hand dug deep into Cali's hair and he pulled gently at the roots. She moaned.

"Shh," Mike whispered into her ear. He pressed his body behind her.

Precious pulled back with a smile on her face; the wicked one Cali loved, because it held so much promise. Cali leaned back into Mike's body, still holding onto Precious's hands.

"You two like it, don't you?" Cali asked the question already knowing the answer.

Precious was bouncing on her toes, her body practically humming with energy. Cali could feel Mike's excitement in the way his fingers dug into her shoulders.

"You can say no," he said again. Precious nodded.

"We have to make this decision together. This is our first real decision as a family."

Cali's brain and heart stuttered at the word "family." She let go of Precious's hands and turned around to wrap her arms around Mike's waist. He squeezed her shoulders while Precious rubbed her back.

Just then, the realtor pushed open the bedroom door. "Oh, is everything all right?"

"Everything's great," Precious said, in her brightest voice. "We definitely want the apartment. What's the next step?"

---

They had to spend an hour and a half filling out paperwork. The realtor had promised to call as soon as she heard back from the landlord, and hopefully — fingers crossed — they'd get the apartment and could move before their lease ran out in August. If they didn't get the apartment, they'd keep looking, or they would convince their current landlord to let them stay.

Mike wasn't particularly worried about the outcome, because he was enjoying the ride. For the first time since he'd moved to New York, he wasn't consumed with fear about the future. There was something infectious about the combination of Precious's belief that if you planned thoroughly enough, everything would be okay, and Cali's need to feel every bit of every moment. It allowed him to slow down and just be.

The temperature had dipped in the late afternoon, so they decided to walk home. Cali casually wrapped an arm around Mike's waist, and he put his arm around her shoulders. Precious was walking next to Cali, eating a popsicle and throwing furtive glances their way. Cali reached out to twirl her fingers around the tip of Precious's ponytail.

Precious's phone beeped. She pulled it out of her back pocket and screamed. He and Cali stopped and turned to her.

"What's wrong?" Mike asked. His arm tightened around Cali's shoulder, but he relaxed at the smile on Precious's face.

She moved in front of them. "I texted my brother and told him about us."

"And he was... okay with it?" Mike cringed at the fear in his own voice.

He could feel Cali's wariness in the tightening of her shoulders under his arm.

Precious nodded and read from her phone.

Of course you're dating your roommates. You're always all over each other on your Instagram. Was this supposed to be a surprise?

Mom's gonna freak.

But you're her favorite. Just cry or something.

Mike laughed, another one of those big laughs that made his abs and cheeks hurt; the kind that made him feel complete.

Precious wrapped her arms around Mike's neck and kissed him, an enthusiastic press of her lips to his that tasted like artificial strawberry flavoring. He smiled against her retreating lips. She moved quickly to wrap her arms around Cali's neck and hugged her.

And then they were kissing in the middle of the street, and Mike couldn't help but laugh.

"Alright, you two, we're almost home. And now we have to brainstorm how to tell my parents."

They pulled away from each other and Mike's heart swelled at the love in their eyes.

"Don't worry," Cali said. "They already love me. And how could anyone not love Precious?"

"I don't actually think that's how they'll see it," Mike replied.

Precious turned toward him with wide eyes. "So you're saying I'm not universally lovable?"

He rolled his eyes and smirked. "You two are ridiculous, you know that?"

They wrapped their hands around his waist and pulled him close. "Which is literally why you love us," Cali said in a light, playful tone that, one year ago, had been the stuff of his fantasies, but never reality.

He couldn't help but laugh.

Precious stood on her toes and pressed a kiss to his jaw. "Don't worry, babe. I've been working on some strategies for telling your parents."

Cali laughed, a loud guffaw that attracted even more attention. "Of course you have." She moved to continue walking, pulling Mike forward by the waist.

He kept an arm around each of them.

They walked the rest of the way home, linked together as naturally as ever.

If anyone thought it was strange that the three of them were so entangled, they didn't notice, and they surely didn't care. As far as Mike was concerned, the rest of the world just melted away, and there was only room for three.

# NEIGHBORLY

# 1

Fight night always took a lot of energy. It usually took her all day to prepare. She slept in as long as she could, which was never really long enough. She took her coffee with her into the garage – her makeshift studio – and she spent as much time with her clay as she could. She turned the music up loud and she let her mind and body wander. She tried to forget what was coming; all the people and the noise and the eyes on her. Instead, while her hands dug into the malleable, wet clay she focused on him and how much he was worth all the discomfort and more.

But she always set a timer because she couldn't be late; no matter how much she wished she could stay in her quiet garage that had been the deciding factor in her decision to rent this condo, that she really couldn't afford. She felt at peace here, alone for a few hours a day, but when her alarm blared, she remembered that some things were worth leaving her sanctuary for, even if it took her a bit of time to work up the courage to go.

When her alarm went off, she went to the kitchen and made lunch. Something light; something that wouldn't betray her at the most inopportune moment. She ate and cleaned the kitchen to waste time. Then she dragged herself to her bathroom and showered, scrubbed, and moisturized herself to within an inch of her life. This afternoon, she'd swiped her hand across her fogged mirror and looked at her reflection – really looked – for a full minute. She wondered if he saw her the same way when he looked at her. She knew the rest of the world didn't and that hurt more than she was comfortable admitting, even to herself. So she washed her face, brushed her teeth and even did her makeup, with her eyes averted, not ready to confront the sore spot just below her heart.

When Heaven moved into her small bedroom, she put off getting dressed by making the bed. She put on fresh sheets and fluffed her pillows, already yearning to crawl back between those covers as soon as possible. When she opened her closet, she tried to remember what she'd worn to the last few events. She had a system: if she could remember wearing it to another fight, she couldn't wear it. It made things easier, but also frustrating. She didn't have the kind of budget to support this kind of variety, but after being shredded on a popular celebrity forum for wearing the same dress to two events in three months, she'd vowed to never make that mistake again; to never embarrass him that way again. So, she shopped more than she felt comfortable to keep her clothing options as varied as she could, even though she always wore a dress or skirt. Never pants. That was his only request and one she was happy to oblige. Very happy to oblige.

After shuffling some hangers around, she remembered that she'd bought a dress for this fight, because it was a special event. The midnight blue velvet bodycon dress still had the tags attached. She ran her hands over it and shivered. She wondered if he would have the same reaction when he touched her. She bought most dresses with him in mind, but this one especially. Blue was his favorite color and this shade matched his ring gear perfectly. It was the kind of tight that was almost obscene. It clung to every curve of her breasts, thighs, stomach, even the rolls at her sides. Her dress dipped dangerously low on her chest. So low, she'd have to be careful. Or not. The fabric would be a soft contrast to his rough hands and even just imagined his calloused palms and the soft velvet against her silky skin made Heaven's thighs clench. This feeling was more than enough to warrant leaving her garage and the night had barely just begun.

She snatched the dress from the hanger and carefully pulled it over her head. Heaven felt the usual mix of fear, anxiety, anticipation and lust that was unique to fight night. She walked back to the bathroom to make sure she hadn't ruined her hair or makeup and make sure the dress looked okay. It looked more than okay. She could imagine what he would think when he looked down from the ring and saw her. she could already imagine how his gaze would make her feel. And even amidst the emotional turmoil, she craved it.

For the past three years Heaven had endured roaring blood thirsty crowds so loud her ears rang for hours after the fight had ended. She learned to pretend that she couldn't see the side eyes the other girlfriends and groupies aimed at her because they hated that someone like her got to walk down the aisle with him, that he looked at her before he entered the ring and that every fight he won – no matter how bruised and battered – he found her in the crowd, sometimes with swollen eyes, kissed his gloves and extended them to her. He deserved better, they thought. He could do better, they very often said loud enough for her to hear. Better than her. Better than someone who looked like her, who came from where she came from and who use to grimace during his bouts before she learned to stop her discomfort from showing.

Heaven sat on the bed and stepped into the strappy sandals that made her average height and just about chest height to him. She walked to her dresser and carefully arranged her jewelry. Large gold hoop earrings, the nameplate necklace he'd given her on their first anniversary with his name etched there, delicate bangles on both wrists and the diamond promise ring he'd given her two months ago on their third anniversary. He'd saved for a year for it. He was saving for the engagement ring he'd told her. Her jewelry was like her armor and it felt heavy on her hand. She didn't know if she deserved it. She wanted it. She wanted him. She couldn't imagine her life without him. But her stomach flipped when the doorbell rang.

It was Reggie, his best friend and personal assistant. He always drove her to the matches and drove them home. She walked carefully to the front door, breathing deeply to prepare herself. As soon as she opened the door, she couldn't be Heaven, the up and coming visual artist, she had to become Calvin "The Beast" Jefferson's girlfriend. Her name, her work, her needs didn't matter; at least not to everyone who would see her and judge her tonight. All that mattered was that she looked good on his arm. How she dressed, how she behaved, every minute movement of her face would all reflect back to him. And she didn't want to disappoint him. She loved him too much for that.

She took one last deep breath, put her hand on the

door handle, and then pulled the door open. "Hey Reg," she said in a high-pitched croak.

"Oh shit," Reggie yelled with the big, warm smile on his face. "Look who got their foot on everybody's neck tonight."

Heaven smiled, "Fool shut up." She smoothed her hands over her wide hips. "I look okay?" she asked in a soft voice.

"You look better than okay, sis. Our boy's gonna be real excited when he sees you in this. And those girls in row three are gonna be pissed. I bet you end up in the next issue of *The Ring* too. Foot meet neck."

Heaven's stomach flipped when he said that. She didn't want to be in *The Ring* again. Like ever. But that was wishful thinking if she wanted to be with Calvin. So she bargained with herself that if she *had* to show up there it was better to be in the Ringside TKO column with its favorable coverage and perfectly timed "candid" photo instead of the Boxseat Bleeders column, where all of the pictures were grainy shots from the worst angles. Never again, she thought to herself.

But she kept that existential fear to herself. Reggie had other things on his mind. Besides chauffeuring Heaven to the fight, he was also running Calvin's social media and until Calvin was back in street clothes, Reggie was on call for anything else he might need.

Everybody had a struggle.

So Heaven closed her front door behind her and

followed Reggie to his car. She used each step toward the curb to shove her anxieties as deep inside her soul as possible.

She used to sit in the front passenger seat and annoy Reggie during these drives, changing the radio station to fuck up all his presets and laughing about their latest binge watch obsessions. But she couldn't do that. If she got to the venue and stepped out of the front seat, some random person with a blank avi on the betweentheropes.net forum would call her "a broke bitch who doesn't even have her own car." Again.

So, she smiled at Reggie as he held the back door open like her chauffeur and not her boyfriend's best friend. She slid into the backseat and breathed deeply while he walked to the driver's side. She tried to pretend that this was all okay.

"Seatbelt," he said with a smile in the rearview mirror.

She fumbled to put it on with a quick nod.

Heaven couldn't believe she was nervous enough to forget something so basic. She couldn't afford that tonight. She had to do better, be better. She had to be someone he deserved. She said that over and over in her head hoping it would sink in.

---

"How you feelin'? Feelin' good?" his manager, Neil, asked, like he always did before a fight.

Calvin nodded and rolled his shoulders up to his ears, front and back. He watched his body in the mirror in front of him, trying to focus on his form and not the chaos around him. His locker room was crowded and he hated it, but this venue was basically just an oversized school gym so he knew he couldn't complain. At least not yet.

He had one year, five year and ten-year plans – professionally and personally – and he knew this gym, like this fight was just a steppingstone. He worked his day job as a UPS delivery driver and worked out at the gym damn near all evening, spending much less time with Heaven than he liked. But he made that sacrifice, because in a year he wanted to move from amateur boxing to pro and he wanted to propose. In five years, he wanted to buy Heaven the family house neither of them had ever had, with an art studio out back where she could work. He wanted to be able to fight less but earn more so they could spend time together with their future kids. So even though his trainers and managers were making it hard for him to relax right now, Calvin didn't complain, because this would all be worth it someday.

"Alright let's tape him up," his trainer, Pete, yelled.

This was it; showtime. Suddenly, Calvin's entire body went tight with anticipation. He turned from the mirror and stuck his hands out, rolling his neck from side-to-side.

"You got this," Pete said, as his assistant started wrapping his right hand and wrist.

"I got this," Calvin parroted. It wasn't just rote mimicry, Pete was right. He did have this. He'd done the work on his body and his mind. He knew his opponent's style and history. And even though Calvin knew he was better, he trained as if he wasn't. For six years Pete had been drilling home the idea that the only person who could beat him was him. If he thought he couldn't win; he wouldn't. If he got cocky and lazy, he was just handing his opponent the fight. The fight didn't start in the ring, it started weeks, sometimes months, before. It took years to get it, but now he did. "I got this," he said again, as the assistant moved to his left hand.

"Gloves," Pete yelled and another one of his assistants came to help the first shove his fists into his favorite gloves. He trained with better gloves; he could afford better gloves, but these were special. He cleaned them himself after every match and had had them repaired more times than he could remember. They were the only gloves he would fight in; a gift from his mother. She'd saved up for six months for them and they were the first real investment anyone had ever made in his dream. And now that she was gone, he wore them to keep her close, taking her with him into the ring every time.

The locker room door opened and one of the venue staff stuck his head in, "Go time, fellas."

The room started to buzz but Calvin didn't let their nerves carry him away; not yet.

"Aye, my girl here?" he asked generally.

The guy from the venue shrugged but Neil jumped up. "I'll check," he said quickly and hurried from the room.

Calvin turned to Pete who looked him up and down before speaking. "What's the plan?"

"Same as usual," Calvin said meeting his trainer's eyes. "Tire him out. Take an opening when I see it. Protect my pretty face."

Pete stared at him for a few seconds before he smiled, "Smart ass."

Calvin tipped his head back and laughed before answering for real, "Gutierrez favors his left hand. He's also big and doesn't like to move. I gotta keep him mobile, don't let him corner me and stay the fuck away from his hard ass left hook. And protect my pretty face."

Pete nodded, "Good. Let's go."

Calvin nodded, bumped his gloves together and exhaled. Pete and his assistants led him from the room and down the hallway. They stopped just at the entrance to the gymnasium. Calvin could hear the crowd, but he zoned it out, craning his neck, looking for her.

Pete and his assistants moved out of the way and

there was Reggie, pushing through the crowd, clearing a path. When he stepped to the side, Heaven came into view, just barely five-five in her too tall heels. His eyes moved from the top of her head down, slowly, even though he really didn't have time for that. But this was a ritual, just as much as taping his hands and putting on his mother's gloves. Pete always asked him to remember what he was fighting for right up until he stepped into the ring, then he had to forget it all to get the job done.

So, Calvin liked to see Heaven and sear her dark eyes and pouty lips, round hips, thick thighs, and even her cute toes in his memory as his heart began to beat faster and the blood rushed through his vein, pounding in his ears. Some boxers needed to be hyped up, they yelled and screamed, devolving into animals before they stepped into the ring. Calvin didn't need all that bullshit. He just needed to see Heaven, to look her in the eyes and watch her shiver, her nipples hardening to points while he watched her to give him the rush he needed. He just needed her to remind him what he was fighting for.

He stood still as she walked toward him and everyone else disappeared. They might as well have been as far as he was concerned. Heaven was the only thing he could see.

She stopped just out of his reach and he grunted. She smiled, knowing what that grunt meant. Closer. She bit her bottom lip and inched toward him. He kept his gloved hands at his sides. He could still wrap his arms around her if he wanted, but he preferred to deny himself. That was part of the ritual too. He wasn't one of those dudes who didn't have sex for three days before a match, but the day of... yeah, he liked to deny himself; and her too. It made this moment better. When she stepped close enough to rub her nipples against his chest. When she grabbed at his forearms. When she lifted onto the balls of her feet. When she brushed her lips against his jaw. The denial made this all so much more.

Calvin grunted again.

She smiled against his skin and moved her mouth to his. Her smile wasn't shy now and those big doe eyes that had caught his attention the first time they met weren't so innocent anymore. They were deep, dark pools of excitement, lust. The muscles in his arms tensed and he waited. Her lids fluttered and then she swiped her tongue across the seam of his lips.

He could have opened his mouth and met her tongue with his own or sucked hers into his mouth. But it was the denial – putting off the pleasure of this kiss until later– that gave him the kind of fire he needed. The kind of fire that got him his ring name.

She lowered herself down to her heels and smiled up at him.

He grunted again and smiled just as his entrance music started to play.

She squeezed his arms and he licked the taste of

her from his lips. They didn't need to say all the things they felt, that wasn't what this moment was about. The touch, the taste, the looks. From the moment he'd met Heaven, they hadn't needed words.

Heaven squeezed his arms one more time and then turned. His fists clenched in his gloves as he watched her ass move in that tight ass dress the same shade of blue as his shorts and gloves. He licked his lips again. He kept his eyes on her until she and Reggie disappeared into the arena.

"How you feelin'?" Neil asked.

"Ready," Calvin growled. Because he was.

---

Most athletes were obsessed with rituals and Calvin was no different. He prayed before he entered the ring. He always entered left leg first. He pumped his gloved fists together three times while the ref went over the rules. They bumped gloves, he stepped back, held his breath and then waited for the bell to sound.

He also watched his fights over and over again afterward. Pete liked it because it gave them the opportunity to go over his form for the next opponent. But Calvin needed it because sometimes he felt as if the matches were an out of body experience. He was there, but not really. sometimes the matches ended and he would come back to his body and wish he could disappear again as all the punches and jabs he'd been too zoned out to register crashed in on him. But even on the worst nights, his mind coming back to his body was the biggest adrenaline rush. The fight didn't get him going, the end did, especially when he won.

But he hadn't just won this fight. He'd decimated his opponent in the third round. Gutierrez had lumbered around the ring, swiping at him, sometimes connected, trying to take him down in a KO. He was cocky. It was annoying. So when he started the third round a bit slower than normal, Calvin had known his opening was coming and he danced a little faster, moving forward and back in a circle, first counterclockwise and then clockwise and back again. Gutierrez swiped at him with his left hand, but Calvin was waiting. As soon as Gutierrez's right hand moved, Calvin danced left and hit him square in the temple with his left hand, which was just as lethal as his right. Gutierrez had staggered back and Calvin had followed him, hitting him left and right in his head and body and then getting one more good shot in before the ref stepped between them. They were in the ropes. Calvin danced away. Gutierrez stumbled back.

Calvin watched as the ref yelled at Gutierrez. The man struggled to stand, took half a step forward and then stumbled again. The ref kept yelling. Gutierrez swayed left, right, and then he was down. The crowd erupted. Calvin couldn't hear the ref call the fight for him. But he didn't need it. Pete and Neil were in the ring in a heartbeat. The ref raised his right hand, Pete raised his left. The crowd cheered louder. Calvin tried to smile around his mouth guard.

When the ref let him go, his trainers surrounded him, but his eyes moved to his corner. Heaven was on her feet, cheering and clapping until they made eye contact. She pressed her lips shut and continued clapping. Calvin struggled free from his team swarming around him in celebration and kissed each of his gloves before extending them toward her. She smiled with wet eyes and then bit her bottom lip. Calvin's eyes shifted to Reggie. His best friend nodded and began to shuffle Heaven from the front row. She hated the crowd and he didn't want her to have to push through the masses to leave. Also, Calvin liked rituals and this one was his favorite, even more than the fight itself. So much more.

---

Heaven had never had a relationship like this. Calvin was only her third boyfriend and the first guy she'd dated as a real proper adult. She was eighteen when they met. He was nineteen. She'd been at the mall, visiting her favorite art shop, looking at the new watercolors she couldn't afford.

He was working his regular delivery route. His brown uniform caught her eyes. And then she'd been enraptured by the way his sleeves seemed barely able to contain his muscles, ogling him without meaning to. Without even realizing it. When he'd turned around, he'd caught her staring, their eyes met and her face warmed. His eyes widened as they traveled down her body. She pulled at the hem of her t-shirt, trying to cover the small muffin top spilling over the top of her jeans. He'd smiled at the gesture and licked his lips.

He walked past her, pushing a dolly full of large boxes. He was so close she could smell the spicy scent of his cologne, she had to bite back a moan. And then she'd swiped at the sweat beading her upper lip. No man should be that fine she'd thought and then ducked into the closest aisle on shaky legs.

She'd kept peeking toward he front of the store, watching as he brought his packages into the store. He never looked her way and she got careless, openly ogling him as she stepped in line to buy the pack of erasers she'd hastily grabbed.

She watched as he handed his clipboard over to the store manager for a signature and then he headed toward the exit. Heaven had turned quickly away, only to turn and check out his ass in his perfectly pressed brown shorts one more time before he was gone forever.

But at the door, he'd turned and made eye contact with her, smiled, and then winked before pushing the door open and leaving for good.

Heaven had grabbed one the closest craft magazine and fanned herself. The cashier rang up her purchases while nodding sympathetically. "Girl, I feel you," she'd said as Heaven handed over a five-dollar bill.

That should have been it. Just a story for her to tell her friends about the sexiest UPS driver she'd ever seen. But when she'd walked out of the store, there he was, leaning against the side of his truck. Waiting for her. She'd stumbled over her tongue giving him her phone number. He was the perfect amount of hot and sweet from the beginning, just like they relationship they'd built together.

Except after a fight.

Reggie pulled the locker room door closed behind her. She shivered in the empty room and waited. It was eerily quiet even though she could still hear the crowd roaring in the distance. She could hear her breath and the rush of blood in her veins. Her skin was hot, her pussy was wet. Every time; it was like this every time. And no matter how much she hated being on display during the fights, Calvin always made it up to her, even if he didn't know that's what he was doing.

She knew when he was close; the cheering crowd still echoing down the hall, reverberating up her feet, between her thighs and across every inch of her skin. Heaven dropped her purse on the bench and stood in the middle of the room; ready for him. When it opened, she saw Calvin and Pete and then Reggie, but only Calvin entered the room. They all knew the drill.

"See you later, champ. Heaven," Reggie said as he

pulled the door closed. Calvin turned the lock and the quiet was all-encompassing. Or maybe it was just that Heaven tuned everything not in this room out. Calvin's panting breaths as he stalked toward her; the thud of his gloves hitting the bench next to her purse; the smell of him — soap, sweat and the slight metallic notes of blood — as he circled behind her.

She didn't look directly at him. She kept her eyes just over his head and followed his movements by sound, letting the vibrations of his energy course through her body. She felt him, big and hard and warm behind her, and she reveled in all that residual power from the fight rolling off him and through her. She loved this moment.

Heaven moaned when Calvin finally touched her.

His big hands clapped against her outer thighs. The sound of his skin hitting hers was like a klaxon call. His blunt nails raked up her soft skin before snagging the hem of her dress and pulling it up her legs. She felt the cool air on her wet pussy and whimpered. He licked his lips in her ear at the sound, or maybe because he could smell her now. Smell how turned on she was. Smell what it did to her to watch him in the ring.

Calvin threw an arm around her stomach and turned her quickly to the mirrored wall to their left. She gasped as she took in their reflection. He towered over her, his bare shoulders and arms covered in sweat. His left eye puffy, but not fully swollen, and his eyelids hooded with desire. She knew that look. She adored that look.

"Look at yourself," he said in that deep whisky voice that had made her pussy weep the moment they met.

She clenched her thighs and swallowed hard and did as he said.

Heaven hadn't been a virgin when she met Calvin. She wasn't innocent or particularly inexperienced. But three years with Calvin had only opened her eyes to all she could have. To all he was willing to give her. Before him, she never would have imagined that anyone could turn her out like this. Have her waiting for him in a dress so tight every roll and curve and thigh dimple was on display. Have her waiting for him with an already dripping pussy. Have her standing in front of a mirror, her dress hiked up to her hips, her bottom half bare, and not feel one inch of shame. What was there to be ashamed of?

He moved his mouth to her ear but kept his eyes on her reflection. She watched him watching her as his hand moved over the curve of her stomach to the seam of her thighs. His other hand gripped her waist so tight it hurt, but it was the perfect amount of pain. His touch was always so perfect, precise. He was nothing if not great with his hands.

"Spreads these big ass thighs for me, sweetheart," he growled in her ear.

She moaned and did as he said. Happily. Immediately.

He didn't wait until her feet were wide enough; his adrenaline wouldn't let him. He shoved his hand between her legs and Heaven's knees went weak at that sharp touch. She moaned as his fingers caressed her slit.

"Wet as fuck," he mumbled into her hair.

"Always," she moaned, trying to ride his hand. He wouldn't let her. The hand at her waist held her still. She tried to circle her hips and her ass bumped against his erection. There was nowhere else she wanted to be besides caught between his hand and his dick.

But also she wanted more. "Please," she moaned.

He laughed in her ear. "Please what, sweetheart?"

"Please," was all she could say because she wanted too much. She wanted his fingers, his tongue, his dick inside her right now. She needed it.

He laughed louder and slipped two fingers into her pussy.

She smiled, exhaled, and shivered all at the same time at the beautiful intrusion.

"Better?" he asked.

She shook her head, because his fingers weren't moving. They were just inside her, not even filling her fully. Not enough.

"Baby," she whined. "Stop teasing me. You never tease me after a fight."

He let go of her waist and dragged his hand up her body heavily, over her stomach, up her rib cage. He squeezed her breast and then flattened his palm over her sternum and slid his strong hold up her circle her neck. He didn't squeeze, but he knew she liked the weight of his hand just there. It made her feel safe and secure.

She clenched her pussy around his fingers to thank him.

He pushed his fingers inside her just a little bit more and the heel of his hand settled onto her clit.

She moaned.

"I got good news, baby," he whispered into her ear.

"When? The fight just ended," she gasped. She wrapped her hands around his waist, grabbing his ass and pulling him closer.

He grunted when his dick pressed into the soft cushion of her ass. "On the way back here," he said. "You wanna hear it?"

"Will you fuck me first?" she ground out.

"No," he said with a laugh. She knew he would.

"Then tell me and then fuck me. And then tell me again because I'll probably forget."

"Nah, you're gonna remember this."

"Baby," Heaven whined.

Calvin kissed her cheek gently, lovingly and then he started pumping his fingers into her. In and then out and then back in again; forceful thrusts that reminded her that here is where she belonged. His heel ground against her clit and Heaven shuttered in aroused relief.

His whispered breath against her skin was so much more than she could handle and she didn't want him to stop. "Pete said the sponsorship came through," Calvin whispered against her cheek.

"Oh my god," she rasped in excitement and arousal.

"All our sacrifices. All our hard work. You holding me down for three years," he whispered and slipped a third finger inside her. "It was all worth it. I can quit my job and train full time. I can be home more. We can take a damn vacation. We can move into a bigger place. I can fuck you to sleep at night and wake you up with my face between your legs." He whispered all their sweetest dreams and filthiest promises against her skin as he started to grind his dick against her ass.

"Baby, please," Heaven whined. She didn't know what she was begging for, but she took comfort in the fact that he would. She moved her hands to the waistband of his shorts and pushed it inside. She squeezed his ass with one hand, loving the way the muscles felt under her fingers. But she felt triumph when she squeezed her hand between their bodies and began to rhythmically squeeze his dick in her palm.

He grunted into her ear and started moving his fingers in and out of her so fast. The quiet room filled with the wet sounds of her sex. "We did it, sweetheart," he said just as he settled his thumb over her clit.

She was so fucking close, but she didn't want to come like this. Not when they were celebrated more than just tonight's fight. Not when his dick was hard and pulsing in her hand. "Baby, please," she whispered again.

He kissed her cheek one more time and pulled his fingers from her clit. She'd asked for it, but she still whined at the empty feeling. But he kept his hand at her neck. He walked her forward, toward the mirror.

"Bend over."

She did so gratefully, her hands on the mirror, her fingers spread, trying to grip the glass with all her strength. Heaven heard his shorts fall, and his grunt when his squeezed his dick. She watched him line his dick up with her pussy.

They both moaned when he moved the head of his dick up and down her slit.

"Oh god," she breathed, her breath fogging up the mirror.

They watched each other as he pushed into her slowly, her wet sex sucking him in deeper. His chest rumbled and she became one long moan. It was so much. So perfect. He pushed into her inch by slow inch. This moment was worth it all.

His wet hand grabbed her waist again and his hand flexed at her throat.

"We did it, sweetheart," he said again, finding her eyes in the reflection.

"We did it," she said. "Oh fuck, we did it."

Their eyes were locked as he started to move into her. it was slow at first, gentle. This wasn't the norm. this was because of the good news. Because Calvin was going pro. Because they were starting the next phase of their life together. But it couldn't last.

All that adrenaline from his fight, all the denial of their day apart, all the pent-up anxiety at being on display just to support him. All that lust and love they felt for each other. The energy from the fight and the cheering crowd. It took them under, and their bodies took over, bringing them back to why they were really here, why Calvin always had Reggie rush her back to the locker room when he won and he always locked the door behind them.

His hips moved faster and faster. Her moans grew louder and louder. He grunted every time he pushed into her. soon they were rutting against each other, her sex dripping and gripping him tighter. His hands holding her, grasping her harder. Their eyes intense and intent on each other. The room filling with the sounds of their flesh slapping against each other.

Heaven cried out when she came, and her legs went weak. Calvin wound his arm around her waist again, holding her up while he fucked her through one orgasm and toward another. And then another. And then his own.

She turned her head to him and finally their mouths touched. The kiss was soft, always so soft even when he fucked her so hard. She loved the taste of his sweat and moans. The feel of him releasing inside her and leaking down her inner thighs.

"I love you," Calvin breathed into her mouth.

"I love you," Heaven replied and then sucked his tongue deep into her mouth.

# 2

## Six Months Later

1415 Green Circle Dr.

That was the address scribbled on a piece of paper next to Heaven's coffee machine this morning in Calvin's scratchy handwriting. There had also been a time, next to it: 2:15. She'd seen the note at 11:45, but what if she hadn't. She'd asked him that in three separate voicemails and in a text message. He only replied to the later.

"I'd have called," was all he'd said. That's it!

What if she'd felt like water instead of coffee this morning? What if she'd slept in later? What if she'd had a coffee date with a friend? These were just some of the questions she was going to lob at him just as soon as she arrived at wherever the fuck Green Circle Dr. was.

They'd been looking for their first apartment for months, but it was difficult. Calvin wanted to find a place cheap enough that he could cover it on his own – with the money from his sponsorship and his winnings – so Heaven could save what she made from selling her jewelry online and sometimes subbing as an art teacher to invest in her work. But Heaven wanted them to be full partners in their first home together. Needless to say, this had made house hunting a struggle. It had been so bad that they'd even stopped speaking to one another for nearly eighteen hours.

Heaven was still emotional thinking about it. She and Calvin never fought and she'd hated it. In fact, she'd hated it so much that she was considering suggesting that they *not* move in together; at least not yet. She loved Calvin too much to let anything get between them, even if that thing was supposed to bring them closer together.

So when she pulled up to the curb outside of a neat little duplex that looked as if it had been recently painted in shades of gray with black accents, she took a few moments to collect herself. She looked around and didn't see Calvin or Reggie's cars. She checked her watch. It was 2:15 on the dot. It wouldn't be the first time that one of Calvin's training sessions had run long, so Heaven didn't sweat it. Instead, she decided to look at this little reprieve as a chance to figure out how to suggest to Calvin that they put the move on hold.

Someone knocked on Heaven's passenger side

window. She screamed and immediately locked her doors.

When she turned there was a man crouching on the curb looking apologetically at her through the window.

"My bad. I didn't mean to scare you. Are you Heaven?"

She bunched her eyebrows together, "Who wants to know?"

He smiled, "My name's Stephen. I'm the landlord. Calvin told me to tell you that he's running late."

Heaven pressed the button to lock her car again. "Why wouldn't he just call me to tell me that? Why would he tell a total fucking stranger?"

The man smiled, "He said you'd say that and to tell you that your "Do Not Disturb Setting" is on again."

Heaven frowned. She reached for her cell phone but kept her eyes on the man.

"Huh," she breathed to herself. He was right.

She turned her car off and unplugged her phone. When she unlocked it, she had three texts from Calvin and a missed call.

Have a meeting with Pete. Gonna be late.
Landlord's name is Stephen. He can show you around.
Or wait for me.
I'm sorry, baby.

Heaven exhaled. When she looked up at Stephen

he was still crouched down and smiling at her. "We can wait for Calvin if you want. I'm good either way."

Heaven forced herself to smile at him. "No, no, it's okay." She unlocked her doors. "I'm coming." Better to view the apartment and use it in her speech to Calvin, she thought to herself.

Heaven took a deep breath to steady her nerves and then pushed the driver's side door open. When she stepped onto the curb, she turned to look up and down the street, trying to get a feel for the neighborhood, but the suburbs all looked the same to her. She bit into her bottom lip and frowned. She wouldn't have chosen this place. She'd wanted to live somewhere downtown, maybe in a loft, some place where they could get views of the city and maybe even be close to Calvin's gym so they could see each other more. She'd wanted them to be in the middle of things, because she knew that's what people would expect of a young boxer like him, with all his swagger and charisma.

But, nondescript though it was, the cul de sac was quiet and since she usually worked from home, she liked that.

Stephen moved in front of her, standing at the edge of the lawn. He waited until she took a few tentative steps forward before sticking out his hand to shake. "Nice to meet you, Heaven."

"Nice to meet you too."

"You ready to see the place?" he asked, tipping his

head back to the house.

She nodded, bit the inside of her cheek and followed Stephen to the porch. There were three wooden steps up to a wide porch, with two doors at either end.

Stephen turned to her and tipped his head back. "Lemme just grab the keys."

She nodded and he darted into his front door.

When he returned, he still had a big friendly smile on his face. It helped to put her at ease. "My wife and I are just next door. I can handle most of the handyman stuff, so if you chose this place and had a problem you could just walk across the porch."

"That's convenient," she admitted as she followed him to the other door.

He unlocked the front door and then pushed it open. "After you," he said.

When she walked inside what could be her and Calvin's new home her smile tightened. Not because this side of the duplex was terrible. It wasn't. Actually, it was amazing. Directly in front of the front door was a skinny staircase that led up to the second floor alongside the wall the two sides of the house must share. To the right was an open plan living and dining room, separated from the kitchen by a combination breakfast bar and kitchen island. The house was at the butt end of the cul de sac and looked out to the edge of a nature preserve and from every window Heaven could see there was nothing but nature and blue sky.

"Don't you want this view for yourself?" she asked, as she rushed to the big pucture window across the living room.

Stephen closed the front door with a chuckle. "Actually, not. My wife is kind nosy and there's a better view of our neighbor's garden from the other side of the duplex."

"Garden?" Heaven asked with a confused look over her shoulder.

"We think he's growing weed," Stephen said with a shrug and a smile.

It made Heaven laugh in spite of herself.

She turned and walked tentatively into the kitchen. The medium brown wood floor that provided the only real border between the kitchen and the rest of the room looked original and pristine. And the slate tiles in a kind of rusty brown accented the dark and light patterns in the marble perfectly. Everything was state of the art and seemed to be recently renovated, maybe even brand new.

"We just finished renovations," Stephen said as if he could read her thoughts. There was pride in his voice. "Oak floors, stainless steel appliances, new carpet upstairs. New paint. There are two big bedrooms upstairs and a basement with washer and dryer hookups. It's one big basement, but we separated yours from ours with a door, so you two would have privacy even down there."

"Amazing," she said.

"Come on, I'll show you the backyard," Stephen said, excitedly.

She followed him down the skinny hallway past a closet under the stairs and a small kind of bonus room – too small for a bedroom but maybe just big enough for an office – and a door just by the backdoor that Stephen indicated led to the basement. He unlocked the back door and this time proceeded her out onto what looked like a brand new deck.

"This is amazing," Heaven said.

"Built it damn near myself," Stephen said with a laugh. "All my crew was either sick or on another job the whole time I needed them."

"Crew?"

"Oh, yeah, I work in construction, especially home renovations."

"Oh, that makes a lot of sense. It's beautiful."

"Thank you. So, we share the front and back porches," he said, "Y'all would be welcome to come and cook out with us whenever or stay to yourselves. Either is cool. I keep the grass tidy in the front and back, that's all included in your rent." He turned to her and tapped his forehead, "Mowing the lawns help me keep the mind clear, you know?"

Heaven nodded, but she didn't know. What she did know was that there was no way they could afford this place. So, why had Calvin chosen it?

They'd been looking at studios and one bedrooms downtown and every single one had strained their budget and was starting to strain their relationship. A loft was their best hope for a place that would also give Heaven a place to store her art materials, although realistically she might have to put some of her things in storage or sell them outright.

In fact, that had been the cause of their fight. Heaven had offered to offload her clay and ceramics wheel, and Calvin had refused. Then Heaven had suggested that she could pick up a full-time gig so they could increase their budget and Calvin had nearly blown his top. And the apartment they'd been viewing hadn't been nearly as nice as this one. It was a dark basement that was certainly not zoned for habitation and maybe poorly insulated and then three hundred dollars over their budget to boot.

Heaven had worried they would break up over that place. So why in the hell was Calvin trying to provoke another fight with a duplex that was probably twice their budget?

"You ready to see the best part?" Stephen asked with a mischievous glint in his eye.

"You mean the kitchen wasn't it?"

Stephen barked in laughter, "I'm gonna tell my wife you said that. She designed it, so that'll make her day. But nah, come on."

She followed him down the deck onto the lush lawn. They headed across the yard toward a small shed she hadn't noticed at first.

"Your man asked me how much to throw this place

in," Stephen said as he opened the door for her to step inside.

"I built the shed just for extra storage if we needed it later. But Calvin said you're an artist?"

Heaven's eyes widened and finally she couldn't stop the tears from clouding her vision and falling down her cheeks. She turned in a circle, just barely seeing the room through her tears.

There were windows at each end of the long room. She could imagine that there was good light in here most of the day. The walls were the patchy white of plaster and the floor was rough concrete. It was the perfect space for a studio. She could already see herself here, her easel in the corner close to the window, her clay in the far corner away from direct sunlight. She could imagine losing herself in her creations with her jazz and blues playlists turned up as loud as her Bluetooth speaker could go just like in her garage. She could see herself feeling free here and making this blank canvas her own. And knowing that Calvin had thought of giving her a space of her own made her heart constrict and well with love..

She swiped at her wet cheeks and turned to Stephen.

"It's not much space," Stephen said in a wary voice, clearly uncomfortable at her tears. "And I can paint the walls whatever color you want."

"No. It's perfect," she said. "But there's no way we can afford this."

Stephen smiled in relief. "You get a break when you're out here in the sticks. Rent is nine hundred dollars."

"What?"

"Water is included, but the rest of your utilities you'll have to set up."

"Are you serious?"

"Yeah is that... Calvin didn't tell you the price."

"No," she shrieked. If he had she might have felt less anxious on the drive over. But if he had she might have looked at this place with skepticism, picking it apart and wondering if he was lying or if they were being scammed. "How much is the shed?" she asked, nervously. Their total budget was only $1,100.

"Oh nine hundred includes the shed. It' be eight hundred without it."

Heaven's mouth fell open. "Fuck."

Stephen laughed, "Is that a good fuck or a bad fuck?"

"That's a we'll take it fuck!"

"He thought you might say that."

Heaven was starting to wonder if Calvin had actually been pulled away by Pete or if he'd just wanted her to see this place and fall in love with it. either way, she had. "I hope you don't have other people looking."

"We do. Did. When Calvin came, he put a deposit down. But it was contingent on you liking the place."

"You agreed to that?" she asked warily.

"Fuck yeah, I did. I saw The Beast knock Dewayne

Moore out cold in two rounds. I'd have held it without the deposit."

Heaven laughed. "So you're a boxing fan."

"Big time. Besides, I remember what it was like when me and my wife were just starting out. I'm happy to give a young Black couple a hand up. Y'all seem like good people."

Heaven smiled softly to herself. Surely, this wasn't the first time she'd ever heard someone give her relationship a compliment, but it was the first time she'd ever met a reasonable boxing fan. She already had a good feeling about Stephen, now she had a great feeling about him.

"Okay, I've got the lawnmower in the corner," Stephen said, pointing, "but I'll have that outta here before you two move in."

She nodded happily at him.

"If there's anything you need hung in here you can just let me know and I'll get to it on my day off."

"Thank you," she said and then smiled. "Your wife is a lucky woman."

At that Stephen's face lifted, "Make sure you tell her that when you meet her and every time you see her."

A few tears slipped from the corners of Heaven's eyes as she burst into laughter. "When can we move?" she giggled.

# 3

## A Few Days Later

Tasha's back ached.

In truth, it had started aching almost as soon as she'd sat down for her first client – a mani/pedi that had kept her hunched over for nearly an hour – and it had only gotten worse. As she eased her car into their driveway, she could hear Stephen admonishing her – not for the first time – that that's what she got for not giving herself a break or asking someone else at the shop to handle her pedicures at least. She frowned because he was right. She'd never tell him that though. Besides, he knew he was right, so why give him the satisfaction of confirming his "I told you so," was Tasha's petty internal logic.

Every week Tasha meant to listen to him and spread her clients out, but then she didn't. She couldn't. If she was going to be at the salon, she wanted to be making money. And sometimes, even when she didn't pack her appointments, she ended up taking every walk-in she could. And unfortunately, she always ended up paying for it, physically.

She took a deep breath and pushed her door open and began the slow, painful walk to her front door. At least once she answered it, she'd have Stephen's welcome to look forward to. The way he'd surely glare at her as he told her off for neglecting her wellbeing while letting her lean against him as they walked upstairs. He'd grumble and run her bath water. And then he'd slowly undress her. She tried to keep that bath in mind with each step she took, imagining sinking into the tub and letting Stephen wash her body and massage her back and feet. And then he'd lock eyes with her and finger fuck her to a gentle orgasm and her back would finally relax. And then, when she was fully relaxed, Stephen would start to tell her off again, for the millionth time, that she needed to take better care of herself. Tasha's favorite way to spend an evening.

As she was gingerly walking up the paved path to their front porch, the door to their rental unit opened and Tasha stopped short. It took her a few seconds to understand why door might open; a faint memory of Stephen's text message about their tenants moving in today came to mind, but she had a clearer memory of the full acrylic set she was doing at the time. And it took her a few seconds more to realize she was staring at the woman walking from the open door, down the front steps and around the porch to the recycling bins. Her gaze zeroed in on the elegant curve of her new tenant's ass. She wanted to shove her face in between those cheeks. She was being wholly inappropriate. But the need that gripped her in that moment was so strong her muscles tensed and her back ached.

Tasha was still standing there when her tenant turned from the recycling bin and yelped in surprise.

Tasha smiled. Her tenant smiled back.

She was adorable. Round face, bug wide brown eyes, cute button nose and a set of thick lips that were absolutely Tasha's type. In fact, from what she could see, everything about her new tenant was her type, especially that thick waist. She was never this inappropriate and she was internally embarrassed at herself. She guessed she must have been more tired than she realized. So, she forced herself to soften her smile, extend her arm, and not wince as her back muscles protested the sudden movement. She was happy that her voice sounded normal and calm, rather than tired or hungry, which was actually how she felt.

"You must be the new tenant," she said.

The woman's face relaxed as she nodded and took Tasha's hand. "I am," she said in a gentle purr of a voice that made Tasha's sex clench. "My name's Heaven."

*Jesus*, Tasha thought, *this woman cannot be real.* "That's a beautiful name," she said.

"Thank you."

"There are two of you, right?" Tasha asked.

Heaven nodded, "Yeah, my boyfriend Calvin. But he's not here right now. He's been at the gym all day."

Tasha lifted an eyebrow. "All day? He left you to move by yourself?"

Tasha smiled, "No, we had movers. But he's a boxer. He's training for his next fight. He's going for his first title match soon, so every minute counts."

"Oh okay. And what about you, Heaven? What do you do?"

Tasha didn't mean to step forward, closing some of the space between them, or run her thumb over the back of Heaven's hand. She didn't mean for her voice to drop or for her eyes to zero in on Heaven's mouth. She didn't mean it, but she didn't regret it either. Especially not when Heaven's lips parted, and she caught a peek of her pink tongue and white teeth inside just before she spoke. It was one of the sexiest things Tasha had seen in a very long time.

"Oh, I'm an artist," Heaven said, but in a self-deprecating tone that contrasted sharply with the pride in her voice when she'd told Tasha about her boyfriend's career.

Tasha didn't like that. She lifted her eyes to Heaven's and smiled, "Is that why your boyfriend wanted to rent our shed?"

Heaven nodded and beamed. "It's gonna be my studio."

"I'd love to see some of your work some time," Tasha said. "If that's okay."

Heaven ducked her head shyly.

Tasha wouldn't have thought it possible to be smitten and so horny she felt as if she might ignite at the same time and yet she was.

"Maybe," Heaven whispered.

Tasha became obsessed, in that moment, wondering if she whispered like that when she had sex with her boyfriend. Tasha wondered if Heaven would whisper to her like that as she crawled between her thighs. So inappropriate.

"Whenever you're ready," Tasha said, "I'm just next door." She didn't mean to make it sound like an innuendo, an open invitation. But, it was.

Heaven beamed, "I'll think about it."

"Please."

They stood there, staring at one another for a few seconds longer, still clutching one another's hands. Tasha wanted to hang on. She wanted to invite Heaven to the other side of the duplex. She wanted to crawl into her bath with Heaven and touch her. She wanted to lose herself, forgetting her physical discomfort for a few minutes or hours as they touched each other.

But that would be the most inappropriate thing she could do, especially before they'd even moved in fully.

So she forced herself to let go of Heaven's hand. They turned and walked up the steps together. Tasha moved right and Heaven moved left. Her hand on the door handle, she turned to Heaven's door. The other woman turned to her. They smiled at one another and then Heaven stepped into her apartment and quietly closed her front door. Tasha watched the empty porch where Heaven had been for a few seconds more before slipping her key into her own lock.

"You're late," Stephen yelled from the kitchen. "You're lucky I didn't start dinner on time."

Tasha dropped her keys into the bowl on the small table by their front door. She hung her bag from the hook on the wall, toed off her shoes and walked as quickly as she could to their kitchen.

"Tash?" Stephen called, his back to her as he rummaged in the refrigerator.

"I'm here," she said.

He turned and smiled. He was so fucking beautiful. It was a different kind of beauty than she'd seen in Heaven. Stephen's beauty was all in the angular planes of his face, the five o'clock shadow of his beard, his soft lips. They weren't plump like Heaven's, but she knew that he could make her knees weak with just a kiss. Could Heaven? Stephen's beauty was also in that easy smile he never failed to welcome her home with, the love in his eyes, and the way he knew her; knew what she was thinking and feeling before she could even express it.

"You met Heaven?" he asked as he turned fully.

She nodded.

"Can you wait?" He'd already started moving toward her slowly.

She nodded and swallowed. "But I don't want to." She felt his soft, burring chuckle at her fingertips, over her nipples, and inside her sex.

She let him back her against the wall, using just his built chest as leverage. She moaned when he pressed against her, giving her the secure feeling of being trapped that she so desperately needed. That was part of his beauty as well; that he knew what she needed and gave it to her. No questions. No judgements. Just the easy press of his knee between her legs and his hands along the column of her neck.

He licked along her bottom lip.

"She's fucking adorable," Tasha whispered.

Stephen nodded as he kissed her chin and jaw and then her earlobe softly.

Tasha began to grind against his thigh. "Oh god, that ass."

Stephen laughed in her ear and kissed her just at her hairline. "Is this gonna be enough?" he asked, pressing his leg even more firmly against her aching core.

She shook her head quickly. She wasn't sure if his question was about this moment — Can you get off on just the pressure of my leg? — or if this was about the impending dilemma of Heaven next door — Can you get off on just knowing that she's there? — but the answer to both was no.

Tasha knew herself and she never lied to Stephen. That had always been the core of their relationship, a kind of honesty she'd never thought possible. They had the kind of trust that was the result of nothing fancier than good fucking hard work. They were the kind of couple who cringed at even the thought of #relationshipgoals because what worked for them was so beautifully specific that it fit like a favorite sweatshirt — a little worn at the edges, a torn seam or two, but a fit so perfect it felt like home. So, Tasha knew she needed more of Stephen right now and Heaven would become a particular point of distraction, but so did Stephen and they could worry about all of that later.

Because what mattered most to Tasha in this moment, was the strong feeling of her husband's hands on her waist as he moved her back into their living room, his big body hot and reassuring behind her. His thumbs dug into the small of her back and she moaned, her aching muscles spasming at the beautiful pressure. She felt his smile as he leaned over to whisper in her ear.

"I knew it," he said, but left it at that. At least for now.

Her stomach pressed against the back of the couch and she turned to smile at him over her left shoulder.

Stephen kissed her gently as his hands slid forward to unbutton and unzip her pants. When he pulled away, she tried to lift onto her toes and twist her body to get his lips back, but sometimes Stephen knew what she needed better than she did. So he shook his head and pushed her pants down over her hips.

He kissed her shoulder and then bent down, pulling her slacks free.

She stepped carefully out of the legs and moved to grab her underwear, but he stopped her.

"Nah, you can keep those on," he said, and then bit her left ass cheek playfully.

Tasha's giggle was part moan.

Stephen playfully smacked her other ass cheek and then bit that one as well.

Tasha heard him chuckle an then she felt his hands on her shoulders. He pushed her over the back of the couch. He held his hands on her shoulders until she relaxed against the pillows with a long sigh. Tasha sunk into the couch and Stephen ran his hands from her shoulders to her waist and back, giving her a quick massage as he went.

She whined the pressure of hands disappeared.

He chuckled. "Calm down."

She gasped at the sound of his belt loosening and his zipper rasping open.

He moved his foot between her legs and pushed them further apart. His hands settled onto her hips. He pressed his face between her legs.

"Oh god," she moaned. She tried to arch her back, but his hands on her waist pressed her forward, stopping her from irritating her stressed body any further.

She loved him so much. Tasha spread her legs wider as Stephen's tongue circled her clit and then pressed in between her lips. He licked up to her opening and then back again. He suckled her pussy, holding her down as she squirmed. He used his mouth to get her close, but not off, because he knew that wasn't what she needed. Not right now. No matter how much she pressed her ass back onto his face.

She groaned in relief and squirmed in anticipation when he used her waist as leverage to stand, putting a delicious pressure against her sore back.

"I love you," she breathed. "No please fuck me." She reached behind her, her fingers grasping for his dick.

He laughed and angled his hips not toward her opening, but for her hand, letting her grab him and pump his dick before moving it toward her clenching pussy. He knew how much she loved putting him inside her.

They both groaned as his dick tapped her clit before pushing into her at just the right speed to tease to make Tasha nearly come undone with lust and frustration.

When his hips were pressed against her ass, they stilled. Their small living room was quiet but for the sound of their ragged breaths and the muffled music from the other apartment next door. Heaven's music.

"I want her big thighs wrapped around my head," Tasha moaned and the dam broke between them.

Stephen began to pump into her with long, sure, strong strokes. His balls slapped against her ass, his fingers dug painfully and soothingly into her waist and her pussy clenched and gushed around him. Soon the room wasn't quiet. It had filled with his grunts and her moans and cries and the sound of their couch slowly moving forward with their effort.

She cursed and called his name and told him all the filthy things she'd thought about doing to their new tenant during their brief acquaintance.

Tasha wondered if Heaven could hear. Not her words, but her moans; not the squelch of her wet sex as Stephen pumped in and out of her, but their mingled cries when she came, pulsing around his cock and his own groans as she dragged him with her over the edge.

She rested her cheek against the couch cushion as he softened inside her. She laughed softly when he pressed his wet forehead against her back. Her pussy spasmed around his dick again. He groaned weakly.

"She's got a boyfriend," he said after a while.

"And I've got a husband," Tasha replied.

"Not every couple is as open as we are," he said.

"I know," she whispered sadly.

"Just be careful," he said and then kissed her shoulder. "I don't want you getting hurt."

He stood and his dick slipped from inside her. He helped her stand and then their evening routine returned to normal; to a time before she'd met

Heaven. Tasha leaned against Stephen's side as he led her upstairs. Instead of a bath, he turned on their shower and then helped her finish undressing. He helped her into the shower and followed her. They washed each other sensually. She stroked him to another orgasm as they kissed hungrily. And then he fell to his knees and ate her to a wobbly-kneed orgasm.

Tasha's back felt more relaxed than it had in weeks. She made a mental note to find a way to thank Heaven for that. And then she shivered at all the possibilities.

# 4

"Baby," Heaven groaned into her pillow, snuggling into Calvin's embrace, running her nails over his arm wrapped around her middle.

She'd gone to bed alone last night but waking up wrapped in his arms was the best balm to her soul. She'd hated to spend her first night in their new house alone, but she knew what Calvin was like when he had a fight coming up. She considered herself lucky that he'd slept in long enough so they could wake up together, since he normally liked to be up and out the door before the sun rose, and that was assuming he even left the gym. If his trainers didn't give Reggie a detailed schedule and meal plan so that he wouldn't spend all his time working out and training, she would have he'd train himself to death. Before they started dating, he'd even been known to sleep in the back of his trainer's gym so he only had to sleep for a few hours between workouts.

When she'd met Calvin, he was so single minded that he barely dated and hardly even went out with his friends. His entire life was driving for UPS, sleeping and working out. Even his meals were tied into his training. But once they started dating, almost everything had changed. He still spent hours in the gym – especially after he was able to quit delivery driving – but he always made time for Heaven. Some days he went into the gym earlier so he could take her on a date. He stayed later one day so he could spend the next with her. And no matter how close his next fight was, no matter how frantic his nerves, he promised her that once they moved in together, he'd come home. Every night. So even though she'd gone to bed alone last night, she'd woken up wrapped in the cocoon of his arms; her ass nestled against his semi-hard dick. Calvin always kept his promises.

"Baby," she whined, running her foot up his left calf.

Calvin jerked his knees closed over her foot before she reached the back of his leg and she smiled. He was ticklish. He laughed, a hoarse, grumble of a sound was sexy as fuck.

"Please," she moaned into his ear and then erupted into excited giggles as he moved her quickly onto her back and crawled over her. His big, calloused hands spread her knees wide and he smiled down at her with such happiness it stole her breath away.

"Morning," he rasped in a voice thick with sleep.

She sucked her bottom lip into her mouth and reached for the waistband of his boxers. He let her, watching the movement of her hand hungrily. She lifted onto one elbow, pulled his dick mostly free and stroked him as she purred, "Good morning."

"You miss me?" he asked, licking his lips.

She nodded and squeezed his dick.

His hips jutted forward.

"You miss me?" she whispered.

He nodded as the head of his dick became slightly wet with moisture.

Heaven swirled the beads of precome around with her thumb and smiled up at him, "You wanna show me how much?"

Calvin's smile was predatory, a dark promise, hungry, eager to please her, have her, take her. She loved when he looked at her like that. She loved seeing her own feelings reflected in his gaze.

He hooked his hands under her knees and pulled until she fell onto her back. He let go of her left knee and pushed his underwear over his hips.

She held her breath and her heart hammered against her chest. When his wet tip touched her lips, they both exhaled hard breaths. Calvin licked his lips, teasing her clit until he pushed the mushroom head of his erection against her opened. They moaned in unison at just that contact. But he didn't push into her hard and fast like she wanted. Instead, he pressed into her slowly, but not too deep, before retreating again. He repeated teasing her with shallow thrusts until she was scratching at his chest in need.

He laughed out loud. "What? You thought just cause I'm tired I'ma jack rabbit you? On our first morning in our new place?" His right eyebrow lifted, arching so beautifully. "You thought I wasn't gone make this special?"

"Baby," she moaned.

"That's not gone work on me, Heaven." He punctuated her name by pressing against her opening and biting his own bottom lip when she moaned. "Nah," he whispered to her, but also maybe to himself, "I'm gonna make this special. Give you that good dick you deserve."

"Fuck. Me." She said the words through clenched teeth just as she crossed her ankles together behind his butt and tried to pull him forward. Calvin was strong and steady, emotionally and physically, giving her the kind of security she'd always craved. Sometimes, he would spin this teasing out, ratcheting up her desire slowly, making her pant and squirm and beg for him before he fucked her good and hard, reminding her that he would always give her exactly what she wanted; what she needed.

But maybe this time he was as horny as she was

because he only teased her for a bit before pushing fully inside of her. He still entered her slowly, but forcefully. She sighed in relief before groaning in anticipation.

Before Calvin, Heaven had always felt ashamed at how happy sex could make her. Her previous partners had often made her feel ashamed, as if she shouldn't want sex too much, as if it should make her happy, as if she should play coy about wanting to come and make them come as much as possible. As if there was something wrong or dirty about her desires. But Heaven had never felt shame with Calvin. Not when she sighed happily when he was inside her or as he secretly played with her while out at the club with friends or when he took her rough and fast after one of his fights. Calvin loved every second of her wanting him and gave as good as he got. She had never felt freer or more protected than when she was with him and it had nothing to do with the damage he could do in the ring. Calvin was the love of her life.

Calvin settled his thumb right over her clit and began to pump into her with those deep, long strokes that made her wild, while toying with her.

"Oh fuck," Heaven moaned.

He smiled. "Mmmmhhhm. This what you wanted, baby?"

"Yes," she gasped, pulling her nightgown over her chest so she could play with her breasts while he fucked her. "Mmmm, yes baby."

Calvin licked his lips while he watched as his hungry gaze settled on her pebbled nipples. Heaven smiled up at him and he slammed into her harder; his thumb still making lazy circles over her clit. Her pussy spasmed around his dick. He closed his eyes, trying to keep himself together. It was adorable. She rolled her nipples between her thumbs and forefingers and pinched them, just a bit, not enough to get her off, but enough to stoke her flames higher.

She was panting, watching him fucking her, feeling his finger on her clit, his dick moving in and out of her. But she wanted more. And one of the best things about Calvin was that he was always willing to put in the work to give her what she wanted. So, when she gripped her breasts, pointing her hard nipples up at him and moaned again, "Baby," he opened his eyes and didn't miss a beat.

She missed his finger on her clit but there was nothing better than feeling Calvin's big, thick fingers digging into the soft skin at her waist as his head bobbed back and forth between her titties, his tongue leading the way. Heaven clutched the back of his head to keep him close – not that he would be coming up for air anytime soon – and pulsed her pussy around his dick, encouraging him to fuck her just a bit faster, just a bit harder.

The room filled with the sound of their headboard hitting the wall.

It reminded her that she needed to get Calvin's

help to attach it to their frame correctly. But right now, the rhythmic banging of wood hitting plaster made Heaven think a curious thought. She wondered if Tasha and Stephen could hear them next door.

That thought should have made her ease Calvin away just in case the answer was yes. They should have changed position so they didn't disturb their landlords this early in the morning. And maybe even she should have lowered her voice just in case that carried between the walls of their apartment as well. But she didn't. Heaven tightened her legs around Calvin's body and begged him out loud this time to do as he promised and give her the good dick she deserved.

His mouth latched onto her left nipple, licking, sucking and scraping gently with his teeth and her back arched into his touch. And just before he fucked her over the edge of her orgasm, she remembered the way Tasha's breasts had strained against the V-neck t-shirt she'd been wearing last night, so tight it had looked as if it was painted on, her nipples hard diamonds pointing straight at Heaven. And then she came with a hard cry. Thankfully it was Calvin's name on her lips.

She maybe should have felt bad for something else then; for thinking of someone else while Calvin was inside her. But the effervescent euphoria of her orgasm didn't leave room for shame. There was only room for that banging of their headboard as Calvin lifted to his hands and held her still at the waist as he slammed into her with those deep thrusts. There was only room to smile seeing the vein in his neck bulge and pulse as he worked overtime to stave off his own release to get her off again. And then she was floating, pulsing gasping, clutching, leaking wet and warm around him again as he cried out his own release.

When he collapsed on top of her, sweaty and gasping, holding her close, their heartbeats pounding against their chests in greeting, Heaven had felt what she always felt with Calvin: loved. It made everything else seem less important. Her worries, his upcoming fight, a vague sense of shame and betrayal. Nothing mattered more than that this was their first morning in their new. Why ruin this euphoria for nothing? Just a fleeting thought that didn't mean anything at all.

"What you getting up to today?" Calvin asked as soon as Heaven came down to the kitchen.

She waited until he was done blending his protein shake to answer. "I'm gonna try and organize my new studio," she said with a giddy smile on her face as she wrapped her arms around his waist, "and then open my Etsy store again."

Calvin wrapped an arm around her shoulders and pulled her close. He kissed her forehead. "Sounds like a plan," he said and then took a sip of his shake.

"And what about you?"

He smiled down at her, "I'ma do what I always do."

"Train train train," she said with a playful roll of her eyes as she stepped out of his grasp. Heaven moved to open the refrigerator but Calvin's hand covered hers. His other hand settled over her stomach and he wrapped his body around her back.

He gently pulled her closer to him, the gentle bulge of his dick pressing into his ass. "You know I'm doing all this for us, right?" he whispered against her cheek.

"I know."

"I'm trying to secure our future."

"I know," she said, turning to face him.

"I don't ever want you to have to choose between your art and our bills. I told you the day we met that I just wanna make your life easy and your knees weak," he smiled down at her with the dirty grins he loved.

"That's it?" she asked with a seductive smile.

"I mean," he said and then dipped his head to kiss her.

Heaven smiled against Calvin's lips and lifted her hand to the back of his head. His teeth grazed her bottom lip and then he stroked her tongue with his. She moaned into his mouth and his hand started to move over the curve of her stomach down to the apex of her legs. Heaven was growing wet in anticipation that they would christen another room in their new house, when their ringing doorbell interrupted them.

Calvin pulled back and frowned down at her. "That's Reggie," he breathed in annoyance.

"Tell him you're 'bout to fuck me back to sleep," she whined and pressed her ass against his bulge.

Calvin squeezed her stomach. "I wish I could," he said and then kissed her forehead.

She sighed sadly as he moved away. She missed the warmth and coiled strength of his body immediately. He walked back to the counter, screwed on the cap of his smoothie cup and then turned back to her. He held her chin between two fingers and tipped her face up so they could make eye contact.

"You get your studio together and when I get home I'ma put you on this counter and eat you for dinner. Deal?"

Heaven couldn't help but smile. "Deal."

Calvin smiled and then dipped his head to press his mouth to hers.

"Have a good day," she whispered against his retreating lips.

"You too, baby."

She turned and watched him walk to the front door. He picked up his gym bag and slung it over his shoulder. He smiled at her one more time before he opened the door.

"Rise and shine, mothafucka," she heard Reggie yell. Heaven dissolved into fits of laughter.

"If you don't shut the fuck up and lower your voice," Calvin said in mock irritation.

"Morning, Heaven," Reggie yelled.

"Morning, Reggie," she yelled back.

"Alright let's go before you get us kicked out of this fucking suburb."

She smiled as Calvin walked out of their door and closed it gently behind him.

She walked into their nearly empty living room to the front window. She opened the blinds and watched Reggie excitedly speaking to Calvin as they walked to the latter's car. Calvin threw his bag into the backseat and slammed the door. He opened the passenger door and turned to the house. He smiled when he saw her standing at the window and waved at her, pouting his lips as if pressing a kiss to her mouth.

She waved back and stood there watching them until Reggie's car disappeared out of their cul de sac.

God, she loved that man.

---

Tasha didn't work on Mondays and thank god. She might have been able to pull herself together after a regular workday but after letting David fuck her over the back of the couch and then half the night, she felt like she'd run a marathon and was out for the count. Stephen, however, had bounced out of bed as if he'd gotten a full eight hours of sleep. He'd even sang at the top of his lungs in the shower. Tasha had glared at his back until their front door closed, and then she'd star fished on their bed and gone immediately back to sleep.

When she finally woke up, she'd crawled out of bed, took a shower and then sunk into the hottest bath she could stand. This was the favorite way to start her days off and rest her lower back. And because David was so considerate, he'd pulled her bath salts from the linen closet and placed them next to the bath for easy access. She let the morning while away as her bath water cooled.

When she was relaxed and moisturized, she pulled a loose t-shirt dress over her naked body. The idea of getting dressed any more than was necessary made her want to fall back to sleep. In the kitchen, she sighed happily when she saw that David had set the coffee machine up for her. All she had to do was press the brew button. She watched her coffee brew and smiled to herself at how lucky she was to have David and be loved so thoroughly by him. She was still smiling when she stepped onto the back deck. She'd just settled herself into one of the deck chairs, when the door at the other end opened and Heaven stepped out.

"Oh hello," Heaven said in a shocked, shy voice. "Good morning."

"Good morning," Tasha replied, working to keep her eyes on Heaven's face and not let them wander. "How are you two settling in?"

"Alright. Neither of us had much furniture before, so we're mostly unpacked."

Tasha smiled, "Is this your first time living together?"

Heaven's shy smile deepened and the dimples in her full cheeks became deep crevices that Tasha had an intense and inappropriate urge to dip just the tip of her tongue into.

Heaven nodded and inched forward.

"Would you like to have a seat with me? I can make you a cup of coffee." Tasha offered, indicating one of the chairs across from her around the table even though she really wanted Heaven to sit next to her.

"Oh, I don't want to interrupt you."

"No interruption. I don't mind the company. But if you wanted to have a moment alone that's just fine."

She shook her head, "I was actually just going to check out the shed. Stephen said he'd fix it up as a studio for me."

"Oh that's right."

Heaven had inched closer to the table.

Tasha gestured again to a chair and took a slow sip of her coffee as the other woman finally sat. "I'd love to see some of your work."

Heaven shook her head and her smile turned shy again. "No, I'm... it's just okay."

Tasha tilted her head to the side and looked at Heaven with a new eye as she bit the inside of her cheek in concentration. "I doubt that," she finally said. "But there's no pressure."

Tasha watched as Heaven seemed to fidget under the compliments. She didn't want to overwhelm her so she took another sip of her coffee and waited. But she didn't move her eyes from Heaven's face.

"I'll... we'll see," Heaven mumbled.

"You want some company looking at the shed?"

"Oh no," Heaven said, happy for the change in subject. "You don't have to do that."

Tasha fixed Heaven with an intense stare. She wasn't certain what Heaven saw in her eyes but her mouth fell open the tiniest bit. "I don't offer what I'm not willing to give." Tasha hadn't meant anything sexual by that, but the desire she'd felt last night flared up as she watched the other woman watch her. Tasha's tongue darted out to moisten her lips and Heaven's eyes darted down to take in the motion.

Tasha wasn't trying to seduce Heaven, but if David were here, he'd make a knowing correction that she wasn't not trying to seduce her either. And maybe Heaven wasn't closed off to being seduced.

"Okay," Heaven said in a wistful voice.

"Good," Tasha replied. "Lead the way."

---

This wasn't the way Tasha had expected her day off unfold. She'd planned to enjoy her coffee on the back patio, clean the kitchen and spend a few hours reading or catching up on some tv. In other words, she'd thought she'd spend this day off as she'd spent every other day off: relaxing and waiting for Stephen to get back from work.

Following Heaven across the small expanse of grass to the shed, was much better than that. Even if nothing happened, she thought. Even if this was a slight detour from her plans. Even if nothing came of this, there was still something so exhilarating about the sway of Heaven's hips in her pants as she walked and the adorable way she kept turning over her right shoulder to smile, nervously, at Tasha.

Heaven pulled the shed door open and peered inside.

"Stephen said he can paint or put up any shelves if I want?" Heaven asked.

"Yeah, he liked working, even when he's not working. Give him a project and he's in heaven."

Heaven turned to look at her with a look that Tasha interpreted as a kind of wistful stare. She stepped forward, crowding the entrance, but not touching Heaven. She was aware in that moment that she was naked underneath her dress. It should have made her feel self-conscious but there was something about the growing heat of the day, the soft cotton of her dress and the nearness of Heaven's body that burned away even the possibility of anxiousness or shame.

"You seem nervous," Tasha whispered.

Heaven smiled and nodded. It was an interesting

moment of honesty and vulnerability and Tasha found attractive. Even more attractive than her body.

"I've been crafting in spare bedrooms and my mom's garage for years. Painting at my friend's studio when she's not using it. I've been dreaming about having my own space to just... create. And now I do but..." Her voice trailed off and she bit her lip.

"You're scared?"

Heaven nodded again. "What if I finally have all this time and space to focus on my art and it's not good?" she admitted in a whisper.

"What if it is?" Tasha said nonchalantly, with a shrug.

Heaven's eyebrows bunched as if she'd never considered that possibility.

Tasha leaned against the door frame and smiled. "You never know until you try. Isn't that what everyone says? So you try and you see. But considering what your boyfriend was willing to pay to get you this space and the fact that you're already selling your work online, you probably don't have anything to worry about. Not that you asked me," she said, and crossed her arms over her chest.

She saw Heaven's eyes dip to her breasts and tried to ignore that look even though she didn't want to.

Heaven's eyes quickly shifted away. She licked her lips, staring off into the backyard. Tasha took that moment to watch her, noting the smooth skin of her face, the beautiful curve of her full lips and button nose, the soft flutter of her eyelashes. She bit her own lip.

After a few seconds of silence, Heaven turned back to her and smiled. It was soft and timid but Tasha wanted to get lost in it. She wanted to taste it, run her lips along that curve of her mouth, sip at the crease of her lips. Tasha wanted Heaven.

"Thank you," Heaven whispered.

"Anytime," she replied without hesitation.

---

She's naked.

Heaven couldn't stop thinking those two words.

Tasha was naked underneath her long t-shirt and it was all Heaven could think about as she walked around the small studio space. She was supposed to be thinking about where she'd put all of her materials – maybe in the north corner, away from the windows and out of direct sunlight– and where she might need shelves – maybe on the east wall because the light was good and she'd definitely want to paint here. She was supposed to be imagining her pottery wheel in the south corner and she could bring her Bluetooth speaker out here and listen to her podcasts and music while she worked. She could even picture an online order fulfillment station just by the door if she could find the right tiny desk for her laptop. She was supposed to be dreaming of kissing Calvin goodbye at the front door and then slipping out the back to work.

She was not supposed to be trying to decipher every dip of cellulite on Tasha's ass and imagining dipping her tongue into them. But she was. And it was exhilarating if also disconcerting. She'd been with women before, but she hadn't even been attracted to anyone of any gender since she'd been with Calvin. Never looked at any of the other boxers when she went to his fights. Never gave the Starbucks barista with the curly mohawk even a second glance when she tried to flirt. For three years, she'd only had eyes for Calvin. And yet here she was, losing track of her thoughts daydreaming about what it might be like to touch the curve of Tasha's hip.

Tasha turned to her with a wide smile on her face. Heaven pressed her lips together and took in a deep breath through her nose.

"Stephen gets home most days around four. You're welcome to come over whenever you're ready and tell him what you need him to do."

"What time are you home?" Heaven asked, even though she didn't mean to. She could have kicked herself. "I-I mean just in case you're home earlier." It was a pathetic save but Tasha nodded kindly at her.

"I don't get back until about six, most days. Stephen's fine. He doesn't bite. But you're welcome to knock on our doors whenever you like."

Heaven swallowed. “What do you do?” she asked, completely off track.

“I’m a nail tech. I work at a salon downtown.” she said and then her eyes dipped to Heaven’s hands. Heaven cringed and clasped her hands behind her back.

Tasha laughed. “You know you have to show me now, right?”

“They’re terrible. You’ll probably think I’m terrible.”

“Because of your nails? Believe me, it’s not that deep.” Tasha held her hands out with her palms up in clear invitation. She walked toward Heaven with slow intent.

But all Heaven could focus on was the soft sway of Tasha’s breasts as she walked. She wanted to groan but she swallowed it down and lifted her hands tentatively placing them onto Tasha’s upturned palms, she held her breath.

Tasha dipped her head and ran her thumbs over Heaven’s knuckles soothingly. Heaven watched as Tasha inspected her hands carefully. She peered up at Heaven through her inky eyelashes and smiled. “They’re bad,” she said.

Heaven cringed. “But you’ve got strong nails, chipped but not too jagged, and your cuticles are better than most. Beautiful, healthy nail beds,” she ended in a soft whisper.

"You don't have to lie," Heaven said, still looking away.

"I don't lie," Tasha said, clasping Heaven's hands in hers.

Heaven turned as Tasha pushed her hands together and brought them to her chest. Heaven couldn't stop the gasp that fell from her lips. her hands were so close to Tasha's breasts and those nipples. Her own nipples hardened at the thought. "I never lie," she continued. "It's one of the things my husband loves about me." Her eyebrows lifted, "That and my ass." She bit her lip as she held Heaven's gaze with her own.

Heaven swallowed.

"All you need is a good manicure," Tasha said as she inched closer, Heaven's hands still clasped in hers.

"I never get manicures," Heaven whispered. "The clay and the paint. There's no point."

Tasha's eyes dipped to Heaven's mouth and Heaven took that moment to do the same. Tasha sucked her bottom lip between her lips and let it out slowly, her bone white teeth scraping along the deep brown of her skin.

"The point is that it's a nice treat," Tasha whispered back. "Everyone deserves that every now and then." Her eyes lifted to Heaven's again but they were hooded, sultry and they made Heaven's blood churn in a way she'd only ever experienced with Calvin. "First one's on me. Whenever you're ready, come and knock on my door and I'll be happy to take care of you."

Heaven wasn't sure if she nodded or said 'okay' or just mumbled something nonsensical. She wasn't sure if she'd waved at Tasha when she left, but she did know that she went to the window to watch her ass jiggle in that t-shirt. And she knew that she waited exactly five minutes to leave the shed, because she set an alarm. She knew she walked on shaky legs to her backdoor and she didn't run, even though she wanted to. And most importantly, she did run from the backdoor upstairs to her and Calvin's bedroom.

The sheets still smelled like him, but she was too horny to worry about that. All that mattered was that she ripped off her clothes and plunged her fingers into her pussy; she was soaked. She couldn't bother waiting to dig in the as yet unpacked boxes in her closet for her vibrators and it was the touch she wanted. Tasha's hands on hers had been like fire and every word she'd whispered to Heaven felt like flames all over her skin.

She didn't tease herself. She knew she couldn't have survived it. so she circled her clit with one hand while fucking herself desperately with the other. She came and then came again. And then again. She felt like one long shuddering mess of need that her own hands couldn't sate. And for the first time in years, it wasn't Calvin's name on her lips when she collapsed onto the bed and fell fast asleep.

It was Tasha's.

Tasha's favorite day off activities included sleeping, dozing on the couch, soaking in the bath or napping with a bit of snacking in between. By the time Stephen got home, she was relaxed, hungry for whatever he was going to cook for dinner and horny. They had a routine.

But Heaven ruined that. Instead of relaxing, Tasha was amped. There was something about being in that small, warm shed nearly naked with her that made her blood simmer. Not boil like it had last night after meeting her for the first time. That might have been better. Instead she felt a low-level arousal that created a sheen of sweat at her hairline and made her restless. She'd tried to enjoy the rest of her coffee, but it had gone cold. She'd dumped it down the kitchen sink and didn't even consider making another. Instead she rushed up to her bedroom.

She ripped her dress from her body and nearly dove into bed. She would have preferred to use her fingers so she could imagine they were Heaven's, but her nails were too long for her to touch herself the way she wanted; as deep as she wanted. The way she wanted Heaven to touch her.

She had to fish around in Stephen's bedside table to find her favorite toy. It was long, about the same girth as her husband and, most importantly, when she put it on the fourth setting – persistent vibration with strong intermittent pulses – she could come in a heart-beat. This toy was an investment in a guaranteed orgasm. Tasha spread the first lube she found in her bedside table onto it and spread her legs, praying she would come soon, immediately, now.

But she didn't.

She moved her toy over her lips and tickled her opened before dragging it up her vagina and circled her clit and then pressing it inside of her sex. It should have worked. There wasn't much she loved more than teasing herself sexually and true enough her arousal slowly ratcheted up and up and up. But no matter how high she turned the setting or how much pressure she used to fuck herself or played with her clit, she couldn't get over the crest.

And then she heard it.

She sat bolt upright in bed and used her thumb to shut off her toy as she turned to stare at the wall behind her and Stephen's headboard. Her room was silent but she trusted her ears and her pounding pulse and the slow pulsing ache between her legs. She knew what she'd heard. It was her name. It was Heaven's voice. It was a shouted moan.

She moved closer to the wall and even sat up on her knees to press her ears against it. She listened for who knows how long – too long, her rational brain tried to tell her – but she couldn't move. And it didn't matter. The next moan was louder. Longer. Clearer.

"Tasha," Heaven moaned and Tasha had to swallow the answering groan that rose in her throat unbidden.

She stared at the wall and tried to think of what to do.

What she wanted to do was so clear in her brain. If life were uncomplicated, she'd get out of bed, pull her dress back on – probably inside out – and walk across her porch to knock on Heaven's door. She'd kiss her instead of saying hello. She'd let Heaven lead her to the bedroom on the other side of the wall and she'd spend the rest of her day off naked in bed with her new tenant and next-door neighbor.

But life was not uncomplicated. She and Stephen had a very clear protocol for these things and as it had always served them well. She had to wait. She had to talk to him. And then talk to Heaven. And then there was Heaven's boyfriend. Tasha hadn't met him yet and she was glad of that because it might have made the slow winding of her waist as she settled onto her back again strange. And it certainly might have intruded on the beautiful moment when she eased her vibrator into her vagina, Heaven's face emblazoned on her closed eyelids. He wouldn't have stopped her, but it might have been odd nonetheless to be able to put a face to the name as she fucked herself – first slow with a little vibration and then harder, faster, with those intermittent pulses – to a wet orgasm so good Tasha's toes curled and she clutched the pillow beneath her head and cried out.

As she drifted off to sleep, she thought of what she would say to Stephen and Heaven and maybe even

Heaven's boyfriend for a bit. But then her mind drifted off again when she used the pads of her fingers to gently circle her clit.

She wished the orgasm had been less intense so she could have called out to Heaven in hopes she'd hear.

She wondered what Stephen would think when he came home and she was relaxed, hungry but hornier than normal.

# 5

Heaven was desperate for Calvin to come home. She could have painted or checked the stock for her Etsy store re-opening, but every time she thought about her art, she thought of the shed, and then an image of Tasha's breasts jiggling under her dress and she would lose herself daydreaming about it; about her.

So, she channeled that restless energy by unpacking the kitchen. She hung up some of Calvin's clothes, knowing that if she left it up to him, he'd dig around in suitcases and boxes for days, maybe even weeks, until he ran out of socks. She organized their medicine cabinet and did some online window shopping. All the while she wanted to crawl back into bed and touch herself again.

But she didn't.

In a rush, she stripped the bed and walked down

to the basement. She shoved her and Calvin's sheets into the washer, hoping the cycle would wash away the guilt she felt deep in her chest. It didn't, but the fresh sheets did make her feel less... well she didn't really know what she felt. Not really. There was guilt and arousal, those feelings she understood. But there was something else underneath it that she couldn't quite name and she didn't want to, she decided. Not yet.

She'd just finished remaking their bed when Calvin called.

"Whatchu doin'?" he drawled in that deep, sexy voice she loved and made her feel younger and sexier and smitten all over again.

"Waiting for your big head ass to get home," she said with a broad smile on her face.

"Oh yeah? Well whatchu wearing for when I get home?"

She looked down at her leggings and t-shirt before answering. "Nothing," she lied.

Calvin laughed, "Lying ass."

She giggled.

"I'm leaving the gym in a bit, but I'm not coming straight home."

"Why not?"

Heaven could hear the excitement in his voice when he answered, "Got a meeting with Big Al about a fight."

"Big Al?" she breathed and dropped onto the fight.

"Big Al," he said again. "I think he's gonna finally schedule the title shot, baby."

"Baby," Heaven squeaked.

"I know. But you know how he is so I might not be home until late. I just wanted to call and tell you that so you weren't waiting around for me. Or didn't throw all my shit out on the lawn."

"I'd start with your ring gear," she said seriously, still smiling.

He huffed out an amused breath, "I know you would, that's why I called."

"Thank you."

"You're welcome." His voice dropped, "But since you was lying about being naked earlier, you should make that up to me."

Heaven rolled her eyes, "Is that right?"

"Mmmmhmm," he moaned.

"And how should I do that?"

She couldn't see him, but she knew the kind of seductive smile that would probably be on his face. And experience told her that the smile would be paired with a heavy bulge in his pants. She licked her lips.

"I'll let you know when I get home," he said.

Her smile dropped, "Boy you better not wake me up."

He laughed, "Gotta go."

"Calvin," she warned, "you better the fuck not."

He'd already hung up.

---

Tasha was in the kitchen and that was probably what tipped Stephen off that something just wasn't right. That and the fact that even though he'd called out to her when he got home, she'd been so distracted she hadn't heard him.

She jumped when his lips grazed her shoulder. "Shit, you scared the fuck outta me," she breathed. Her heart was pounding in her chest.

"Welcome home, honey," he said, in a poor imitation of her voice.

She leaned back into him and relaxed when his arms wrapped around her waist. "Welcome home, baby," she said.

He kissed up her neck. She tilted her head to give his lips access to her jawline, the underside of her chin and then her lips. She opened her mouth on a sigh and he slipped his tongue between her lips. He smiled as he kissed her slowly, gently, thoroughly. His tongue explored every inch of her mouth, his lips pressed forward and retreated, massaged her own lips open and then his teeth grabbed her bottom lip.

She groaned and frowned as he pulled away.

"You miss me?" he asked and placed a soft peck on the tip of her nose.

She nodded. "You have no idea."

He smiled down at her and then his left hand gripped her stomach briefly, in a hard, possessive clench. They stared into one another's eyes as the hand moved down her abdomen to the crease of her legs.

Tasha pulled her dress up to give him easier – faster – access to her aching pussy. She spread her legs and sighed again as his big, rough hand cupped her sex. And then she whined and ground her hips into his hand, silently begging him to rub her or slip one or two or three of those big fingers she loved inside of her and quick.

But he didn't, because Stephen knew her better than she knew herself.

"How was your day off?"

She swallowed, still moving her hips, loving the feeling of being caged by his big arm and hard body. "I saw our new neighbor again."

Two of Stephen's fingers swiped up her lips and just barely grazed her clit. She hissed.

"That so?"

She nodded.

"She get you this wet?"

Tasha nodded again.

"Have you been like this all day? Frustrated?"

She shook her head. He smiled.

"Did you fuck yourself while I was gone?" he asked, a dirty smile spreading his lips.

She nodded. "To sleep," she answered in a breathy moan because his fingers had begun to rub her wet lips slowly, up and down, in insistent strokes. She could feel the growing bulge in his pants behind her. Tasha moved her hips faster against him.

"She just smile at you or did something happen?"

The question was like being doused in ice cold water. She pushed his hand from her pussy – albeit reluctantly – and turned to him. "That's not how this works," she said in a hard tone.

He brought his fingers to his mouth and sucked her essence from them with a smile. "I didn't mean anything sexual," he finally said. "I know you'll talk to me before that."

"I would," she said. "But..."

Stephen lifted his right eyebrow and she smiled. She loved that eyebrow lift. It was the first thing she'd noticed about him the day they met. He'd been walking through the mall where she used to work with a friend. She'd been walking in the opposite direction, rushing back to the shop from her lunch break. His friend had said something to him that made him frown and then lift that same eyebrow. She knew now that that lift could mean anything, but then she hadn't known what it meant, and it'd intrigued her. Her steps had slowed and she'd stared. He'd seen her and turned his head to stare back. That eyebrow had seemed to lift even higher when their eyes met. His frown turned into a smile and she'd smiled back, something she never did to strangers.

They passed each other. She'd turned around to see that he had done the same. An hour later, he walked into her salon and asked for a manicure. She'd been doing a full acrylic set. He sat in a chair and waited. Another manicurist finished before Tasha and offered to do his nails. She heard him clear as day as he responded in a deep, almost gravelly voice that was kind and sexy. "No, thank you. I'm waiting for her."

She'd looked up and their eyes met again. And that eyebrow lifted – this time she thought it was playful – and she smiled at him as her face warmed. She hadn't rushed her client out of her chair, she was too professional for that. But her stomach had tightened the littlest bit in anticipation. When he was finally in her chair, she'd had to concentrate on making sure that her hands didn't shake during the first touch of their hands.

"Have you ever had a manicure before?" she'd asked, even though she knew the answer.

His light brown face had flushed just a bit. "No."

He was adorable. He made her blood rush. "I can tell. What do you do for work?"

"I'm a construction site manager."

She nodded, "Construction is hell on your hands, especially your nails."

"True."

"So what inspired you to get one today?"

"You," he'd said quickly. Matter-of-factly. It was the sexiest thing she'd ever heard.

She put his hands in the bowls of warm water on her table and looked up at him. The shop wasn't busy but My was next to her, working on a gel manicure, so she lowered her voice. "Good. I don't let men with hang nails touch me."

He smiled at her. She didn't know him but she knew the emotions in that smile. It was dirty, promising and it made her stomach clench even harder.

He licked his lips. "Then get me ready," he whispered back to her. His nails had never been out of shape since.

The lift of his eyebrow was similar today in their kitchen. He stepped closer to her. He put both hands on the counter on either side of her and leaned down. "But…?"

"There's something there," she said in a soft whisper. "You sure?"

She bit her bottom lip and nodded.

He stepped closer and took one of her hands. They unzipped his pants together and she slipped her hand inside. She didn't bother teasing him or herself. She didn't have that kind of restraint right now. She didn't want that kind of restraint, not with him. She moved her hand into his boxers. He was hard and the tip of his dick was wet with his arousal. He groaned when she took him in hand.

"I forgot my underwear," she whispered as she started stroking him.

"Forgot," he huffed in knowing disbelief.

"I didn't expect to see her. I was in the back. I just wanted to enjoy my coffee."

"And then?" he asked, dipping his head to kiss her right temple softly, lovingly.

"And then she came outside and we went to her shed. I just wanted to see what she wanted you to fix back there."

"And?" he breathed.

"Still not sure. She looked around but I was too busy-"

"Looking at her," Stephen finished for Tasha.

She lifted onto the balls of her feet and whispered against his lips, "Have you seen that girl's ass?"

He smiled and she licked his spread lips. "I might have noticed. That it?"

She squeezed his dick and he groaned. His eyes closed and his back bowed. "It shoulda been but..."

"But...?"

"But when I went upstairs to fuck myself, I heard her."

He opened one eye, "Heard her?"

"You maybe did need to put another layer of insulation between the wall like you thought," she said.

He rolled his eyes, "Fucking Diego, I told him."

She squeezed him again. "Be mad at him later." He seemed torn so she switched their positions. She pushed him against the counter and started to lower to her knees. He shook his head and grabbed her underneath her elbows. He walked her from the kitchen to the dining room table.

"If you hurt your back while giving me head, I'll never forgive myself."

She smiled and lowered into one of their dining room chairs. "I love you; you know that?"

"I figured," he said playfully. He unbuttoned his pants and pushed them over his hips, giving her barely enough time to extract her hand. She laughed and then grabbed him again, this time with both hands. She held him at the base and then stroked her hand down and then up his dick. She licked the head slowly, swiping her tongue through the slit and then she sucked him into her mouth. Just once, just enough to get him wet and then she started stroking him again.

"Keep going," he breathed, looking down at her with hooded, intense eyes.

"I went upstairs to fuck myself with our favorite toy."

"That serious, huh?"

"I needed to come. Bad," she smiled up at him. "But then I heard her moan."

"She needed to come bad too?"

She nodded and dipped her head to suck him into her mouth again. This time she bobbed her head twice before slowly releasing him.

"You're gonna kill me," he breathed, his hands politely on his hips as he watched her.

"I'll get you close, but you're not going anywhere

for a long time. I'm gonna be fucking you in an old folk's home, you hear me?"

He gasped as she dipped her head again. She needed to tell him the best part. She would. But he tasted so good and she'd been so horny all day. For him. For Heaven. Even though she'd tried to keep him on track, she'd gotten distracted as well.

She sucked him wildly, not slowly like she planned. She gripped him at the base, squeezing rhythmically and following her mouth with her other hand, twisting as she stroked him. His breathing was ragged and loud and he was bending over her, coming undone at her touch. She always loved that, the way she could break him down so thoroughly. But she waited until he was on the brink. Until he moved his hands from his hips and dug his fingers into her hair, his hips jutting forward, needing to be deeper in her hot mouth. And then she pulled back.

His moan was reedy, strained with need and her pussy clenched.

"She called my name," Tasha whispered to Stephen. She clutched him hard with both hands and began to stroke him furiously. "When she came, she called my name and I heard her."

That was it for him. And for her. He turned her head and pulled her mouth to his as she stroked him to orgasm. He cried out in her mouth as his come splattered over her chin and hands. He gently – as gently as he could – pulled her from her chair and eased her onto their dining room table. He stepped between her legs and pushed into her quickly.

Tasha's head fell back in aroused relief. She moaned as Stephen licked his come from her chin and ground into her in long, hard strokes. He held her legs open with one hand under her right knee but used the other hand to support her lower back.

That simple, beautiful, act of care was everything Tasha loved about Stephen. She'd never had a relationship like this before. She'd never been with anyone that made her feel so safe and so free. She slid her hands up his chest and around his neck and then pulled his mouth to hers. She tasted him on his tongue and her pussy gushed and clenched around him.

"You can say no," she whispered against his lips.

"Why the fuck would I do that?" he asked, punctuating his question with hard thrusts of his hips.

She smiled against his mouth. "I really do love you."

"Yeah?" he breathed and kissed her again. "Then show me. Come for me. Come all over this dick for me baby."

Tasha wrapped her legs around his waist and did as he directed. She never could deny Stephen anything.

---

Heaven liked lists. She liked to be organized and prepared for anything. She'd been composing a list in her head for Stephen about where he could hang shelves in her studio. There was also a squeaky closet door in their spare bedroom that she wanted him to look at. Now she had to figure out how to tell him that the walls were thin; maybe too thin. But she was nervous.

How to explain that she could practically hear them in their apartment when they spoke loudly without explaining that she'd heard them fucking? Could she say so without hinting at exactly what she'd heard? Would he guess that she'd listened? That she'd hung up the phone with Calvin and then sat on her couch daydreaming about his wife. That when she'd heard Tasha's laughter she'd unconsciously moved toward the closet under the stairs.

How to tell them that she'd heard him moan and began to rub her thighs together at the thought of what his wife was doing to him. That she'd touched herself – first through her leggings and then shoved her hand in her underwear – as all the possibilities had unfurled in her mind. How to explain that she'd slipped two fingers into her cunt when she'd heard Tasha moan? And that when he'd told Tasha to come on his dick, Heaven had come too. A shuddering, wet, leg-shaking orgasm, not because of his command, but because of Tasha's moans and knowing that only a couple of thin walls and not enough insulation separated them from coming together.

# 6

Heaven woke up alone. She turned over in bed and ran her hand over Calvin's cold pillow. She yawned, reached for her phone and smiled at the nearly twenty text messages from Calvin.

At Big Al's downtown club
This is gonna be a long night.
This mothafucka is wildin

The next messages came an hour later.

At Big Al's club on the Eastside

He punctuated this message with a string of eye roll emojis.

This fucking night won't end

Heaven smiled as she crawled out of bed and padded to the bathroom, reading all of Calvin's messages to her as she went. She could imagine him smiling, his entire body coiled tight in anticipation but not being able to show it. Calvin hated clubs. He didn't even really like going out unless he was with her or Reggie. That was the only time he let himself relax. He didn't like crowds, unless he was in the ring and they were cheering for him. He also rarely drank; not because he was opposed to it, but because he was always training and he hated wasting calories on alcohol. If he was going to break his strict diet, he either wanted his mother's fried chicken, Heaven's jambalaya or carrot cake. A glass of whiskey on New Year's Eve was the most he was willing to indulge.

She knew the only thing that got out last night was the promise of a fight. And the only thing that could keep him out all night was a shot at the welterweight belt. He'd been waiting his entire career for this. Five and a half years of work, of keeping his body in exquisite condition, hadn't been for nothing. He was ready. He was always ready. As she walked downstairs to the kitchen, she could just imagine him standing off to the side while everyone else drank and partied, texting her how annoyed he was to be there, hungrily waiting for the moment when Big Al was ready to talk business. She frowned over the kitchen sink when she realized that his messages ended three hours ago with no text about the fight and no Calvin at home.

And just as her thumb was hovered over the button to call him, their front door opened.

Calvin walked into their apartment with a scowl on his face and dark circles under his eyes.

She smiled at him, “Good morning.”

He shut the door and dropped his gym bag on the floor. “The next time I tell you I’m going to see Big Al, we’re gonna have to work out an escape plan,” he said in a dry and raspy voice. He headed straight to the refrigerator and pulled the pitcher of water out.

“You mean like women do when they’re on dates with strangers? Should I call you and say our dog had to go to the emergency vet?” she asked and then waited as he poured a large glass of water and downed it in two gulps.

He began to pour another, “I don’t care what you say. House on fire, meteor in New York, hi, whatever. But I’m never going to meet that motherfucker without knowing how to get out of there in three hours or much less.” He drank another glass of water and then leaned against the counter. “That man took me to half his clubs and kept pouring drinks even though I didn’t drink any of them. And every time I started talking about the fight, he changed the subject.”

"Oh no," Heaven sighed. "You didn't get the match?"

Calvin put his hands up, "Nah I got the damn match. It's in three months. But do you know when he told me the date? Guess?"

Heaven wanted to laugh at her very calm boyfriend's annoyed face. It was such a rare sight. "I don't kno-"

"Three fucking am this morning. That man was dragging us around on some dumb shit power trip for *five hours* before he told me the date. You know why?"

Heaven shrugged and shook her head.

Calvin crossed his arms over his chest, "Because that motherfucker just signed Steve Macias to his roster."

Heaven squinted and then, "Oooooh."

"Yeah," Calvin snorted in disgust. "So, the dude I'm fighting in two months – right before my title shot – is his new fighter. He was probably trying to see if he could throw me off my game."

"'Cause if you lose to Steve-"

"Big Al's sneaky ass is gonna swoop right in to give my shot to Steve's green ass. Motherfucker," he breathed.

Heaven watched as he stroked the bridge of his nose, which he only did when he was exhausted. Even if Big Al hadn't gotten him drunk and completely off his game, he'd still kept a man so dedicated to his health that he was asleep most nights by nine, out all night.

"You need to sleep," she whispered, walking toward him.

He shook his head. "I need to shower and get to the gym."

She grabbed his hand and moved it from his face. "No, you need to rest. You can go to the gym later if you need to, but right now you're gonna go upstairs, shower, and sleep. And when you wake up, I'll make you some baked chicken and vegetables and if you're still tired, we're gonna sit on *our* couch and watch a movie."

"Heaven," he started.

"We've been in this house for three days and you've barely been here. And I never tell you what to do, so you better know I mean this." She saw as his shoulders relaxed and he gave into her with each loosening muscle. "I know you like to fight, but not here. Not me," she whispered.

He put his big, rough hands on either side of her neck, his thumbs grazing her jawline. "Never you," he whispered back.

She smiled up at him. "I haven't showered yet," she said.

His head tipped sideways and he grinned at her with just a slight tilt of his hips on the right side. "You wanna take a shower with me?"

She nodded and pulled out of his grasp. She snatched his left hand and led him toward the stairs. He followed her willingly, his free hand smoothing here and there at her waist, her hips, her ass. She looked at him over her right shoulder. "If you're good, I'll ride you to sleep," she whispered.

At the top of the stairs, he grabbed her waist and pulled her close. He whispered into her ear. "I'm gonna always be good to you, Heaven. You know that?" He began to push her forward toward the bathroom with their bodies were connected, front to back.

"Oh, I know," she giggled pushing back at the growing bulge in his pants, "that's why I'm so damn good to you."

His raspy laughter in her ears made her nipples hard and in the bathroom, his heated stare as she undressed made the fact that she'd woken up alone more than okay; she knew he would make up for it. And he did.

The shower was foreplay, hot and quick. Their soapy hands and washcloths rubbing over each other's bare skin made Heaven's gut tighten even as she watched Calvin's previously tense body relax. They washed their faces and brushed their teeth, side-by-side at the sink, their hips touching and their eyes glued on each other in the mirror, a smile spreading both sets of lips.

Heaven let Calvin lead her back to the bedroom

and he yawned as she pushed him onto his back. But his eyes were alert, deep dark pools of wet earth brown as she crawled on top of him. She pressed a soft kiss to his lips and bit at his chin, licking the small patch of hair there. But she leaned up to look him in the eye and reached between their bodies to angle the head of his dick toward her entrance.

"You should let me eat you first," he whispered to her.

"You're tired," she said.

He lifted his eyebrows and ran his hands up her thighs. "I don't even have to move."

She smiled and moaned and then squeezed his dick before releasing it. He helped her move up his body, her big thighs straddling his head.

"Hold onto the headboard," he whispered as he pulled her hips down, smothering his mouth with her sex.

"Mmmm," she moaned as his tongue swiped up and down her lips, opening her, wetting her.

Calvin's hands were rough. Old calluses healed and sometimes split open again and then re-healed, even rougher than before. Over the years, she'd grown to love the way those callouses felt against her skin; on and in all of her most sensitive places. And because Calvin was the kind of lover she'd never had before, he noticed that she loved it. He used those rough patches of skin in the same way he used his lips, tongue, dick;

stroking her, getting her warm and then hot and then hotter still. This morning was no exception.

Calvin licked at her – his tongue swirling her clit now – as his hands traveled up her legs to cup the swell of her stomach and hold her in place as he teased her. Her hips began to circle as the tip of his tongue played at her opening and then he licked up her slit again.

Heaven's hands tightened on the headboard and her back bowed. She moaned when he sucked her clit into his mouth.

His hands moved up her chest and he lifted her breasts.

She moaned loudly as he circled her nipples with those callouses before twisting and plucking at them. "So good," she mumbled to herself. She felt his smile against her pussy and it made her wetter.

Her eyes fluttered closed but opened quickly. She thought he'd heard a rustling on the other side of the wall.

On any other morning she would have let him eat her slowly, grinding her pussy into his face, smothering him with her thighs and wet cunt just the way he liked. She would have shuddered and gushed over his mouth and then came again as he lapped at her, cleaning her up as she came and came again. But he was tired, even if he wouldn't admit it right now. Calvin loved to take care of her, but every now and then she had to take charge; take care of him.

So reluctantly, she leaned on the headboard to crawl off his face.

"Hold up, I'm not done yet," he said in ragged breaths, his mouth and goatee wet with her arousal.

She smiled down at him. "You can eat me as long as you want," she said, "after you wake up."

He grunted in dissatisfaction. She smiled down at him and then threw her leg back over his waist. She moved her now wet pussy up and down his dick and he groaned, flinging his head back onto his pillow. Once more she reached between them, grabbed his dick and angled it to her opening.

She sank onto him immediately.

And then she knew she hadn't imagined that rustling, because she heard it again.

Calvin's hands landed heavily on her waist. Heaven forced herself to refocus on him as he helped her ride him slowly.

She began to shift forward and back and around slowly. So slowly she could probably have done this for hours. Her hands flat on his chest, her pussy clenching at him as she rode herself to orgasm after orgasm but never gave him quite enough stimulation to come, keeping him just on the edge of arousal. They both loved when she did that. But again, he was tired. So, she leaned back, spread her thighs just a little bit wider and she increased the pace.

He closed his eyes, moaning softly as he fully relaxed and began to drift to sleep.

Even though she wanted him to sleep, she was horny now and had her own needs. "Watch me," she whispered to him.

He smiled and sucked his luscious bottom lip into his mouth. She clenched around his dick at that smile and those teeth sinking into the beautiful brown of that lip, which probably tasted like her.

He opened his eyes, dug his fingers into her waist and then he lifted his hips to meet her. "You miss me?"

She scratched at the coarse, curly hair on his chest and began to move just a bit more. "I woke up alone."

"I'm sorry," he said.

"Don't make it a habit."

His hips jutted up, pulling a shocked moan from her mouth. "You ain't gotta worry about that," he said.

"Good. You miss me?"

He sat up and wrapped an arm around her waist while the other grabbed her behind her neck. His eyes trapped hers. "I miss you whenever I'm not with you," he said, not for the first time.

She wrapped her arms around his shoulders, leveraging the grip to spread her legs that much more and fuck him harder.

"You're gonna beat Steve Macias," she said, panting. "You know that. I know that. And Big Al knows that."

"Yeah?" he grunted.

"Yeah. And then you're gonna beat Winston King and take that title," she moaned around that last word.

He groaned, one restrained exhalation that for someone like Calvin was a sign that he had damn near come undone.

"And when you get that belt, you're gonna fuck me with it around your waist." She moaned. He grunted. "I want you deep in me while the venue's still full. We might even hear Winston crying in his locker room." Her words had become one long, desperate moan.

Their hips were meeting, retreating and meeting again, wild and fast. Heaven's words came faster, punctuated by ever louder moans. And Calvin alternated between grunting as she fucked him and groaning as she squeezed him tight with her arms and her pussy. Their bodies were covered in sweat. Heaven figured she'd have to change the sheets again. She didn't care.

"I wanna feel that heavy belt while I'm throwing my ass back at you, you hear me?"

"Yeah, fuck," Calvin breathed. "I hear you. Fuck, I love you."

She let go of his shoulders to push him back on the bed. There was no slow winding on him now, they were both too far gone. She planted her palms on his chest and they slammed their hips together, moaning, screaming, panting.

"I love you," he screamed when she came, wet and clenching around his hard dick. She shuddered in his arms as he came soon after.

"I love you too," she whispered against his lips.

There was gentle moments of silence. Heaven was

still on top of him and they were staring at one another with shocked, sated eyes. The moment was rent when a loud moan on the side of the wall – a sound Heaven knew instinctively was Tasha's – sounded in their room

Heaven and Calvin's eyes widened and then they burst into laughter.

Heaven crawled off him and settled against his side. She put her head onto his chest. the rumble of his laughter nearly covering the sound of his hard-beating heart.

She pulled their comforter over their bodies. She brushed some of the sweat from his forehead and kissed his hairline. His eyes were already drifting closed.

"I love you," she whispered again against his skin.

---

"I definitely need to put some more insulation between the walls," Stephen said, his hips bouncing off Tasha's ass. She was on her hands in knees, facing the wall as he fucked her in long, strong strokes.

She tried to imagine Heaven and Calvin on the other side of the wall. She wondered if Heaven was on her knees like she was. Or was she riding him? Was Calvin massaging her breasts or gripping her hips like Stephen was holding her.

But as she began to moan, her sex quivering and

her orgasm so near she could practically taste it, mostly she just wondered if Heaven was thinking of her. The idea of that combined too perfectly with her husband's dick inside of her. Her arms buckled and her face fell to the bed.

"Fuck, baby," she screamed into her pillow.

She groaned as Stephen's body covered her back. She shuddered beneath him as he ground into her, touching new sensitive parts of her pussy.

"You screaming for me or for her?" he whispered into her ear.

She groaned and squeezed his dick inside her. "Both of you," she said because it was the truth. And because she knew it would drive him wild.

And it did.

His back straightened. He gripped her hips and began to pound into her so hard she had to fist their comforter in her hands to anchor herself. And he fucked her like that through one and then another and then one more orgasm before he pulled out and came all over her ass in a messy spray. She always loved when he did that. And if her body weren't so spent, she might have come again. But all she had left in her was a deep, teeth-clattering full-body shudder.

The sun was just barely up in the sky. Normally Stephen would have been in the shower by now and Tasha would have been downstairs making coffee. But Heaven and Calvin had woken them up with their moans and their morning plans were all askew. But

Stephen could go in a bit late and Tasha could grab her coffee on the way to the salon. Right now, they were happy to catch their breaths in their now quiet bedroom, the aftershocks of their orgasm stretching out.

Out of nowhere, Stephen's hand came down hard on her ass; just hard enough to pull a groan from Tasha's throat. "Getting some tenants in next door was my best idea this year," he said.

She smiled against her pillow. He crawled from their bed and she turned onto her side to watch him. She supported her head with one bent arm and stretched the other out along her side. Her eyes ran over his body, the hair on his chest wet with a thin sheen of sweat and his softening dick covered in her arousal. She licked her lips and he groaned.

He was watching her. "As much as I love all this sex, I'm gonna have to get on that insulation sooner rather than later."

She frowned.

"Don't shoot the messenger," he said with a chuckle. "Besides, I know you, and you're not gonna be okay with just eavesdropping like a pervert. Not when she'd close enough to touch."

Tasha's pussy shivered at his words.

"If you want her, step one is to tell her. Isn't that what you always tell me?"

She rolled her eyes, "Don't use my words against me?"

He leaned over the bed and brushed his lips across her cheek. "Ain't it annoying?" he said as he walked from the room, laughing.

She frowned at his retreating back even though she knew he was right. Her eyes shifted to the bedroom wall they shared with the other side of the duplex. She took a deep breath and sighed as she let it out.

# 7

The move had been stressing her out for weeks before the moving truck had even shown up at her mom's house and for weeks after. She'd been unable to create while living amid boxes and felt rudderless without the familiar of creation. So this morning, she got up well before sunrise and set about unpacking the last few boxes scattered around the house. She was ecstatic to put the final broken down bodes into the recycling bin. Now that she was free, she waked immediately from the front of the duplex, through her apartment and straight into the backyard to her shed studio.

There was something so cathartic about laying out her jewelry inventory on the newly installed shelves that Stephen had put nearly as soon as she'd asked. She unpacked her pens and pencils, organized her paints and set up her easel. The sun was just cresting over the horizon when she sat onto a stool and officially reopened her Etsy store. And then, instead of worrying if any of her customers would return, she sat at her easel and painted without a clear vision or goal while her music played – loud enough to fill the small space, but not to disturb their landlords.

Heaven let herself be distracted by that familiar glide of her brush across the canvas, the smell of paint and thinner, even the slight tension in her shoulders as she tried out differing pressure in each stroke, reacquainting herself with the freedom of creation and trying not to hunch her shoulders. Sometimes her mind wandered to other things – Calvin's training and his upcoming fights and sometimes Tasha – but she forced herself to get back on track each time her mind strayed.

After she didn't know how long, a knock at the shed door pulled her from her work. "Come in," she called, knowing deep in her gut who would be there.

Heaven felt as if she'd conjured Tasha from her daydreams. Tasha stepped tentatively into the room, a bright smile on her face, a tight V-neck t-shirt and a pair of cropped black leggings hugging of her curves; so many curves that Heaven had once dreamt about tracing them with her hands and her tongue. She'd woken up so wet and horny that morning that she'd made Calvin late to the gym. Not that he complained.

She swallowed and blinked, "Hi."

"Hi," Tasha replied. "Am I interrupting?"

Heaven shook her head quickly – maybe too quickly – and stood from her stool. "N-no, you're not. I'm just... just messing around."

Tasha's right eyebrow lifted as she looked around Heaven at the easel. "That's you messing around?"

Heaven turned to look at the canvas and sucked in a shocked breath. She'd thought she was just painting freely while she thought, and she had been. But apparently her thoughts had been centered on the thing she was actively trying to avoid. Heaven's style was usually more abstract, but this piece was not. The figure on the canvas was easily recognizable to her eyes; thick thighs, rounded hips, a beautiful expanse of flesh above the waist, large, rounded breasts with dark circles and nipples. The canvas was filled with dark brown skin that was as close to Tasha's complexion as Heaven could get from memory. The nude didn't have a head, it was a closeup study of the form, but if it had had one, it would have been Tasha's – aquiline bridge of the nose with a beautiful rounded nub, large, elegant nostrils, Disney princess eyes topped by lashes so long they made Heaven's heart flutter when she blinked and full lips, slightly fuller bottom lip than the top.

She knew the painting was Tasha and her stomach clenched at the thought that Tasha would recognize herself; or at least the version of herself that Heaven had created in her imagination.

"It's beautiful," Tasha whispered.

Heaven jumped. She'd been so entranced with her own work – and worry – that Tasha had moved across the room and was now so close. Heaven could feel Tasha's body heat at her right elbow.

"Th-thank you," Heaven said, too nervous to turn around, but enjoying the way the other woman's body felt nearby.

"Do you use models?" Tasha asked.

Heaven shook her head quickly. "No, I normally... I normally don't paint people," she admitted.

Tasha moved around her, closer to the painting. Heaven watched as she bent down to study it. "You did this from memory?"

"My imagination," Heaven corrected.

Tasha straightened and turned to her. There was a small grin on her face that Heaven couldn't read but made her heart beat just a bit faster.

"I like the way you think," Tasha whispered. It sounded seductive, but Heaven wondered if maybe that was just her own arousal making something out of nothing.

Heaven ducked her head to hide her smile. Tasha stepped forward.

"Your hands," Tasha said, reaching toward Heaven, but stopping just before they touched.

Heaven spread her fingers out and cringed. Her fingers were covered in paint, the skin between her fingers was ashy and her fingernails were dry, cracked and split. She shook her head and moved her hands behind her back. She raised her eyes to Tasha's and laughed, although it was strained, embarrassed.

"Don't look at them," she said, cringing.

Tasha's face softened into a sympathetic smile. She stepped forward, so close that Heaven could smell the light floral scent of her perfume and feel just the tips of her breasts touching just the tips of hers. Heaven sucked in a soft gasp and Tasha's smile broadened and she licked the corner of her mouth.

Heaven gasped as Tasha's hands touched her arms, tentatively at first and then she leaned into the touch. Her hands pressed down Heaven's bare arms and slid toward her hands. She grabbed Heaven's wrists and then moved them around. Heaven was saddened as she stepped away. It had only been a short moment, but Heaven had enjoyed it more than she was comfortable acknowledging; as if she had been yearning for it for weeks.

Because she had.

But Tasha was still holding her hands. Her thumbs smoothed over the dry, stained skin of Heaven's hands and palms in smooth circular motions. "I've seen worse," Tasha said, tipping her head up to smile at her through those inky lashes.

"I should take better care of them," Heaven said, ashamed.

"Or," Tasha said, "you could have a trained professional take care of them for you."

"No, I couldn't-"

"Of course, you can. I'm right next door. And I'd be happy to do the first manicure for free."

Heaven shook her head for a second, but Tasha's grip on her flexed. She sucked her bottom lip into her mouth and Heaven's body tensed and stilled.

"It's part of my business strategy," she said, stepping forward. "I lure you in for the first free manicure and then I get you hooked by the hand massage and how good your nails look when I'm done."

"That works?"

Tasha nodded. "That's how I got my husband."

Heaven didn't know what to make of that. She knew what she wanted to make of it, even if she shouldn't. She wanted Tasha to be flirting with her. She wanted Tasha to keep touching her, to kiss her. She wanted Tasha, even though she knew she shouldn't. But Tasha shouldn't be flirting with her, she reminded herself. Tasha was married and whatever soft heat seemed to be arcing between them was probably nothing but Heaven's own overactive imagination.

But what if it wasn't, she thought? "Okay," she said quickly, before she could stop herself.

Tasha's smile was beautiful. Heaven briefly daydreamed about lifting onto her toes to kiss her, but she didn't; she wasn't that bold. She was already too close to the invisible line separating propriety and wanton abandon. And however someone might describe Heaven, reckless was not a descriptive option. At least not normally.

"Okay?" Tasha asked.

Heaven nodded, too afraid to speak.

"Good! I actually came out here to invite you and Calvin tonight. Now that you two are settled in hopefully."

"Oh yeah, yeah we are," Heaven replied, her heart beating at the mention of Calvin's name.

"Great. So dinner? We'd love to cook dinner for you two." She tipped her head and grinned. "Well, Stephen would love to cook you dinner. I'll tell jokes and make the drinks."

"Calvin doesn't drink," Heaven blurted out. "Well, rarely. But he's training right now so he can't. And actually, he has a really restrictive diet, you shouldn't waste your time."

"Oh nooo, Stephen loves a challenge. If you tell me what he can and can't eat, he'll spend damn near every free moment working on the recipe. How about this?" Tasha said, seeming to bounce on her feet in excitement. Heaven's eyes only dipped to her jiggling cleavage briefly. "How about you come by in a few hours. I have some errands to run, but when I'm back I'd be happy to get these nails together. And you can tell me about Calvin's diet. Sound good?"

It sounded great, but not because Heaven necessarily wanted the manicure or because she was looking forward to breaking down Calvin's diet so close to a fight. But Tasha was still holding her hands. Her thumbs were still stroking Heaven's palms and Heaven's sex had begun to clench and pulse as she imagined Tasha's thumbs touching her there, lower, dipping in and out of her with those soft movements. Her beautiful nails carefully grazing across her wet lips. Followed by her tongue.

"Okay," Heaven said in a breathy whisper.

Tasha beamed and then took Heaven's breath away. She dipped her head and brushed her lips across Heaven's cheeks. Her lips were so soft, the touch so feather light that Heaven knew she'd be touching herself remembering it for a long time to come.

"Come by whenever you're ready," Tasha whispered, her minty breath fanning over Heaven's cheeks.

Their eyes met and Heaven nodded. Tasha's eyes dipped briefly to Heaven's mouth. For a second Heaven let herself imagine that Tasha was thinking the same thing she had been for the past few moments, wondering what it would be like to kiss her, taste her. She imagined that the softness in Tasha's gaze wasn't just neighborly kindness but arousal, lust. She let herself wish for something she knew she shouldn't.

And then the moment was over. Tasha squeezed her hands one more time and then let them go. She stepped quickly away and began to walk toward the door.

"See you in a bit," Tasha called over her shoulder. She stopped and turned at the door. She chewed on her lip for a second and then seemed to decide. "If you ever want a model," she said, tipping her head to Heaven's easel, "I'd happily volunteer."

Heaven was nodding before Tasha even finished offering. She kept nodding as Tasha smiled and exited the shed. It was a bad idea, she knew, but it made every part of her feel so good.

---

Calvin bounced down the stairs just as Heaven pulled the special high protein, gluten free breakfast muffins from the oven.

"Aw yeah, smells good as fuck in here," he said, the sound of his heavy steps booming along the hardwood floors.

"It's just muffins. Don't get too hype," she said.

He wrapped his arms around her middle and shoved his face into the crook of her neck. "If my girl is cooking for me, I'll get hype if I want to," he mumbled against her skin. "How was your morning?"

She leaned into his hold, "Good. I got a few orders. Started a new painting."

He kissed her just behind her ear. "You were worried no one would come back to your store, huh?"

She nodded. He kissed her again.

"I wasn't," he said. "I know how good you are."

She shifted and he loosened his grip just enough to let her turn in his arms before clutching her close. "You're really good to me."

The smile spread slowly across his lips and his eyes closed just a bit before he tipped his head to the side, toward the oven. "And you're damn good to me."

Heaven rolled her eyes. "It's *just* some muffins."

"Nah, I've been drinking my meals for damn near a week. Those ain't just muffins. That's fucking gold," he laughed. And then he did a thing that Heaven loved. He tilted his head to look at her down the bridge of his nose. His eyes were hooded and his mouth was tilted into a grin. "And you're fucking gold. I wish you could see yourself the way I do."

She sucked in a breath and tried to blink away the tears suddenly pooling in her eyes. "You're being really fucking charming right now." She squinted up at him. "Why?"

He laughed and quickly shifted his hold to the back of her legs.

"Calvin," she screamed, as he picked her up and deposited her onto the counter next to the sink.

His hands moved to her hips and waist, his strong fingers digging into the flesh, massaging her. She was so short that the height only put them at eye level. "I saw Stephen's wife leave the shed earlier."

"Tasha?" Heaven asked, wistfully. "I thought you were sleep."

"I got up to pee and I just happened to look out the back window on the way. She looked damn happy," he said, looking at her.

Heaven's heart was beating in her chest. There was

no way Calvin could know what she'd been thinking earlier and yet, she was terrified that he did. "She um... she offered to give me a manicure and she invited us to dinner tonight."

"Oh word?"

"Yeah, but we don't have to go. You're training. And you need to watch what you eat. I told them that."

Calvin squeezed her thighs under his palms. "And what'd she say?"

"Um...," Heaven licked her suddenly dry lips. "She said Stephen could work around your diet."

"Then what's the problem?" he asked as his hands moved up her thighs.

"I-" Heaven didn't know how to answer this question without exposing her deepest desires. But that wasn't why her voice failed her. For a second, she lost the ability to speak, when his thumbs nudged the top of her sex.

It was a brief touch, but it short circuited her brain.

But just as quickly as he'd touched her, his hands moved; one at her right knee and the other at the small of her back. He pulled her closer to the edge of the counter and pushed her legs apart. And then his hand moved from her knee, up her inner thigh and he cupped her covered pussy with his palm.

She whimpered.

"Something you want to tell me, sweetheart."

Heaven didn't lie to Calvin so she clamped her lips shut, but he pulled them apart when his fingers started to massage her clit. She gasped and moaned. Her head fell back and her eyes closed as she started circling her hips.

"You wanna tell me why she was so happy this morning?"

She shook her head, "I don't know. She just asked abut the manicure and dinner."

"What about before that?" Calvin asked.

Heaven's hips stilled, her eyes flew open and she frowned at him. "Before that?"

"When you were fucking me to sleep this morning," he said cryptically.

"I- We should tell Stephen the walls are thin."

"We can. But I meant," he said, dipping his head to lick her bottom lip. "Do you wanna talk about your pussy spasming when we heard Tasha moaning this morning?"

Heaven gasped again in shock, but then moaned again when Calvin cupped her and crushed his mouth to hers. His hand was heavy at her back, encouraging her to grind against his palm. He wanted to get her off.

And even though she didn't know what to make of this moment, she wanted to let him get her off. She wanted to come so bad.

She whined when he broke their kiss.

He licked his own lips with a smile. "Tell me."

She shook her head.

He shook his as well and then he moved both of his hands between her thighs.

"Calvin," she gasped when he split her leggings at the crotch.

He pushed her underwear to the side, pushed two thick, calloused, strong fingers into her wet core and started fucking her deeply.

"Oh fuck."

His other hand moved to the back of her head and pulled her face close. But this time he didn't kiss her. Instead, he growled his words against her lips. "Tell me."

"I want her," Heaven groaned, shocked to hear the desperation in her own voice. "But I shouldn't. I love you."

He rolled his eyes and settled his thumb over her clit.

She cried out and he kissed her quick.

"One thing doesn't have to have a damn thing to do with the other," he said matter-of-factly.

Calvin was a still, strong pillar, while Heaven was a shivering, panting mess in her arms. Even though they were talking about Tasha, she'd never been more attracted to Calvin before.

"I'd never cheat on you," Heaven whispered desperately.

"Good. I'd never cheat on you either. But I'm also not trying to hem you in. We can be adults about this."

She wasn't sure if it was his fingers or his words – but probably both – but she was so close to coming she could barely think straight. "Another," she groaned. "Give me another finger."

He chuckled in that deep sexy groan before pulling his finger out and then hooking three fingers into her cunt this time.

Heaven wrapped her arms around his neck and whimpered against his lips.

"If I said you could fuck you, would you?"

"Yes." She was too far gone to even hesitate.

"Would you?"

"Would I fuck Tasha? Girl you seen that ass?" he teased.

"Not Tasha. Someone else. Do you want to be with someone else?" It took her forever to ask the question. Each word came slow interrupted by panting breath after panting breath.

His fingers slowed inside her and he seemed to really be considering the question. "No," he finally said. "Not right now. If that changes, I'll let you know. But right now, this is about you and Tasha." His hands sped up inside her.

She shook her head and shuddered. "There's no me and Tasha. I don't think she wants me. Shit," she screamed as he started rubbing hard circles over her clit.

The time for talking was over. Before she could

even process what was happening, Calvin had lowered to his knees and replaced his thumb with his mouth.

Heaven leaned back on the counter and lifted her knees to give him better access to her pussy. And he rewarded her immediately for the effort.

She came in a wet instant.

Calvin's fingers slowed incrementally inside her as he moved from sucking at her clit to licking up and down her lips.

"Oh my god," she groaned.

Eventually he stood, his face wet and his fingers in his mouth. He looked at her down his nose, her chest heaving and her legs spread obscenely. "She'd be an idiot not to want that pussy," he said matter-of-factly. "Lemme clean up and then we can both eat."

She groaned.

He chucked as he jogged back upstairs.

# 8

Tasha was nervous. Tasha didn't get nervous. Not anymore. Not over a simple manicure. But this wasn't a simple manicure; it hadn't been when she offered it and she doubted it would be simple now. At least not for her. so she was pacing around her small living room, waiting for her doorbell to ring, terrified that it wouldn't but also terrified that it would.

She could still remember the way Heaven's hands had felt in hers; small, a bit rough but pliant. And she wouldn't be forgetting the way Heaven's cheek felt against her lips

Stephen had cackled loudly in her ear when she told him about her conversation with heaven. "You gonna be okay?"

Tasha rolled her eyes. "I'm not gonna jump her mid-manicure if that's what you're worried about."

He laughed, "It wasn't, but now I'm wondering if I should be."

"Shut up. Don't tease me."

He opened their front door and turned to her. "Okay but if you need me, just call."

"What am I gonna need you for? You gonna help me paint her nails?"

"No, but after..." he said, letting his voice trail suggestively. Her stomach and sex had clenched.

"Keep your phone on," she'd whispered.

And now she was eyeing her phone wondering if she should call him and have him talk her nerves down.

But then there was a tentative knock on the door; soft as if the person on the other side was afraid she might hear. Tasha walked slowly to the door, even though she wanted to rush. She grabbed the door handle but stopped to take a deep breath before she pulled it open.

Sometimes at work Tasha had to force herself to smile. No one wanted to come back to a frowning manicurist. Or a quiet one; especially not a quiet, Black one. They might just decide she was mean even if she gave them the best manicure of their lives. She had to spend so much of her day sitting damn near ramrod straight, smiling and chitchatting that by the time she was home she could hardly bear to do any of those things unless she was deeply moved. It was part of the reason she'd fallen for Stephen. Even at her most weary, even when she didn't want to, he could make her laugh and smile. He never asked for more than she could give. He filled in all the silences and absences in her life and made her feel safe and warm; something she hadn't had in abundance before they'd met.

And when she opened her front door, Heaven's nervous smile moved her.

"Hi," Tasha breathed.

Hey."

She stepped back and opened the door wide, "Come on in."

"Thanks." Heaven was in a cute t-shirt dress that hugged her in all the right places and gave a peek of her dimpled knees.

"Come on. I set up a station in the kitchen." Tasha had to force herself to look away and close the door. She accidentally brushed Heaven's hip with her right hand as she walked past.

She turned to look over her shoulder and had to swallow a groan and quickly whip her head around again.

Heaven had been staring at Tasha's ass.

Tasha walked to the kitchen, using each step to try and bury the smile on her face. There was nothing she could do about the pit of arousal in her gut, however.

"Have a seat," she said, gesturing toward the kitchen table. She tried not to remember how Stephen had taken her on that table weeks ago and how every time she'd cleaned it since then, she'd thought of nothing but that and Heaven's hands in hers. "Do you want anything to drink? Coffee? Water? Juice?"

"Water." Her voice cracked.

"Coming right up."

"So, I thought I could throw a pedicure in the mix. Get you hooked on the double service so you'll come back for more. What do you think?" She sounded much surer of herself than she felt.

She put a glass of water in front of Heaven with a smile. Then she turned back to the kitchen sink. She let the spout run until the water was just past warm and filled two bowls. When she turned back, Heaven's water glass was near empty. "Do you want some more?"

Heaven shook her head. "Not right now," she whispered.

Tasha set the bowls down on the middle of the table. "So, about that pedicure?" she asked sweetly, in that up sale voice she used at the salon.

"Are you sure?"

"Yeah. A good pamper session never hurt nobody."

"Um..." Heaven's eyes darted to her bare knees. So did Tasha's. "Okay. If you're sure."

"I'm sure," Tasha whispered. She swallowed thickly before turning to the sink to fill the foot basin with piping hot water. She was careful not to aggravate her back by filling the bowl too full. And she walked carefully to place it at Heaven's feet.

She'd kicked off her flip flops and placed them inside.

"Too hot?" Tasha asked.

"No, so good." There was a luscious smile on her lips.

Tasha licked her own lips hungrily.

She moved to the kitchen table and sat across from Heaven. She took a second to position the cushion she'd brought from the living room at her lower back for comfort. Then she grabbed a small bottle from the basket of tools she'd placed there for the manicure. She twisted the top off and dropped a few drops of essential oil into each bowl.

Tasha reached out, palms up, gesturing for Heaven's hands. Because she was looking right at her, she couldn't ignore the hesitation. The way Heaven's eyes dipped and zeroed in on Tasha's hands and the deep breath she took before she tentatively lifted her hands and placed them palms down in Tasha's made Tasha's breath catch.

They exhaled slowly together when their palms touched. Heaven looked up at her and smiled nervously. Tasha smiled back, a warm smile that she hoped would reassure her, as if to say it was okay, she wouldn't hurt her. All those things were true, but she wished she had a nonverbal way to tell her that she was nervous too. That she loved the way their hands felt together. That she would take good care of her in this manicure, pedicure and... beyond, if she wanted.

But she didn't know how to say that with just her eyes and her smile so she smoothed her thumbs back and forth across the backs of Heaven's hands before she slowly placed them in the warm water.

"This is to soak your cuticles, so I can clean them up," Tasha said softly.

Heaven nodded.

"Have you thought about what color you might like?"

Heaven shook her head. "I don't... it'll probably just chip while I work."

Tasha smiled. "We can do a gel coat. It'll last longer. What's your favorite color?"

"I don't have a favorite color actually."

"Really?"

"What's," Heaven's voice trailed off and she briefly sucked her bottom lip into her mouth. "What's your favorite color?" she asked in a small voice.

Tasha couldn't stop the small gasp that escaped from her lips. "Yellow," she whispered softly.

"You think yellow nails would look good on me?"

Tasha's smile widened, "I think any color would look beautiful against your skin." Heaven's head dipped slightly. "But I have the perfect color yellow for our skin tone," she said quickly, digging into the box of nail polish until she found what she was looking for.

She held it out for Heaven to see. The other woman shrugged. "If you think it'll look good on me."

"I do," Tasha said quickly. "I really do."

That seemed to make Heaven smile. "Okay," she said.

"Okay."

Tasha and Heaven smiled at one another shyly for a few too many seconds before Heaven dipped her head again. Tasha decided to get the manicure started if only so that she didn't scare Heaven off and also because of the own hunger she felt to touch her again.

She folded one of the towels she'd placed on the table into a square and placed it on the table between them. She lifted Heaven's left hand from the water and placed it on the towel, drying it with firm pats of the towel. When it was dry, she lifted her head to see Heaven watching her. They smiled at one another again, or maybe they'd never stopped smiling.

Tasha held Heaven's hand in her left, their palms touching, as she reached with her other hand back into her small box of tools. For a fraction of a second she forgot what she was looking for, but she took a deep breath and mentally shook herself. She snatched the cuticle tool from the box and began to work gently on pushing back and then carefully clipping Heaven's cuticles until they were nice and neat.

"My nails are in such bad shape," Heaven said.

"I told you, I've seen worse. This is nothing." She looked up at Heaven. "Besides, you're an artist and they're just nails."

Heaven lifted an eyebrow – the move was so

different from the way Stephen did and she liked that. "Just nails?"

Tasha laughed and reached for Heaven's right hand. "I love nails and hands but no one has to love them as much as I do." And then she raised her own eyebrow. "And you really don't have to worry about them if you come and let me get you together," she said.

Heaven smiled, "So I'm guessing you're a great saleswoman."

Tasha shrugged, "A girl's gotta eat."

"Oh, and you're humble. That's cute." Heaven laughed.

Tasha chuckled but couldn't give herself falling over to laughter because she was so overcome with watching the way Heaven's laughter looked on her. She laughed with her entire body. Her beautiful round cheeks pushed her eyes nearly closed; her mouth was spread wide to show her teeth and her tongue. But really it was her chest that consumed Tasha's gaze. Her full breasts bounced methodically up and down and then jiggled just a bit side to side. Tasha licked her lips and then dropped her head.

"How long have you been doing nails?" Heaven asked unexpectedly.

"Ten years," Tasha said as she began to work on Heaven's cuticles.

"How'd you get started in it?"

Tasha smiled but didn't look up. She didn't trust

herself. Not just yet. "When I was little my mom had these long nails. She got them done religiously every two weeks with bright colors and airbrush designs and jewels. You name it and she had it." She looked up now, "They were her only really splurge. We didn't have lots of money. We were always just barely getting by. My mom worked two, sometimes three jobs to keep a roof over our heads. And the only luxury she ever allowed herself was a regular acrylic fill and a fancy paint job."

Tasha dipped her head again. "But when I was about fourteen, my dad stopped paying child support and my mom's manicure money had to go to important stuff, you know, like the electric bill and food." Tasha put Heaven's hands back in the water to let them soak a bit more before she finished cleaning up her cuticles. She sat back in her chair and looked at Heaven. "I still remember when I realized that we were really poor and not just regular broke. One day my mom could afford to rent a house so me and my brother each had our own rooms and then the next day we were living in an apartment and my brother and I still had our own bedrooms, but my mom was sleeping on the couch in the living room.

But I remember that moment mostly because one day she had these gorgeous, long claws that curved and were these deep eggplant purple and the next day she had short, unpainted stubs. It all hurt but for me there was something about seeing my mom without her nails that hurt the most. It was like seeing a queen without her crown and it sucked. So, when I got my first work permit, all my friends went to get jobs at like Burger King or McDonald's and I went to the local nail shop and started cleaning up until one of the nail techs agreed to take me on as their apprentice. When my friends went to college, I went to cosmetology school." She smiled now, "And every time I needed someone to let me practice on their nails, my mom was the person I always asked. I still do her nails now, for free of course 'cause she gave me life or whatever," Tasha said, playfully rolling her eyes.

Heaven laughed. "That's sweet."

"What about you?"

"You mean how did I not get into nails?"

Tasha rolled her eyes again. "No, I mean how did you get into art?"

"Oh," she shrugged, "I've always been into art. It was the only subject I didn't basically fail out of in school. And I just..."

"You just what?" Tasha asked, reaching for both of Heaven's wrists and lifting them from the water. She dried them on the towel but kept her eyes on Heaven's face.

"I feel free when I paint or sculpt or even when I'm making jewelry. I feel like nothing else really matters, like I don't have any stress or anxieties or worries when I'm creating."

"That's beautiful," Tasha said.

Heaven shrugged again.

"How did you meet your boyfriend?" Tasha asked and reached for her nail file.

Heaven's entire face lit up. "I was at the art store," she began with a broad smile on her face. "And he was making a delivery."

Tasha looked at her with confusion.

"He used to be a UPS driver." She rolled her eyes but not in frustration but desire, Tasha knew that look. "He was so fucking sexy in his uniform."

Tasha laughed and then bent her head over Heaven's hands, beginning to gentle file her nails into shape.

"We saw each other in the store and I was basically drooling over him and he was looking at me for whatever reason."

Tasha's nail file stilled and she lifted her head again. "I can think of lots of reason to look at you." She hadn't meant to say it. She absolutely had meant to flirt with Heaven – of course she had – but she'd decided to be vaguely flirty, to give them both an out just in case she'd been reading Heaven wrong this entire time. But there was something about Heaven dismissing her beauty that had pushed her right past plausible deniability into overt. "You're beautiful," she whispered.

Heaven swallowed. "So are you. But I..."

"It's okay," Tasha said quickly. "I just wanted you to know that."

"It's not okay," Heaven said, pulling her hands from Tasha's grasp.

That move hurt but Tasha made sure to school her features not to betray that. IT wouldn't be fair.

"It's really not okay," Heaven said again. "I have a boyfriend and I love him but..."

"But?"

"But ever since we moved here," she said hesitantly, "I can't stop thinking about you."

Tasha wasn't strong enough to school her features this time and she smiled so wide her cheeks hurt.

"Don't smile at that," Heaven said quickly, nervously.

"Why not? I've been thinking about you too?"

"You have? You shouldn't." Heaven shook her head.

"Why not?" Tasha asked again, laughing.

"You're married," Heaven said, whispering as if Stephen were hiding in the pantry.

Tasha laughed and reached across the table. She tentatively placed her hand over Heaven's fisted hands. "And I love my husband with my entire self. But that doesn't mean that I can't think about you," Tasha said carefully.

"I'm not a cheater," Heaven replied.

"Neither am I," Tasha said. "My husband and I have an open marriage. He knows that I've been thinking about you."

"And he's okay with that?"

Tasha pulled Heaven's hands back to her. She placed her right on the towel and began to massage the left. This was out of order. She liked to clip and shape the nails, then massage and then paint, but she wanted to put Heaven at ease. "He's more than okay with it. Does Calvin know? That you've been thinking about me?"

Heaven swallowed loudly and shook her head.

"And what does he think?"

"That," she licked her lips quickly. "That I should tell you how much I want you."

Tasha's entire body froze. "And now you have."

"He also said that he's okay with me exploring if I... if you..."

"If we...?" Tasha added with her biggest smile yet.

---

Heaven wasn't certain what to expect of this manicure besides neater nails. She had that and she couldn't help but smile at her mustard yellow nails as Tasha moved around the kitchen. She wasn't certain that she'd make this a regular thing, but she had to admit that the bright color made her happy in a simplistic kind of way that she couldn't have predicted.

And even better, focusing on her nails allowed her to ignore the thick sexual tension between them. They'd pretended as if they hadn't just admitted to a mutual attraction while Heaven went through

Calvin's detailed pre-match diet. Heaven guessed Tasha had let her steer the conversation away from their admissions because she didn't want to scare Heaven away. She was scared, but she didn't have any desire to run away. And that was the scariest thing of all.

"Okay, let's see about these toes," Tasha said. Heaven watched as the other woman carefully sat on a low stool at her feet.

And it was only in that moment that she realized a pedicure would require the other woman to be in this position.

"Um, you know, that's okay. You don't have to."

Tasha rolled her eyes. "I've never had to force anyone to let me give them a pedicure. Come on, put your foot up here," she said, tapping the platform above the foot bath.

Heaven tentatively lifted her foot from the water. She tensed her thigh muscles and wished she had had the foresight to imagine that this moment was a possibility. If she had, she would have changed into another pair of leggings after throwing the ones Calvin had ruined away.

She had no excuse for why she hadn't worn underwear.

Heaven's face heated when Tasha's eyes dipped to her lap, but the woman focused her gaze immediately on her feet. Heaven exhaled and let herself relax. And for the next fifteen minutes, she enjoyed the feeling of

Tasha's expert hands buffing her heels, clipping her toenails and even massaging her feet.

She was so relaxed that she'd forgotten to vigilantly keep her thighs together and had even slumped down in her chair. Heaven only realized her error when she heard Tasha's choked gasp.

Heaven scrambled to sit up. "I'm sorry," she said in a rush, pushing the hem of her t-shirt dress over her knees.

"It's okay," Tasha said in a tight voice, her head bowed as she massaged the almond scented lotion into heaven's feet.

"It's so not. I can't believe-"

"Heaven," Tasha said, lifting one of her hands to heaven's calf. "It's okay."

Tasha held Heaven's gaze as her fingers drew low circles on her calf. Heaven's entire body felt hot and loose. Her knees spread in slow degrees as Tasha's fingers inched up her leg. There were so many chances to say no, to stop this, to leave, but Heaven didn't take any on them. Instead, she scooted closer to the edge of her seat and spread her thighs.

Tasha licked her lips hungrily in anticipation.

Heaven was holding her breath and only fully exhaled with a moan when Tasha's fingers kissed the hood of her clit.

"Oh my god," Tasha breathed.

There was something about that exhalation that seemed to clear a path for heaven from fear into action. She reached down and grabbed Tasha's wrist. "Wait."

Tasha tried to wrench her hand back. "I'm so sorry."

But heaven held on. "I said wait. Not stop."

Their eyes met again. "O-okay."

Heaven licked her lips. "I've only been with Calvin for three years."

"I understand," Tasha said.

"But I... haven't felt attraction this strong since I met him. And I don't want to let it pass without... exploring it."

Tasha swallowed and gasped. "I want to explore it too. Just in case there's any doubt."

"But..." Heaven said again.

"But?"

Heaven smiled. "But Calvin's my partner. We do everything together."

Tasha's eyes lit up. "That's how it is with Stephen. I understand."

"Good. So we'll see you tonight for dinner."

Tasha nodded and then stood with a wince.

"Are you okay?" heaven asked.

"I'm alright. I'm just... the stooping is terrible on my back."

"Tasha," heaven breathed. "Why did you do this if you knew it would hurt?"

She rolled her eyes and smiled, "Stephen's been

asking me that for years. But this time I had a good excuse."

Heaven bit her lip and then looked away, trying to hide her smile. She carefully slipped her shoes back on and stood. Tasha had moved in front of her and she couldn't help herself. She reached out and ran her thumbs along Tasha's jaw gently. For a moment she enjoyed the way the color complimented their skin tones and Tasha's work.

"You should take better care of your back," she whispered.

Tasha's eyes were hooded with desire. Heaven knew her face probably looked the same.

"Stephen tells me that too."

Heaven couldn't stop herself. She tipped onto her toes and brushed her lips along Tasha's mouth. It wasn't a kiss. Just a soft touch of skin and they breathed the same air for a brief second.

"Does Stephen also tell you that he can't wait to taste you from head to toe," heaven whispered, shocking Tasha and herself.

Tasha laughed and smiled. "He doesn't tell me. He just does."

Heaven groaned. "I'll remember that."

# 9

Tasha had been on pins and needles ever since Heaven left her apartment. By the time Stephen had come home from work, she'd have to crawl into his lap and ride him until they were drenched in sweat. And then she'd curled up in his lap and fell asleep while he watched football. The orgasms and her husband's grumbling as his favorite team lost had settled her nerves a bit for a short nap. But only a bit. But she was still a ball of nerves as she showered, dressed and tidied the living room, waiting for their neighbors to arrive.

Stephen, on the other hand was chill, if not downright giddy.

By the time the house looked presentable, the house smelled like goodness and bell peppers and Jagged Edge was playing loudly on the stereo.

Tasha followed Stephen's off-key voice to the

kitchen and leaned against the door frame. She smiled while watching her husband two-step and stir a pot of something on the stove. "You're turning into your father, you know that?"

He turned to look at her over his left shoulder and winked. "My daddy still running around here like a rolling stone in his Cadillac. There are worse men I could be?"

She smiled, "Oh you tryna be a rolling stone now?"

"We rolling together," he laughed and turned back to his bubbling pot.

She rolled her eyes, "What are you making?"

"A masterpiece," he said.

She was about to tell him to dial down his ego when the doorbell rang. Tasha's stomach flipped and her legs felt weak.

Stephen turned to her and winked.

Tasha turned the stereo down as she walked slowly to the front door, giddily excited about what the night might bring.

---

"You're nervous," Calvin whispered into her ear.

"Shhh," Heaven said.

He chuckled and wrapped an arm around her waist, making her shiver. He kissed her earlobe. She felt his smile against her head. "I'm here," he whispered, just as their landlord's door opened.

"Hi," Tasha said with a bright smile on her face.

"H-hi," Heaven replied in a quiet, shy voice, her eyes skirting away from Tasha's face.

"Thanks for having us," Calvin said in a voice that just oozed charm.

"Please, come in."

Calvin gave Heaven a nudge at her back and she stepped forward. But she turned to glare at him over her shoulder.

Not that he cared, because he simply lifted his eyebrows playfully and winked at her.

Inside the foyer, heaven tried to ignore Tasha's dress but it was impossible. Even Calvin was looking at her, mesmerized. The tight black tank dress hugged each and every curve of her body like it was painted on.

Her skin warmed and her mind ran through half a dozen scenarios of all the ways she could make taking that dress from Tasha's body its own erotic event.

And as if the other woman could read her mind, her eyes lifted and their gazes met. It was barely a handful of seconds, but they seemed to drag on forever. Heaven's plump lips parted on a gasp and Tasha sucked her own lip into her mouth, the implication of her thoughts broadcasting loud and clear, and not just to Tasha.

Calvin's soft grunt pulled them both from that heated moment. Tasha turned quickly away. Heaven turned to Calvin. He was biting his bottom lip and she licked her own.

"My bad," he mouthed.

"That them?" Stephen called from the kitchen.

"Yeah," Tasha said.

"Good, I can put my fish on."

"Don't mind him, he loves cooking."

"That's cool, we love eating," Calvin said.

There wasn't any innuendo in what he said and yet Heaven's brain was completely out on the range and all she could think about was burying her face between Tasha's legs and opening her legs to her in return.

Tasha cleared her throat. "Do you two want something to drink?" she asked carefully.

"Just water," Calvin said quickly.

"Calvin's training," Heaven added, meeting Tasha's eyes again. "He can't drink."

Tasha nodded. "Water it is. And you?"

"I'll have white wine if you have it," she said in a much stronger voice.

"Sure thing," Tasha said. "Have a seat."

---

Tasha all but ran into the kitchen.

"This is gonna be a long fucking night," she muttered to herself.

"Whatchu say?" Stephen asked as she passed him on the way to the fridge.

She stopped and leaned against his back, resting her cheek on his shoulder. "I said I love you."

His chest moved as he laughed and continued to season the filet of fish in front of him. "Oh yeah? Sounded like you said, 'long fucking night' but my daddy got bad hearing too, so maybe I misheard."

She smiled and pressed her mouth against his shoulder. "Your daddy also gets put out by whatever new young thing he's dating every other month. You want that life, old man?" she laughed.

"First of all I'm seasoned," Stephen said.

Tasha rolled her eyes and resumed her path to the fridge.

"I'm perfectly seasoned like this succotash I'm making."

"I'll be the judge of that," Tasha replied as she poured drinks for Heaven and Calvin.

"Hey," Stephen called to her.

She turned and sighed at the warm look in his eyes.

"Relax. It's just dinner."

She nodded and exhaled.

"And if it's not just dinner, I put some condoms in the coffee table drawer just in case."

Tasha smiled and laughed and slapped his shoulder. "Boy if you don't relax your damn self," she said.

Stephen grabbed her around the waist and pulled her body into his. "Ain't nothing wrong with being prepared,." he said, swaying Tasha gently to the music. "That's why I put some lube in there too."

He smiled down at her and Tasha couldn't help but smile so wide at him her cheeks started to hurt. "I do love you, you know that?"

Stephen raised both eyebrows. "Never doubted it for a second." He dipped his head to kiss her. "And you know I love you too."

"You love me enough to hurry up and get dinner on the table so I don't say something stupid?"

Stephen smiled and then slowly shook his head. "I can't rush perfection, woman. You know this."

"Boy," she said and pushed out of his grasp.

She grabbed the bottle of water, wine and a glass of wine for herself. She glared at her husband as she walked from the kitchen.

Stephen started two-stepping while sprinkling some basil over the salmon, smiling at his wife as she walked away.

---

Heaven's life hadn't been sheltered. Not really. Granted, she'd never been a wild child and she'd spent more nights than not at some church function. But she'd found out on the playground that kissing boys and girls was fun and her parents – the kind of couple who stayed together much longer than they should have in the name of not stunting their children's growth with divorce – had been too caught up in their own unhappiness to worry too much about her.

But nothing had prepared her for whatever the hell was swirling in the air of Tasha's living room, Calvin's strong body to her right and Tasha's soft body to her left. She'd had so many dreams like this – especially lately – that she hardly knew what to do with herself. And normally when she was too shy or nervous, Calvin stepped right into the void, threw his arms around her shoulders and took the heat off of her. But not tonight. Besides his hand on her back, he mostly sipped his water and stayed quiet, giving her and Tasha the chance to awkwardly avoid one another's eyes.

"Alright, just about fifteen minutes more and we can eat," Stephen finally said as he walked excitedly into the living room. He had a beer in one hand and another bottle of water for Calvin in the other.

"'Preciate you," Calvin said as they exchanged the water.

Stephen sat on the couch on the other side of Tasha. Heaven watched him press himself against his wife's back and she secretly loved the way the other woman melted into him. As the four of them fumbled over their small talk – and Calvin rubbed small circles on her shoulder – Heaven's body felt as if it might overheat. Her eyes flitted around the room before settling securely on Stephen's hand on Tasha's knee.

"So how's the studio going for you, Heaven?"

It took her a few seconds to realize that everyone was watching her, she was so caught up in watching Tasha. The way her chest rose and fell. The way she scraped her long nails across the back of Stephen's hand. That small dimple on her right cheek. And the way sometimes their eyes caught and Heaven felt certain Tasha knew exactly what she was thinking, how warm she was, how wet she was.

And it wasn't until she locked eyes with Tasha and saw the small smile playing on her lips that she realized the conversation had stopped and so had the music. But Calvin's fingers were still rubbing those circles on her shoulder. And Tasha's hand was still resting on Stephen's over her knee.

Her eyes widened and she looked from Tasha to Stephen to Calvin, who was smiling at her because he knew exactly where her mind had gone. And he thought it was funny.

He liked it.

She elbowed him in his abdomen.

"Oof," he huffed and then laughed.

She turned back to Stephen. "Sorry um... what was the question?"

Stephen laughed. "I asked you how the studio was treating you."

"Oh," she said. "Good. Great." And then her mind conjured an image of Tasha in nothing but a long t-shirt walking around the barren room, the sunlight dappling across a bare shoulder. "Great," she said again as her eyes darted to Tasha's.

"Should we eat?" Tasha said, turning to Stephen with a smile on her face. A small, distracted smile.

"Yeah yeah," he said, standing from the couch. "You two wait here. We'll set the table." Stephen offered Tasha his hand and the two of them disappeared into the kitchen again.

"Calm down baby," Calvin whispered into her ear. "There's no rush."

Heaven shivered violently.

"Maybe I shouldn't," she said, unsure how she even planned to finish that sentence.

Calvin's free hand moved to her bare thigh and he squeezed. "Look at me," he commanded.

And she did. She shivered again when she saw the lust in his eyes.

"I told you on our first date I wasn't ever gone stand in the way of your dreams. Remember that?"

Heaven rolled her eyes, "Of course I do." She'd never forgotten a single promise he'd made her because he'd never broken one of them. Calvin was as sure as he was beautiful and she loved him for all of that and more.

"I also told you I wasn't gonna let you stand in your own way either." His index finger moved from her shoulder, up her neck and skimmed the sensitive skin just under her jaw. He sucked his bottom lip into his mouth and his eyes closed to slits. "So if you're looking for me to tell you to run outta here," he said, shaking his head slowly and chuckling, deep and dirty. "Nah... you on your own on that one. Besides," he said, brushing his lips across the apple of her cheek, "just thinking about you two got me hard."

"Boy, shut up," Heaven said, giggling with him and pushing at his chest.

"Dinner's served," Stephen called from the kitchen.

---

They ate everything.

Stephen reclined in his chair, a toothpick in his mouth and a smug smile on his face watching as the other three practically licked their plates.

"Aye, that was hittin'," Calvin said, a smile on his face. "I normally just eat plain chicken and bland vegetables before a match but *that* was the shit." He dipped his head and lifted an eyebrow at the other man. "You should start a catering business. I'll be your first client."

Tasha rolled her eyes, "Don't gas his big head up this much. I'll never hear the end of it."

"Too late," Stephen said. "And I don't have time to start a new business right now but we can definitely talk. You know, real neighborly."

Calvin sat back in his chair with a big smile on his face and threw his arm around Heaven's shoulders. "Bet."

Heaven hadn't let herself imagine how tonight might play out, but this was shocking in all the best ways. And But shouldn't it have been weird to sit across the table from their landlords, everyone knowing she wanted to fuck Tasha and just talk about how much Calvin liked Stephen's salmon? Heaven felt certain that it should feel weird and yet... it wasn't.

Not even when she and Tasha made eye intermittent eye contact as they ate. Or when Stephen and Tasha cleared the table and Calvin started rubbing those smooth circles against her skin again, but this time on her upper thigh underneath the table. And not even when Stephen and Tasha returned with coffee and green tea for Calvin and those circles didn't stop.

"So how does this work?" Calvin asked as Tasha poured coffee.

The coffee pot overshot Stephen's cup as Tasha's hand shook. Heaven froze but Stephen just chuckled and dabbed at the spilled liquid while taking the pot from his wife's hands and pouring her cup.

"I like that you're not about beating around the bush," Stephen said.

Calvin shrugged. "Not how I work. Besides," he said, his hand moving just a bit higher up Heaven's leg, his pinky playing at the crease of her thighs, "I want my girl to have everything she wants." He turned to her and smiled, "I'm not about making her wait." He said that last word just as his hands pushed between her thighs.

She gasped and he smiled. She was wet.

Stephen's laughter filled the room. "Girl, they remind me of us when we were young."

"I'm still young," Tasha said.

Heaven gasped as they began to banter back and forth, her eyes riveted on Calvin's as he slowly stroked her over her wet underwear. Stephen coughed when Heaven moaned lightly.

When they turned to look across the table, Tasha was leaning into Stephen's side. She looked relaxed, more relaxed than she had all night. The smile on her face was so soft that Heaven squeezed her thighs closed for a second around Calvin's hand before widening them. She heard her boyfriend's chuckle, but she kept her eyes on Tasha, only noticing the small movements of the other woman's arm in Stephen's lap when she began to speak.

"This can work however we want it to," Tasha said.

"How does it normally work for you two?"

Calvin hooked two fingers around Heaven's underwear and stroked her bare pussy. She just barely swallowed a moan.

"There's no normal," Stephen said. Heaven was certain his voice sounded more strained than it had just a few moments ago.

"Sometimes we're together. Sometimes we're apart," Tasha said, licking her lips at Heaven, "the only thing that's consistent is honesty."

"I'm into that," Calvin said and slipped his ring finger inside of Heaven.

She couldn't swallow that moan. And Calvin didn't want her to.

"Is it different," Calvin asked Tasha, his voice thick with lust, "watching her get worked up in front of you instead of listening to her through the wall?"

Tasha smiled and snuggled into Stephen's chest. Heaven heard the distinct noise of a zipper opening. "Yes," Tasha breathed. "But she's not as loud as I thought."

"She's trying to be polite," he said, leaning over to brush his mouth against Heaven's temple.

Stephen shifted in his seat. "We're all friends here. No need to be polite."

"Please," Tasha said in a breathy whisper that made Heaven shiver.

That shiver turned into a bone rattling shudder when Calvin pushed another finger inside of her and increased the pace of his hand.

Tasha's smile was dirty. She licked her palm and the sound of her hand on Stephen's dick under the table became as loud and lewd as the sound of Calvin's fingers inside Heaven.

"Fuck," Heaven breathed, gripping the table.

Tasha smiled.

"How do you want this to work?" Tasha asked her.

Heaven's mind felt muddled with lust. All she could do was sink down in her chair and spread her legs wider. Her knees collided with Stephen's and he moaned. But then Calvin's fingers stopped. They were still embedded in her pussy, but he'd stopped pumping. She turned to him with bunched eyebrows.

Calvin's eyes were hooded with desire but that damn smile she loved was still firmly planted on his face. "She asked you a question," he said.

"You're gonna regret this," she ground out.

He laughed and stroked his fingers inside her in a shallow motion. "I highly fucking doubt it. This is the most fun I've had the night before a match in years."

Heaven moaned the loudest moan of the night as he pumped in and out of her at the same time as he settled his palm over her clit and began to rub in light circles.

"Now go on. Tell Tasha how you want to fuck her," he said with the dirtiest smile she'd ever seen on his face. Not a small feat.

This time Heaven's moans mingled with Stephen's.

When she turned back to Tasha, the other woman was watching her with intent as she jacked her husband off under the table. Stephen's hand had circled Tasha's shoulders and he was massaging her breast over her clothes. Heaven wanted desperately for him to move her dress aside and pull her breast out. She'd been wondering for weeks what they looked like and the thought of Stephen rolling Tasha's nipple between his fingers made her clench tighter than ever around Calvin's fingers.

Another thing Heaven hadn't let herself imagine in the past day was how it might be between them. Not just herself and Tasha but the four of them. But this dinner had illuminated so many things.

"I want to fuck you," Heaven panted.

"Obviously," Calvin said.

"But I want Calvin and Stephen there," Heaven continued.

Tasha's right eyebrow arched beautifully. "To watch?"

"At first."

"And then after?"

"I'm not interested in another man," Heaven said in slow halting words as her orgasm built. "But I like to watch you two. I'd like him to show me what you like."

Stephen grunted and knocked the table when he thrust his hips into Tasha's grasp. Tasha didn't miss a beat in stroking him, but she kept her eyes on Heaven.

"And will Calvin show me what you like?" she asked in a sultry voice.

"Gladly," Calvin answered.

And that was all it took for Heaven. She threw her head back and came wet and messy on Calvin's hand. At Tasha and Stephen's dinner table. In front of them all.

This was the best dinner get together of her life.

# 10

"Hey babe," Calvin yelled from the shower, "can you make me some eggs?"

Heaven nodded for a few seconds before she realized he couldn't see her. "Yeah," she called. "You want anything else?"

"I mean..." he said, and she could tell by the way he dragged that second word out that he was probably smiling mischievously. "You could come in here and wash my back?"

Heaven rolled her eyes. "Wash my back," was code for "let me fuck you so good you won't be mad I got your hair wet."

"Boy, it's fight day. Quit playing. Besides, if you're not out the door in fifteen minutes Pete gon' be all up my ass and I'm too pretty for him to be yelling at me the way he be yelling at you," she yelled. She looked over his gym bag one more time and then zipped it closed. “Grab your bag before you come down,” she yelled.

“Alright.”

Heaven walked from their bedroom, downstairs and into the kitchen. The two halves of the duplex weren’t completely identical and her and Calvin had a breakfast nook, while Tasha and Stephen had a full-fledged dining room, but still the sight of their small kitchen table made her shiver.

Just the memory of Calvin’s thick fingers inside her brought to mind the sound of Heaven’s hands on Stephen and it was almost too much, but not quite enough.

After Stephen had come in his own lap, Tasha had politely gotten the berry trifle Stephen had made for dessert while he cleaned up. Calvin had, of course, skipped it for more tea, but the four of them had found small talk much easier after their sexual ice breaker. The only thing that had ended the night was Calvin’s yawn. He had a fight the next day.

He’d tried to smother it, but she’d seen it. And she’d stuffed as much of the arousal flooding through her veins down and suggested they leave. Tasha had looked as disappointed as Heaven felt.

So disappointed that Heaven had practically jumped Calvin as soon as they were back in their own side of the duplex. The only reason the two of them had made it upstairs to their bedroom was because they wanted Tasha and Calvin to hear them.

They had.

And at some point the sound of their own fucking had blended with the muffled sounds from Tasha and Stephen's side of the apartment. It was amazing. And still, not enough.

As much as the barrier of that bedroom wall had fed so many of Heaven's fantasies, now that their cards – and orgasms – were on the table, she was ready for more. So. Much. More.

But first, Calvin had to fight Steve Macias to keep his welterweight championship matchup with Winston King. Tonight was just the beginning.

She heard the shower turn off upstairs and shook her head to get herself back on track. She opened the refrigerator and set about making scrambled egg whites for breakfast. He didn't like to eat much before a match, but this was their routine. He'd pick at a couple of scrambled eggs and let her babble on and on about whatever she liked to give him a few minutes of distraction before fight day madness got underway.

She was just splitting their eggs between two plates when he came hopping down the stairs and tossed his gym bag by the front door.

"Smells good," he said, strutting toward her.

"You always say that. No matter what I make," she said, rolling her eyes and walking their plates over to the breakfast nook.

When she set them down, Calvin wrapped his body around her from the back. "That's 'cause everything you make smells good as fuck." He kissed her cheek and then shoved his face into the crook of her neck and kissed her softly.

"Better than Stephen's?" she asked with an innocent smile on her face.

She felt his body still. He kissed her again and tightened his arms around her. "Look there's no need to compare y'all two," he said.

Heaven burst into laughter. "Uh huh, I thought so. Sit down."

Calvin pulled Heaven's chair out for her to sit and then sat in their only other chair. She bowed her head while he said a soft, muffled grace and then they ate. Or she ate and he picked at his food and smiled across the table at her.

"You okay?" he asked.

She squinted at him. "Me? You're the one about to go head to head with Macias."

Calvin scoffed, "I'm not worried about that motherfucker. I meant last night. You okay about what we did?"

Heaven could feel her face warm. She dipped her head to hide her smile. Calvin's foot knocked hers underneath the table.

"Come on, talk to me," he said.

Heaven wanted to avert her eyes and look anywhere but at him, but she forced herself to look him straight in the eyes. "I liked last night," she said in a shaky voice, "but..."

"But," Calvin echoed, his eyebrows lifting and the smile disappearing from his face.

"But I want more," she whispered, nervous, unsure.

And there was Calvin's smile again, big and white and charming, and a little bit freaky. "Good. That's the plan."

Heaven smiled but then her smile froze. "The plan?"

There was a knock on the door. "That's Reggie," Calvin said and shot up from the table. He leaned down and brushed his mouth against hers. "He'll be back to get you around seven thirty. I'll see you after I win, aight?"

"Of course," she said.

When he turned away, Heaven stood and followed him to the door. "But what plan?"

She watched as Calvin scooped his gym bag from the floor, slung the longest strap over his left shoulder and opened the door.

"What up, champ?" Reggie said, already reaching for Calvin's bag. "Hey, Heaven."

"Hey, Reggie."

"See you at seven thirty?"

"Yeah. Yes. What plan?" she asked Calvin.

He grabbed her head and pressed her mouth to his. "You'll see."

And then he was gone.

Heaven stood on the porch and watched as Calvin and Reggie walked to Reggie's car. She watched as the man she loved threw his bag into the trunk and then climbed into the passenger seat. As Reggie put the car in drive, Calvin turned to her, winked, and smiled.

"What plan?" she yelled.

She heard his laughter as Reggie peeled away.

---

Tasha was nervous.

"Don't be nervous," Stephen whispered against her temple before brushing a soft kiss at her hairline.

"I can't help it," she whined. "Do I look okay?"

Stephen stepped behind her in the full-length mirror and looked at her reflection. She'd worn this dress for so many reasons. First, the light gray cashmere bodycon dress fit her like a glove and even though it was knee length, it didn't hide any of her assets. Second, she knew Stephen liked this dress. Although to be fair, he liked whatever she wore, but he made no bones about telling her he really preferred her naked. If she would walk around naked all night all day, he'd be ecstatic. But the third reason she'd worn this dress was Heaven.

Tasha knew what she looked like. Her curves were dramatic, her thighs and waist and ass were thick and her breasts were more than a handful, maybe even more than two handfuls. And Tasha seemed to like staring at them all. No matter how horny he was, when Stephen stared at her, Tasha felt loved; his eyes were full of the past seven years they'd spent together and all that was to come. But when Heaven stared at her, she felt as if she was on the verge of being devoured. It wasn't a subtle distinction and it made her blood rush.

Last night, she could practically feel Heaven's eyes on her and was certain that whatever fantasies hidden behind Heaven's eyes might make her blush.

And she liked it. She loved it.

Tasha had chosen this dress because she wanted to know what Heaven's face would look like when she saw her in it.

"I think," Stephen said, "that you look like you might sue anyone who touches you the wrong way but also like you might not be wearing any underwear."

Tasha smiled and then burst into laughter.

"How'd I do?" he asked.

She turned around and wrapped her arms around his neck. "Spot the fuck on," she said and then kissed him.

Stephen moaned into her mouth as his hands traveled around her body to grip her ass and pull her closer to him.

"Do we have time?" she whispered against his lips.

Stephen reared back with a smile, "Time for what? What you tryna get into?"

Tasha opened her mouth but Stephen shook his head.

"No, never mind. Don't tell me. We don't have time. Let's go."

Tasha pouted up at him. Sometimes it worked. Sometimes he was so horny he was willing to be as late as it took for them to both get off as much as they wanted. Sometimes it didn't and tonight was one of those nights.

"You wanna stay here and fuck or you wanna get going and fuck?"

"These are literally the best options," she giggled. "You're so good to me."

"I know," he said, offering her his elbow.

"I'm excited," she whispered to him just before he opened their front door.

"Good. I'm gonna make sure this is everything you've been waiting for."

And if Tasha knew anything, she knew he meant every word of that sentence.

---

Heaven followed Reggie into the stadium at the bottom of the Grand Plaza Hotel. She kept her head tilted down so she didn't have to even accidentally make eye contact with a fan or one of the many vultures who showed up at Calvin's flights trying to poach him from his manager, his coach, his assistant, even his accountant. And most of all, Heaven didn't want to even accidentally make eye contact with any of the other boxers' girlfriends, especially not the ones who thought it was their jobs to keep their boyfriends' in-ring rivalries going outside of the ring. And even worse than them were the ones who were sizing her up; deciding quickly that she didn't deserve Calvin and he needed someone better looking on his arm.

So, she kept her eyes averted and unfocused until she made it to her seat. That's why she didn't see Tasha and Stephen there until she was practically on top of Tasha.

Her eyes widened. "What are you two doing here?"

Reggie answered, "Cal asked me to reserve these seats for your neighbors. That's cool right?"

Heaven's smile was so big her cheeks nearly obscured her vision. Besides the attraction she always felt when she was even just near Tasha, she also felt a sense of relief she'd never let herself hope she could feel at one of Calvin's fights.

"Yeah," she said with a nod, still smiling at Tasha. "It's great."

"Okay cool. I'ma go check on the champ and I'll be back before his intro," Reggie said, urgently.

Normally she'd be so anxious when Reggie left her alone, but as she sat in the empty seat next to Tasha she felt almost as safe as when Calvin was right beside her.

"Hi," she said with a soft smile.

"Hi," Tasha said back.

"Front row seats," Stephen said, leaning into

Tasha's side to smile at Heaven. "You know how expensive these are?"

Heaven laughed as Tasha shook her head. "Don't mind him. He doesn't even really like boxing, but he loves feeling like a VIP."

"Especially when I don't have to pay for it," Stephen said excitedly. "Hold on. Did y'all pay for these seats? Y'all gone make rent?" he asked, squinting at Heaven.

Tasha clucked her tongue but Heaven laughed harder.

"They're comped. We didn't pay. Don't worry, you'll get your rent on the first. Right on time."

Stephen exhaled and smiled. "Good. Tonight would be super awkward if I had to evict y'all after. Especially 'cause we like you. Now that you're here, lemme go see about this bar. What would you two like drink?"

She and Tasha giggled as they gave Stephen their drink orders. They watched him rush away with a huge smile on his face.

"He's a really great man," Heaven said.

Tasha turned to her and their bare shoulders brushed. Heaven swore she could feel each goose bump erupt on her body. They locked eyes.

"He is," she said. "And Calvin seems like a good man too."

"He's amazing," Heaven breathed. "He's the only reason I'd come to this madhouse."

"You don't like the fights?" Tasha asked, leaning forward. Their arms pressed together.

"Not in an 'I hate violence' kinda way. Just...," Heaven's eyes darted around the arena. Right now the noise was just a low, excited and expectant murmur. Calvin's fight was the headliner, but as soon as the mid-card fights started the noise level would begin to ratchet up incrementally until by the time his entrance music started, everyone around her would be pulsing, yelling, screaming. It was the beauty of seeing a fight in person as opposed to on television and Heaven had never been able to really enjoy it. "Everyone has an idea of what a boxer's girlfriend should look like and it's not me," she said. "When I come here I feel like I'm on display for all the people who want to be him and all the people who want to be with him. I feel like they're all piecing me apart and deciding that I'm not good enough."

As she spoke, Heaven watched Tasha's eyes soften and she had to look away. She'd never actually shared how she felt with anyone besides Calvin. At first, he'd suggested that she not come to his fights – or maybe not all of his fights – but she'd shut that down immediately. No matter how uncomfortable she felt, she still wanted to be there for him. She needed to watch him, to see how he performed, to worry about him when he was in the ropes, to cheer him on when he fought back, to celebrate with his fans when he triumphed and to fuck away all that adrenaline when it was all over. That was their thing and she'd didn't want to let strangers or her own insecurities rob her of that.

So, he'd tried his best to provide her with as much of a buffer as he could. Reggie picked her up and drove her to the venues. He made sure she was settled before he ran back to the locker rooms to check-in on Calvin before the fight. He sat next to her and then ushered her to the back when it was over. But Heaven was acutely aware that taking care of her was just one more facet of Reggie's job and adding to his workload made her more self-conscious. And still, his intermittent presence only just made the experience bearable.

Tasha's hand settled on her arm. Her pinky brushed the side of Heaven's right breast. Heaven sucked in a breath and turned to look at the other woman. She sucked her bottom lip into her mouth.

"Does Calvin ever make you feel like you're unworthy of him?" Tasha asked softly.

Heaven had to smile at the ridiculousness of the question. "Never."

Tasha smiled. "I didn't think so. He looks at you like you're the center of the universe. The center of *his* universe."

Heaven nodded. "The feeling's mutual."

Tasha gently stroked Heaven's upper arm. Heaven's eyes darted to Tasha's mouth and she smiled softly. "I don't know if there are other people in here just hoping and waiting for your relationship to fail. I hope not, but people are terrible."

Heaven sighed.

"But I want you to know that that's not who I am." Her eyes darted to Heaven's mouth. "I like you both. You seem good together. Good to each other. And Stephen and I know just how rare that can be." She leaned forward and lowered her voice so only Heaven could hear. "Whatever develops between us, just know that I'm not trying to ruin anything for you. I only want to add, never subtract."

Heaven couldn't help but smile. But also Tasha's hand had stopped moving. She'd pressed her hand purposefully into the side of Heaven's breasts. This touch wasn't accidental. It was purposeful and full of promise. Heaven wondered for a second what people would think if they saw them in this moment. but instead of being terrified of an article in *The Ring*, she shivered at being so visible with Tasha's knuckles caressing her nipple.

"When Calvin wins," Heaven whispered, "he works off all the energy from the fight by fucking me in the locker room."

Heaven saw Tasha's body shiver violently. She liked it.

"I think he invited you and Stephen here to join us. Is that what you want? To watch him fuck me? To fuck Stephen in front of me?"

It was Tasha's turn to lick her lips and take a deep steadying breath. "For starters," she whispered.

"Good," Heaven said, no longer caring who was

watching them, who was judging her, or who was fighting first.

When Stephen finally returned with their drinks and a bunch of stories about all the celebrities he'd seen on the way. Heaven had a hard time focusing. All she could think about was Calvin's fight... and all the fun the four of them could have afterward.

# 11

Calvin was overprepared. At least that's what Heaven had told her more than once during the fight. Tasha didn't know anything about boxing, but she assumed that the other woman was correct as they watched him beat the living shit out of a Steve Macias. Tasha had expected some artful ducking and weaving and jabbing and whatever other terms people used to describe people hitting each other in a boxing ring. Instead, she found herself watching as Calvin danced around the ring – his bare torso glistening in the arena's lights, his muscles rippling and his eyes completely devoid of the charming playfulness of the night before – and methodically took his opponent apart.

Tasha winced with each jab and started looking away as the bruises turned to ruptured skin and the sweat mixed with blood. By the end of the first round, she'd practically wrapped herself around Stephen's left arm. Her husband, on the other hand, was completely engrossed. He patted her hands but never took his eyes from the ring, rejoicing each time Calvin's gloves connected with some part of Macias's body.

And Heaven was worse. Tasha could hardly believe the shy nervous woman she'd been lusting after had turned into a near-ravenous spectator. She screamed and cheered and sometimes growled at the ring. By the time Calvin was knocking Macias out for good, Heaven – sweet, adorable Heaven, whose giggle made Tasha's mouth dry – was mimicking his punches.

She hadn't known what to expect of this fight, but now she did, and she wasn't sure that she ever wanted to come to another one again.

But then the fight was over.

The referee called it. The bell ending the fight sounded and Calvin was walking around the ring, both gloved hands in the air, his mouthpiece obscuring his perfect smile and the crowd roaring for him.

Tasha saw the moment he and Heaven made eye contact. His smile widened around his mouthguard and he winked, kissed each of his gloves and extended them toward her. And then Heaven giggled. Tasha shouldn't have been able to hear it over the sound of the crowd going absolutely ape shit at Calvin's win, but she did. And just like that, much of the apprehension that had clouded Tasha's mood during the fight seemed to disappear.

She turned her head to her left and found Heaven looking at her.

"You ready?" she said.

"Ready for what?" Stephen asked.

Heaven didn't take her eyes from Tasha, "The celebration."

Tasha gut clenched in the best possible way.

---

Heaven was confused.

"Where are we going?" she asked Reggie.

"You'll see," he said.

Heaven bit her lip. This wasn't the routine and she didn't like the deviation.

For the past three years, knowing that Calvin was waiting for her after all of her fights had made the discomfort of attending worth it; more than worth it. It allowed her to tune out the crowd, the side eyes and the flashing lights. It was as if the crowd didn't exist. And having Tasha and Stephen in tow hadn't diminished her anticipation at all; they had heightened it.

They walked from the arena as if there weren't people clamoring to get backstage, as if people weren't on the verge of fighting with one another about the outcome, as if Stephen didn't have to help Reggie get them into the elevator alone, putting his body between her and Tasha and the rushing crowd. But the locker rooms weren't on the thirtieth floor and she didn't understand why they were going here and not to Calvin.

He needed her to celebrate.

Tasha grabbed her hand as they walked down the hotel hallway toward a hotel room Tasha was certain they couldn't afford. Reggie dipped a key into the reader next to the door and ushered them inside.

She turned to Reggie, "What's going on?"

"Compliments of Big Al for the win," he said with a grin. "There's an afterparty upstairs in the VIP suite upstairs, free liquor and a pissed off Macias, if y'all want to come up... later. Cal should be here in a few minutes though. The bar's stocked, but if you need something just text me."

Heaven squinted, "Is he showering?" The question came out harder than she planned, like an accusation and it kind of was. Calvin never showered after a fight unless he was particularly bloody and needed some kind of medical attention. Otherwise, he came to her covered in sweat, the adrenaline coursing through his body.

Just the way she liked.

Her man – muscles tense and overworked, hot and horny – was her prize for coming to these matches. And she – hot and wet and bare – was his.

She didn't know how much of this Reggie knew and she didn't want to. What mattered to Heaven was that she'd spent all the mid-card fights quietly fantasizing about how she wanted this to go and in all of the scenarios she'd created, Calvin was sweaty as ever.

"Everything okay?" Stephen asked gently.

"Everything's fine," Reggie answered. "Don't worry. Your man's not showering, he's just signing some paperwork. He'll be here in a few and y'all can get up to whatever freaky shit y'all had planned in peace." He smiled at Heaven, "Have a little more faith in me. I take this job real real serious."

Heaven exhaled loudly and felt her muscles relax.

"Now lemme get out of here so I can find somebody to fulfill my own freaky fantasies. Anyway, condoms on the bar," Reggie called over his shoulder as he pulled the door closed behind him.

"This some weird shit," Tasha breathed when it was just the three of them.

"Right?" Stephen added excitedly.

Heaven turned to them with a smile on her face and burst into laughter when she saw the incredulous look on Tasha's face. She was about to say something when the door opened and they all turned toward it.

Like last night, Heaven had a moment where she thought this should have been weird. For three years, their post-fight celebration had always been just the two of them; their own dirty little surprise. So it should have been weird to share this moment with other people. But it wasn't.

When Calvin walked through the door, his gym bag slung over one shoulder, a small towel thrown over the other and that same bright white smile slashing across his dark face, Heaven felt what she always felt in these moments: so fucking horny she thought she could melt and catch on fire all at the same time. And he knew it. She could see what he saw in the way he licked his lips, arched his eyebrow and threw his gym bag to the side.

"Congratulations, man," Stephen said excitedly.

"Yeah that was... well honestly that was lowkey terrifying. But at least you won, Tasha said.

They all turned to her and laughed.

"I didn't think I'd be squeamish about this but... I am," she said.

Stephen threw his arm around her shoulders and pulled her into his side, kissing her temple.

Heaven smiled at them and then squeaked when she felt Calvin's overly warm body behind her.

"It's not that bad," Calvin said, his breath rustling Heaven's hair as he spoke. "You get used to it. I mean, if you want to. Ain't that right, sweetheart?" He accentuated his question by pressing his hips forward so the bulge in his shorts brushed against her ass.

Heaven exhaled a harsh breath that turned into a moan when Calvin's hand settled over the curve of her stomach and pulled her back into him. She turned her head slightly. Calvin's mouth skimmed her full cheek.

Stephen's soft laughter broke the silence in the room.

"You know, for two people my wife was worried she'd corrupt, y'all really don't have no problems just getting right down to business. I fucking love that."

"So do I," Tasha said in a daze.

Heaven turned back to Tasha and licked her lips. "We like to live every moment to the fullest. I'm sure you two can relate?"

Tasha's smile was soft and dirty and knowing. "We just might," she said, circling her arms around Stephen's waist as the two of them watched Calvin hold her.

Calvin kissed Heaven's cheek one more time and then led her to the bed. He sat down and pulled her sideways onto his lap. Stephen mimicked his movement, placing Tasha onto his thighs facing Heaven. The implication of it all was so clear: this moment was about the two women and the men were there and ready and – considering the bulge Heaven could feel under her – very willing to assist in whatever way possible.

She reached out to Tasha and again the other woman took her hand quickly.

"I've been waiting weeks to kiss you," Tasha breathed as they leaned toward one another.

Heaven smiled as their faces moved closer and

closer together, the anticipation of it all almost as good as knowing what would come next. But when their lips touched, Heaven knew that wasn't quite right.

It was one thing to fantasize about kissing Tasha and an entirely other thing to actually do it. Her lips were soft and pliable, opening quickly on a gasp as soon as their mouths touched. Heaven smiled as her tongue tentatively licked at the corner of Tasha's mouth. She thought the other woman would let her take the lead. She was wrong. Tasha's tongue darted out of her mouth and swiped along Heaven's bottom lip. When their tongues finally slid against each other with force, they both moaned in excitement as that tentative kiss became deeper and more intense.

Tasha grabbed Heaven's face, her thumbs stroking her jaw. Heaven put her hands on Tasha's legs, which immediately spread in invitation.

Stephen laughed.

Calvin unconsciously thrust his hips up into Heaven.

It was amazing.

Heaven pushed Tasha's dress up her legs. She wanted to take it off. She wanted the other woman naked against her as soon as possible, but she also wanted to draw this night out. She wanted them to take their time. The only rush was the force of their desire, which was strong.

The slower pace won out in the short term.

Heaven pushed Tasha's tight dress up to her hips and pushed her legs wider.

Calvin helped by scooting closer to Stephen.

Heaven pulled back from the kiss but only so she could watch Tasha's shocked, wide eyes, slowly close as Heaven ran her hands from Tasha's knees, up her thighs and then her left hand between her legs. Heaven licked her lips at the warmth there. They groaned as Heaven's fingers met the naked, wet, downy hair over Tasha's pussy.

Calvin thrust up again. "How does she feel?" he rasped.

"Hot. Wet." Heaven's voice was hoarse with lust. She moved her fingers down the cleft of Tasha's sex. She could feel Tasha trembling.

Before Heaven could even think of it, Stephen wrapped a hand around Tasha's waist to hold her still. She felt Tasha shiver against her hand as she slowly circled her clit with two fingers.

"Tell me what you like," she whispered and then dipped her head to lick Tasha's lips.

Tasha held her head close and kissed her slowly, moaning into her mouth as Heaven slipped a finger inside of her.

"Ask him," Tasha whispered against Heaven's lips with a smile.

Calvin's hips thrust again.

Heaven gripped Tasha's right thigh for stability against Calvin's bucking. She moved her finger in and out of her so slowly Tasha had started to squirm in Stephen's lap and his breath quickened.

Heaven turned to Stephen. His pupils were dilated, his chest rising and falling rapidly and his hips were thrusting gently up into his wife's body much like Calvin was into her.

This was so much more than she could have imagined.

"What does she like?" she asked in a deep, lustful rasp; so different from her normal voice.

Calvin's hips thrust again and then she felt his hands on her thighs, massaging her skin.

"She likes to be held down," Stephen said eventually.

Heaven turned back to Tasha. "Yeah?" she breathed. Not a question. Not really. The soft exhalation was as much an encouragement for Calvin to keep massaging her and pushing up against her just like that.

Heaven sat back, settling her weight onto Calvin's dick. He moaned. She pulled her finger from Tasha and the other woman whimpered. And then Tasha and Stephen groaned as Heaven brought her finger to her mouth and pushed it between her lips.

She locked eyes with Tasha and smiled as she tasted her for the first time. She had to suppress the desire to moan when the taste hit her tongue. But apparently all of Calvin's restraint had been exhausted. He grabbed her around the waist and launched himself up from the couch. Heaven giggled, always loving the way his strong hands felt manhandling her during sex.

She loved it even more when he deposited her gently on her knees on the bed, next to Tasha and Stephen. Practically in between Tasha's knees.

"Hold her hands," Heaven's said to Stephen, even though her eyes were on Tasha.

She felt powerful as Tasha happily moved her hands behind her back and squirmed in Stephen's lap when he grabbed her at the wrists. It was wonderful. And so was the shadowed sight between Tasha's thighs.

She moved her hands back to Tasha's knees and spread them apart. Tasha leaned back into Stephen's grasp but smirked over the peaks of her breasts at Heaven.

"You gonna eat me while your boyfriend fucks you?" Tasha asked. Another question that wasn't really a question, just a verbalization of what was happening to concretize this moment for them all and pull more groans from them.

It worked.

She felt Calvin's hands on her hips, gripping her, his strong fingertips digging into her soft flesh. And she could smell Tasha's arousal and just barely see the curly hair between her legs.

"I will," she moaned. 'If that's what you want."

Tasha's laughter was a bright tinkling cutting through all of the intensity of this moment. And then she lifted her right foot onto the bed and leaned dangerously back, knowing that Stephen wouldn't let her fall – baring herself fully to Heaven and Calvin's gaze. The invitation to Heaven's mouth was blatant and sexy and perfect.

And Heaven didn't waste any time leaning forward and flattening her tongue against Tasha's lips.

Tasha's head fell back in a moan that only got louder as Heaven licked at her, teasing her, much like Calvin was teasing her, rubbing just the length of his dick along the cleft of her sex. She was so wet, she could only imagine that he'd be lubricated enough to push into her or jack himself off or whatever he wanted to do. But she'd let him decide, since she was otherwise occupied.

She moved her thumbs to pull Tasha's lips open, exposing the delicate nub hidden at the apex of her sex. She greedily sucked it into her mouth and sucked on it as if she were a dying and desperate person. And maybe she was. This had been so long in the making. Too long as far as Heaven was concerned, especially now that she finally had her hands and mouth on Tasha's trembling body.

Heaven's fantasies had been split fifty-fifty between two general scenarios: the two of them stealing time alone while their partners were away reveling in each other's bodies and the illicit secrecy of an afternoon affair, and then the four of them together. There was no bad option, but in an instant, Heaven was happy that this was their first time. If this turned out to be their only encounter together, she liked that they had all the support they could ever want proven by Stephen's hand unclasping Tasha's dress behind her neck and finally baring her breasts to Heaven's eyes at nearly the same time Calvin decided to stop toying with her pussy and push into her in a long, slow press.

Heaven moaned onto Tasha's clit. She covered her with her mouth, licking and sucking and spreading her with her lips and tongue while Calvin set a steady pace. This wasn't the punishing post-match fuck they normally shared and that was comforting. That was just for them. *This* was something different. Not better or worse just different and wonderful in new ways.

Heaven wrapped her arms around Tasha's thick thighs and sealed her mouth against the woman's sex. The room filled with the sound of Tasha's moans and Calvin's body slapping against hers and, eventually, even Stephen's soft murmuring to Tasha that he had her and it was okay to come.

Somehow that pushed Heaven right over the edge. She moaned and nearly screamed against Tasha's sex which made the other woman's thighs lock around her head as her body spasmed. She came in a delicious wet gush on Heaven's tongue. Calvin fucked her through all of that, a hard, muscled, thick, comforting presence literally at her back.

When Tasha's thighs unclenched, Heaven lifted her head and Calvin wrapped his arm around her breasts and pulled her back against his chest. He grabbed her chin and turned her head, kissing her as the speed of his thrusts increased.

"She taste good?" Heaven moaned against his lips.

"Fuck," he muttered and then yelled. "Fuck. Fuck. Fuck. Fuck," as he slammed into her wildly. She smiled as this man who was always so composed and so in control came undone inside her.

But then she came undone herself when a soft hand snaked between her legs and began to rub her clit.

"Oh god," Heaven breathed.

She and Calvin came like that, his hips thrusting and Tasha's delicate hands and perfectly manicured nails rubbing Heaven's clit.

"Fuck," Calvin said one more time as he pulled out quickly and came all over her ass.

"Fuck," Heaven echoed and then came on Tasha's hand.

It was perfect.

---

Tasha knew tonight would be good and dirty. She'd hoped for it. Prayed for it. Hell it's why she hadn't bothered to wear anything under her dress; real easy access. But even her wildest fantasies hadn't come close to this.

She and Stephen had never been shy about inviting other people into their bed. It was as natural to them as spending a quiet even at home just the two of them. But they'd never met a couple as open and willing and compatible as Heaven and Calvin. She'd spent weeks dreaming of getting close to Heaven, but the added bonus of Calvin joining Stephen in supporting their exploration of one another was a heady rush and it stoked Tasha's desire.

She'd been ready to give Heaven time to recover but the other woman didn't seem to need it. Or if she did, she didn't want it. Instead, while Calvin collapsed onto the bed, Heaven shimmied her dress up her body and over her head with Tasha follow her lead. But she jumped up to still Heaven's hands, wanting to take her bra off herself.

"I love your breasts," she whispered into Heaven's ear as she walked around her. "They were the second thing I noticed about you. Second and third," she said and laughed.

Heaven giggled, "What was the first?"

"That ass," Stephen said, watching them with a prominent bulge in his pants.

Tasha unclasped Heaven's bra and replaced the cups holding her breasts up with her hands. She kissed her way up the side of Heaven's neck to her earlobe and back again as she massaged the large globes in her palms, rolling the stiff peaks between her fingers.

Heaven lifted a hand to Tasha's head, holding her mouth in place as she licked and sucked the sensitive skin behind her ear. Tasha pressed her body against Heaven's, loving the way it felt to finally be skin to skin with her.

"That was the first thing I noticed about you," Heaven said in a breathy moan. "Your ass is perfect."

Tasha licked up the rim of Heaven's ear. "That's what he always says," she replied, her eyes finding her husband. "Do you want to sit on my face?" she said loud enough for them all to hear.

"Jesus," Calvin groaned.

Heaven's adorable giggle was more than just adorable right now. It made all the blood in Tasha's body boil. She seemed unassuming and shy but she was threatening to melt Tasha from the inside out. And she would relish it.

"Yes," Heaven giggled. "God yes."

Tasha's eyes caught her husband's. "You know what I want you to do right babe?" she asked him so sweetly, in the voice she often reserved for the moments just before she gave him a mile-long honey-do list.

And like he did in those moments, Stephen smiled and laughed while shaking his head. He also began to undo his belt.

Tasha kissed Heaven's ear one more time and then walked around her toward the couch. She spared a look at Calvin who was laying on his back, watching Heaven with a pleased smile on his face and his dick twitching.

When Tasha turned to Stephen he smiled at her and pulled her into his arms. He kissed her, slow and passionate. Stephen's tongue explored her mouth as his hands roamed over her body and – Tasha moaned – Heaven's hands joined his at her hips. Her touch was tentative at first, a beautiful contrast to Stephen's heavy, knowing hands on her.

She moaned into his mouth again as Heaven molded herself to Tasha's body, skimming her hands down Tasha's thighs. She kissed her shoulder gently. Tasha thought she could have stayed like this forever, their hands on her, their bodies against her, her husband's erection pressing into her soft stomach. But Stephen had always said Tasha could be greedy sexually; usually with a hard on and a smile.

And he wasn't wrong. Right now Tasha wanted so much she could hardly get her brain to settle. But once again, Stephen stepped in to give her what he needed. He pulled back from their kiss and led her and Heaven to the bed. He put a hand on her back and encouraged her to sit down and lay back. The top of her head just touched Calvin's thigh. And even that touch made her hotter.

Heaven crouched down next to her and palmed

her breasts with a satisfied smile on her face. She ran her thumb over Tasha's left nipple before following it with her mouth. Tasha grabbed her other breast and squeezed as Heaven suckled and bit and licked her breast.

But then she stopped and lifted her head. "Can Calvin hold you down?" she asked innocently.

Tasha rubbed her thighs together and squirmed. A

The bed dipped under the weight of Stephen's body and his hands gripped her hips. She locked eyes with her husband and nodded. She watched him as she lifted her hands above her head and rested them on Calvin's thighs.

The other man's touch was firm but still gentle. She liked how different Calvin's hand felt at her wrist when compared to Heaven's massaging her breasts, especially when it meant that she got to experience Stephen's hands spreading her legs apart. So many hands.

She moaned as Stephen's touch skimmed down her thighs and then back up again, slow and heavy. Tasha lifted her hips toward him, wanting more. And then Heaven moved her right hand over Tasha's stomach and then settled over her clit. Tasha squirmed and groaned loudly under Heaven and Calvin's hands and Heaven's mouth, while Stephen pushed his pants over his hips and stroked his dick slowly just enjoying the view.

"Please," she groaned.

Heaven and Calvin laughed.

Sometimes Stephen would stretch this out, enjoying having her beg, pushing her to her limits. But he was kind tonight. Maybe he realized that she'd been at her horniest for weeks lusting after Heaven, so he only ran the blunt head of his dick up her wet slit a few times before pushing inside of her quickly.

Tasha's back arched up from the couch, her head fell back, her eyes closed and she groaned so loudly she worried for a fraction of a second that someone in the next room might hear.

Stephen pulled out of her only to thrust inside again. And again. And again.

"She's getting loud," Stephen said to no one. Or at least, Tasha thought he was speaking vaguely. She was wrong.

When Heaven's knee depressed the mattress near her ear, Tasha ripped her eyes open. Stephen was sawing into her, his fingers digging into her hips, keeping her as still as possible. And above her Heaven's beautiful pussy hovered over her face.

Tasha lifted her head but couldn't reach Heaven's sex. So she turned her head and licked her right inner thigh and then moaned as Stephen bent her legs at the knees and spread them, opening her wider, fucking her deeper.

"Please," she moaned again.

Heaven put a hand on Calvin's shoulder to steady

herself and Calvin put his free hand on her waist to help. And then Heaven's head tilted down and her adorable, innocent neighbor grinned at her over the bountiful curves of her breasts and stomach as she spread her thighs and lowered her pussy onto Tasha's mouth.

Tasha knew the moment when her tongue finally swiped up the cleft of Heaven's pussy would be imprinted on her brain forever. The bright saltiness of her sex and the force of Stephen's dick pounding into her, touching all her most sensitive spots, and even Calvin's firm grip on her wrists, was a storm of illicit perfection.

She'd been with other women before. She'd had orgies with Stephen before. But this moment was different. As she licked and suckled and tasted every part of Heaven's pussy, and Heaven rode her mouth to orgasm, and Stephen pounded into her with the perfect strokes he'd honed over all their years together, Tasha's body coiled tight until she burst into the biggest orgasm of the night. Even the subtle tightening of Calvin's fingers on her wrists and seeing him move to suck Heaven's nipple into his mouth only made this moment full of so much joy, she couldn't have hoped for it.

They didn't all come together. Instead one person's orgasms triggered another and then another and then another stretched on into another.

By the time they were done, all mostly or entirely

naked, covered in sweat, come and spit, the room felt too quiet and too warm, but also just right.

"That was better than winning the fight," Calvin said.

They were all burst into exhausted laughter.

## EPILOGUE

### Four Months Later

"Paint me like one of your French girls," Tasha whispered seductively.

Heaven rolled her eyes. "I'm not painting, dumb ass. I'm sculpting."

"I know. But 'sculpt me like one of your French girls' isn't really a thing."

"You're so corny."

"You love it," Tasha said.

Heaven lifted her eyes from the mound of half-formed clay in front of her. Tasha was reclining on her side on a bench from Tasha and Stephen's bedroom just for this purpose. The afternoon sunlight was spilling through the window in Heaven's studio, bouncing off Tasha's dark brown skin, making shadows in the crevices of the gentle rolls at her side and in the crook of her neck and at the crevice of her thighs. Calvin and Stephen had hauled the bench into Heaven's studio so Tasha could pose comfortably while Heaven worked on her newest piece, but it was in these moments that Heaven reconsidered the sculpture. She wanted to paint Tasha's body or buy the best camera she could to accurately capture all the beautiful planes of shadows and light in this perfect lighting.

Maybe she would. Maybe she could do all of the above. There weren't any limits on the possibilities.

She looked down at the hunk of clay again and felt a deep settling rather than anxiousness. Tasha had been sitting for her for almost two months, the longest time she'd even been able to have a model. But Heaven didn't have to rush. They were only halfway through their lease and she and Calvin had already decided to renew. They didn't want to live anywhere else right now. They didn't want to live next door to anyone else.

Because of that, Heaven didn't feel any need to rush their sittings, especially since Tasha had refused to accept any form of payment besides Heaven's head between her legs. And that too was an important source of comfort as she looked at the barely formed curve of Tasha's hip in the clay.

Heaven wanted to get this piece right. She wanted to make a sculpture that was as faithful to Tasha's body as possible. She wanted the form her breasts accurately, to get the slope of Tasha's ass mathematically correct and she needed to dapple the statue's thighs with each dip of Tasha's cellulite. This statue was a tribute and this kind of art couldn't be rushed.

That's another reason why, two months into their sitting sessions, all Heaven had to show for it was a curve of a hip. She refused to feel bad about that and Tasha – lounging in the sunlight on her day off, naked and happy – had no complaints.

Instead, Tasha actively encouraged their frequent breaks... in the name of art of course. Like right now, Heaven smiled as Tasha turned from her side to lying on her front.

She arched her back, bent her legs at the knee and crossed them at the ankle. She tilted her head back, making the most gorgeous curve in her body. She turned to Heaven and her lips parted softly.

"How do I look?" she asked.

Heaven answered her by dropping her tools onto the table in front of her and walking to the bench. She climbed onto it and spread Tasha's thighs and then she flattened her tongue along her sex.

"Beautiful," Heaven whispered against Tasha's pussy and then dipped her head to taste her again with greedy swipes of her tongue.

"How do I taste?" she whispered in a breathy groan.

"Beautiful," Heaven said, but the word was mumbled because she was too greedy to lift her head from between Tasha's legs.

But she was certain Tasha got the gist as Heaven

licked her from clit to opening and then up the crack of her ass and back again. Heaven was certain Tasha would understand that she tasted amazing since the room soon filled with Heaven's loud slurping at her body as if the fountain of youth was deep inside her pussy.

But if there was any mistaking it, she made sure to tell Tasha that she looked and tasted beautiful when they repositioned to tangle their legs together and make out. She whispered how good she tasted and how much she loved fucking her as she sawed her perfectly manicured fingers into Tasha's sex and Tasha positioned the pads of her fingers over Heaven's clit, her long nails lightly scraping her pussy.

But if Tasha didn't get it this time, that was okay, she'd tell her next time.

———

"What if he loses?" Tasha asked.

"Shush," Heaven and Stephen said to her.

"Don't even say that," Heaven said, her eyes focused on Calvin's profile

"Positive vibes, babe," Stephen said and kissed her on her cheek.

Tasha turned her eyes to the ring and swallowed all the other questions she had. She didn't want to fuck up Calvin's vibes, but he was sitting on the small stool in his corner looking dazed. He had a bruise on his right cheek and a black eye that would swell soon enough or maybe worse if his opponent hit him there again. His body was covered in sweat and water dribbling from his mouth when his ring manager squirted it into his mouth.

Four months of boxing fights hadn't eased her squeamishness about the matches. If anything, it had gotten worse. Tasha wouldn't have considered herself to be soft, but it gutted her to watch the man who she'd come to care for and who made Heaven so damn happy get pounded semi-regularly. And the manicurist in her hated each time his glove connected with his opponent's face. Even with the padding and tape around his knuckles, Tasha was worried that the cumulative effect of all his fights and practice would screw up all the work she'd done getting his cuticles together.

But she showed up because she wanted to support him and because Stephen and Heaven really fucking liked these brutal displays. Oh and also, she really loved the sex after. But it was hard to focus on the sex while watching the ring manager shove the mouth guard back into Calvin's mouth. He turned his head briefly to them. Tasha didn't have to turn her head to see that his and Heaven's eyes were locked. It was a small movement, but she swore she could detect a slight nod at whatever passed between them. Adorable as ever.

Tasha's heart stopped when the bell rang to restart

the fight. Calvin shot up from his seat. He and Winston King began to circle one another, balancing on the balls of their feet, their hands protecting their faces, but ready to strike.

Stephen mercifully placed an arm around Tasha's shoulders and pulled her to his side. She wrapped her arms around his waist and took comfort in his familiar, clean scent and his coiled muscles. She relaxed just a bit more when Heaven absentmindedly put a hand on the small of her back. The touch was soft, fleeting, distracted; as much to calm Tasha as to take some reassurance as she watched Calvin with an eagle's eye in the ring.

Tasha didn't love coming to Calvin's matches, but in a lot of ways, there wasn't anywhere else she'd rather be.

---

There was a fight afterparty at a local club. They could have gone there or to a hotel. They could have gone anywhere and done anything. But as far as Heaven was concerned there was something so perfectly right about going home together, just the four of them. To celebrate.

"Keep the ice on your eye," Tasha said to Calvin.

"I'm fine," he said, even though he pushed the cold compress back onto his rapidly swelling eye. "I can see my belt. That's what matters."

"Oh really? That's what matters?" Heaven joked.

"You know what I mean," he said and pulled her nearly onto his lap. He pressed his lips to hers and then licked his lips and smiled.

"You did it," she whispered to him.

"We did it," he whispered back.

"Aw, Stephen come look at this adorable shit," Tasha yelled.

"I'm coming. I'm coming," he said. "Keep being cheesy." He walked into the living room with a couple of bottles of beer in one hand and two glasses of wine in the other. "Alright, what'd I miss."

"Y'all done?" Calvin asked, playfully irritated.

"Definitely not, champ," Stephen said.

He was still annoyed but being called champ clearly did a lot to assuage those ruffled feathers.

Heaven kissed his cheek briefly and accepted the glass of wine from Stephen. After he'd passed out drinks, he settled on the couch next to Tasha and Heaven's eyes caught hers.

"So what now?" Tasha asked excitedly.

"Well, he gets a month to recuperate before his first challenge to the belt," Heaven said. "But he'll still have to train and there are probably going to be lots more sponsorship stuff so our rent is covered, huh babe?" she asked turning to Calvin.

He was taking a sip of beer and she waited for him to swallow. He shook his head and Heaven's smile faltered. "Probably," he said, indulgently, "but she was asking about sex. Right?" he asked Tasha, leaning around Heaven.

"Definitely," Tasha answered.

Heaven turned and blushed.

"But you can talk about whatever you want while I'm eating you out. You know how cute I think you are when you're blabbing."

"I also think you're cute when blabbing," Stephen said and then smiled around the mouth of his beer bottle.

"You're alright," Calvin said.

Heaven elbowed him before she could think, he groaned in pain.

"Oh my god," she said turning to him as Tasha and Stephen burst into laughter.

"What if I'd had broken ribs, Heaven?" he asked, laughing.

"I wasn't thinking," she said, mortified.

"You should kiss it," Tasha said, "make him feel better."

"I'm into that," Calvin said, leaning back on the couch.

Heaven rolled her eyes. "Shut up and put that ice pack back on your eye."

She pushed off from the love seat and walked to the couch in front of Tasha. She pushed Tasha's feet apart and stepped between her legs. Tasha too sat back, took a sip of her wine and smiled up at her.

"Are you gonna kiss it? Make me feel better?" Tasha whispered.

Heaven didn't bother answering, at least not with words. She moved to her knees and pushed Tasha's skirt up her thighs. By now, she could recognize the sound of Stephen and Calvin shuffling their clothes aside. Soon enough she'd hear their soft grunts and the friction of their hands around their dicks. At least for a little while. Because eventually all of her senses would be overtaken by Tasha; her taste, her moans, and even the sensory explosion of her thighs covering her ears and blocking off all sound except Heaven's blood pumping in her ears. Her excitement grew as she rubbed Tasha's thighs and pulled her underwear from her body, throwing them into Stephen's lap.

Six months ago Heaven had only hoped that when she and Calvin moved in together, it would bring them closer. She'd gotten her wish and so much more.

## OTHER BOOKS BY KATRINA JACKSON

Welcome to Sea Port

From Scratch

Inheritance

Small Town Secrets

Her Christmas Cookie

The Spies Who Loved Her

Pink Slip

Private Eye

Bang & Burn

New Year, New We

His Only Valentine

Bright Lights

The Family

Beautiful & Dirty

The Hitman

Erotic Accommodations

Room for Three?

Neighborly

Love At Last

Every New Year

Heist Holidays

Grand Theft N.Y.E.

Bay Area Blues

Layover

Back in the Day

Standalones

Encore

Office Hours

The Tenant

Sex Toy Soldier

www.ingramcontent.com/pod-product-compliance
Lightning Source LLC
Chambersburg PA
CBHW070816190726
48292CB00006B/2039